MW01221868

SHADOWFORGED
LIGHT & SHADOW, BOOK II

BY MOIRA KATSON

Cover art by Zezhou Chen.

Thank you to my friends and family,
whose support, encouragement, and feedback
have helped me to take this leap!

Cast of Characters

The Duke's Household

Catwin – servant to the Duke, Miriel's Shadow
Donnett – a member Palace Guard, who fought with
      the Duke at the Battle of Voltur
Eral Celys – Duke of Voltur
Emmeline DeVere – younger sister of the Duke, Miriel's
      mother
Miriel DeVere – niece of the Duke, daughter of
      Emmeline and Roger DeVere
Temar – servant to the Duke, the Duke's Shadow
Roine – a healing woman, foster mother to Catwin

Members of the Royal Family: Heddred

Anne Warden Conradine – sister of Henry, aunt of
      Garad; Duchess of Everry
Arman Dulgurokov – brother of Isra
Cintia Conradine – daughter of Anne and Gerald
      Conradine
Elizabeth Warden de la Marque – cousin of Henry,
      mother of Marie
Henry Warden– father of Garad (*deceased*)
Garad Warden – King of Heddred
Gerald Conradine – husband of Anne; Duke of Everry
Guy de la Marque – husband of Elizabeth Warden,
      father of Marie; Royal Guardian to Garad
Isra Dulgurokov Warden – mother to Garad, widow of
      Henry; the Dowager Queen
Marie de la Marque – daughter of Elizabeth and Guy
Wilhelm Conradine – son of Anne and Gerald; heir to
      the throne
William Warden – Garad's uncle, Henry's older brother
      (*deceased*)

Members of the Royal Family: Ismir

Dragan Kraal – brother of Dusan, father of Kasimir (*deceased*)
Dusan Kraal – King of Ismir
Jovana Vesely Kraal - Queen of Ismir
Kasimir Kraal – nephew to Dusan
Marjeta Kraal Jelinek – daughter of Dusan and Jovana
Vaclav Kraal – son of Dusan and Jovana, heir to the Ismiri throne

Heddrian Peerage

Edward DeVere – courtier; Duke of Derrion
Efan of Lapland - courtier
Elias Nilson – son to Piter; betrothed to Evelyn DeVere
Elizabeth Cessor – daughter of Henry and Mary Cessor
Evelyn DeVere – daughter of Edward, betrothed to Elias Nilson
Henri Nilson – brother of Piter
Henry Cessor – courtier, father of Elizabeth
Henry DeVere – courtier, younger brother to Edward
Linnea Torstensson – a young maiden at Court; daughter of Nils
Maeve d'Orleans – a young maiden at Court
Piter Nilson – Earl of Mavol
Roger DeVere – father of Miriel DeVere (*deceased*)

Other

Anna – a maidservant in service to the Duke
The High Priest – head of the Church in Heddred; advisor to the Dowager Queen
Jacces – leader of a populist rebellion in the Norstrung Provinces

Chapter 1

I knew the dream by heart now. I could hear the snow crunching underfoot, and the hungry moan of the wind, but I felt no cold on my skin. I was home and not home, I would have a chance once more to see the mother and father I had never known, who had given me away on the very day of my birth.

As I did every night, I wavered as I stood in front of the door to their hovel. I could go in and see my father pleading with my mother to keep me, and my mother pleading with my father to give me a quick death, and spare me the betrayal that would otherwise follow me all my life. Some nights, I would walk away, through the village, staring up at the Winter Castle through the billowing snow. Tonight, I pushed the door open and went in.

I watched the familiar argument without comment. I was a shadow in the corner of the room, a young woman that my father could never see. He pushed his way past me every night; I had never been brave enough to see if he would walk through me. Tonight, as I did on many nights, I waited for him to leave. My mother would see me, then—what she saw, I did not know. She did not know me for her daughter, but some nights I truly believed that she had seen across the years, and spoken to me, myself. I waited for her to tell me that I would be betrayed, that my betrayal would be the end, that my sorrow would tip the balance.

But tonight, instead of lying shivering in her pallet bed, she levered herself up and stared at me. After a moment, she motioned for me to come closer and hesitantly, I obeyed her. I had seen this dream every night for a year, and never had it changed. My heart, which had been beating slow and strong with sleep, began to race; I knew this was a dream, but I could not wake, I could not flee. I only knew that I did not want to hear what she would tell me.

"So," she said to me. "The betrayal has come." The sound of her voice came across years, like the baying of hounds, like the trumpeting of the warn horns. "You survived. But it is far from finished."

I woke suddenly, the echoes of her unearthly voice ringing in my mind, and saw the early morning sunlight streaming in the windows. For a moment, I hardly recognized where I was, so jarring was the quiet calm of daybreak after the sound of the storm, and the terror of my dream. I was soaked in sweat and breathing hard, and I lay back and tried to concentrate until the gasps slowed. At last, I opened my eyes.

My clothes were rank with sweat, and I sighed at the thought of going to the laundry. I would be late for my lessons, and Donnett would scold me. Then I remembered that I could not go to the laundry. I could not go anywhere at all. I would stay here, in these clothes until the Duke decided to let me leave this room.

This was the sixth day of our captivity here, and every day stretched interminably. We waited, Miriel and I, for the Duke to make his move, not knowing what events had come to pass outside this chamber. We knew that the court must be in an uproar, quite as shocked as the Duke had been to learn that Miriel was the King's confidant, his friend, his mistress in all but deed. What did they think, now that we had not emerged from our rooms in near to a week? We could not know; we knew only that the Duke was furious with us, and we were growing so tired of waiting for his judgment that I felt we would very nearly welcome the fall of the axe when at last it came.

On the big four-poster bed, I heard a rustle, and I looked over to see Miriel crane her head over the side of the mattress to peer down at me. By the look of it, she had been awake for some time, waiting for me to wake up as well. She raised an eyebrow, as if to ask about my harsh breathing and my sweat-soaked brow, but when I shook my head, she shrugged and inclined her head silently towards the door. I nodded and lifted my clothes off the shelf quietly, and she took her robe from the foot of the bed, and we crept out of the room together—not to her privy chamber, but to the receiving room, where her maidservant might not hear us if we spoke.

Each day for a week, Miriel and I had woken early and gone out to the main room together. She would tie her robe closed and then sit in one of her beautiful padded chairs by the hearth, and I would restart the fire from the last night's embers. When it was crackling again, I changed from my sleeping clothes to my usual black, while Miriel averted her eyes courteously.

Then she would gesture to the other chair—it had become a ritual as graceful as a dance between us—and I would curl into it and stare at the fire. In the half an hour or so we had before the maidservant woke and came out to find us, glaring at us accusingly, we would sit silently and stare at the flames in the grate. Our thoughts went round and round together and both of us knew that there was no need to speak them.

Danger was forefront in my mind; danger, and the fact that we were trapped, helpless, at the eye of a target—no way to run, and nowhere to go even if we could have escaped. In this snare, we thought endlessly on our helplessness, as the Duke undoubtedly meant that we should. When he had found us trapped in Miriel's rooms, frozen with shock at the fact of our escape from death, he had hardly wasted words on us. *Think on your allegiances,* he had said curtly, *think on who you wish to offend.* And he had gone, giving orders to the guards that we were not to be let out.

Now we waited. We were singularly quiet in our confinement; it was one of the things that so unnerved the new maidservant. The old maidservant had disappeared, inexplicably replaced by this dour woman. She had been tasked with watching us, to make sure that we sent no messages, and made no attempt to escape. She was outmatched, completely useless as a guard. If I was minded to, I could have killed her in a moment, and even Miriel was well-versed enough to sneak messages out past her. It was the Duke's guards, and Temar, who kept us confined and cut off from the world. But the woman felt obliged to do her duty as the Duke had instructed her, and she resented us for making it clear that she was ill-suited to the task.

Neither Miriel nor I was minded to make it more pleasant for her; I had taken to sharpening my daggers each afternoon, while Anna looked over at me nervously and Miriel tried to hide her smile. Miriel, meanwhile, affected not to notice that she had been kept in the room by her uncle's order, and took to sending for ridiculous things: a specific book from her uncle's library, a new quill to write with, a length of ribbon to decorate a gown, a lute to practice one series of notes over and over again while Anna gritted her teeth.

All of our jokes were wordless; we shared whole conversations with the lift of an eyebrow, a hidden smile. We moved silently, in concert, and this unity unnerved Anna all the more. We took joy in our unity, for there was precious little joy in our lives. We had no true allies beyond each other, and we had a great many enemies. Miriel had said one day, in a rare break into speech:

"It almost doesn't matter, does it?" I knew what she meant, and agreed with a silent nod. With so many enemies who might kill us, who would kill us—what was the difference in singling out the one who had tried? To follow that lead to its end, oblivious of all else, was to ignore the swarm of enemies that surrounded us. And so, instead of spending my time puzzling over it, I recited, every night, the litany of our enemies: the Dowager Queen, the High Priest, Guy de la Marque, Jacces, the Duke. Every time I recited, I wondered how many more names I did not know.

It was one thing to be practical, and be wary of all enemies, but I held out hope that we might yet learn who had done it—and why. I did not need to tell Miriel to watch the faces of her fellow courtiers when she was finally allowed to leave the room, and she did not tell me to make enquiries to find the servant who had brought us the poisoned food. I was already working to determine what type of poison had been used, and Miriel knew as much. Miriel was always watchful, and I knew as much. Together, if we could find our would-be killer, we could find a motive.

Today, Miriel surprised me by asking:

"What do we want?" I considered the question. We wanted our freedom, but that was not enough. Open the doors to this room, and we were still in the palace. We could not leave—where else was there? Miriel had no family, no allies; she could not live as a peasant. I had nowhere to go, either—Roine was my only family, and she was here at the Palace—and in any case, I could not leave Miriel. It would be to leave a girl to her death, without even the comfort of a companion.

"What do you mean?" I asked, unable to determine what she might be asking. My voice was rusty from disuse. She paused, then shrugged her slim shoulders. Even her simplest gesture was elegant. I thought of my own face, plain and nothing, against the dramatic beauty of hers, and thought wryly that it was good that I was the shadow. She would never fade into the background.

"What's our goal?" she clarified. "My uncle hasn't killed us yet, so he probably won't." She was matter-of-fact; if it bothered her to think that her own flesh and blood would have her murdered, the emotion did not show in her eyes. She could be as cold as the Duke at times. "Which means, we should decide what to do when they let us out of here," she continued. "Every faction has a goal, and we're a faction. So, what do we want?"

I closed my eyes for a moment. It still seemed strange that

her words had not been on a dream: *We're our own side*, she had told me. I could hardly believe it, just as, if I were to close my eyes, I could pretend that there had been no attempt on our lives. If I concentrated, I might pretend that the Duke had never discovered the secret of Miriel's meetings with the King. And if I closed my eyes tightly and blocked out the world, I could almost think I was home, in the Winter Castle, ignorant of the world and free of its machinations. Then I opened my eyes once more and I was trapped in this little suite of rooms, with too many enemies to count, and a fifteen year old girl as my ally against the world.

"It's whatever you want," I decided after a scant moment of thought. I did not add, *but I wouldn't mind running away.* I had the wild notion that we could do it, run away and survive on our own. But that would never do—they would find us someday, and Miriel could never be happy in a hovel, with homespun. Still, it was amusing to picture her living off the land.

The truth was that I did not know how to decide what we wanted. I always told Roine that I could not leave Miriel, but the truth was that I had nothing else in my life, no place to take refuge. There was only the palace, and that was Miriel's world, not mine. And above all, I had sworn to shape myself to her like a shadow. I hated the man who had made me promise that, and I had betrayed him—but the promise had stuck, somehow. Miriel's fate and my own were intertwined, but my fate was tied to the words of a madwoman, and the thought that Miriel might be dragged into my fate was too strange; she was the light, the glittering one, the girl who might be Queen.

"Do you know, the brightest hope in my life was that I could love the King, and be a good Queen to him," Miriel said softly. "And that cannot be. Now I do not know what I could hope for."

It was jarring to hear those words from the mouth of a fifteen-year-old girl, and it made me want to cry. It was like peering down into Miriel's very heart, and seeing the girlish hope for happiness, the simple desire that her duty and her heart should lead her to the same end. Somewhere, Seven Gods alone knew where—not from her mother, not from her uncle—Miriel had come into a sense of morality. When her life had descended into a living hell, what she had clung to was her streak of idealism. She had cherished the dream that her purpose of catching the King's heart could do good for the country.

She had wanted it so much that she had tried to forget the

—

boy she might truly have loved: Wilhelm Conradine, the King's own cousin. She had tried to turn her heart, and she had seen only a piece of Garad: his dream of a golden age, a peaceful age. She had once believed whole-heartedly in a future where they ruled as equals, her at his right hand and her advice healing the nation from its centuries of war.

Now she knew that her heart had betrayed her. Miriel had not understood that a boy of fifteen, emerging from the certainty of his own death and burdened with the weight of kingship, could not be the man she hoped to love. He could not admit mistakes, and his decisions were too weighty to be undone without strong will and a graceful heart, an ability to name himself as wrong. Garad was not that strong, he was too driven to be loved, too driven to be a storybook King with a perfect kingdom. Above all, he was not Wilhelm, the boy whose smile inspired Miriel's own, the boy who shared her sympathy for the rebellion. Garad had been born to power and death; having eluded death, he would not give up even a piece of his power.

And, with the unbending morality of the young, Miriel would never forget this, and never forgive it. Having thought that Garad shared her vision, she had believed that her life might yet be happy. It had been devastating to see the illusion shattered, and Garad's belief in his own idealism did not make it any easier to bear. She felt that she had been made a fool of, and she knew as well as I did that her attempt to escape and set her own course had set her in the full glare of the court as well, at the mercy of the forces there.

And Garad, of course, was the King. He could command Miriel to be his Queen, he could ruin her if she refused—and how could she refuse, what else was there for her? What other man could be what she had hoped for from Garad? No other man in the world, save perhaps King Dusan of Ismir, could give Miriel the chance to be such a force for good, on such a large scale. Garad would command Miriel to his side, and then force her to watch as he betrayed the sentiments she held so dear. He would never see her pain, and I could not say if that made things better or worse. I did not know how Miriel would bear it, save by stripping away her idealism. And what was left then? Only ambition.

She was my ally, and the other half of myself, in ways I could not have explained. But I feared her sometimes. I wondered if she ever feared me, who already had blood on my hands, who watched the world through the eyes of a spy. Even I feared myself. And, if I was not so foolish as to believe that I could keep my hands clean by riding out the storm in the Duke's shadow, I feared what would come when we chose a path.

"What *can* we do?" I asked, to distract Miriel from her melancholy. "What choices do we even have?"

"We don't have any choices yet," she admitted. "But I've thought about it, and being on our own side means that we're always waiting for our luck to turn—for a chance, something that could set us free."

"Free from the Duke?" I asked, and she tilted her head to the side.

"Free from our enemies," she said. "But I've thought...what does it mean that we can't tell who wanted to kill us? And it means that everyone is our enemy."

"We should trust no one," I agreed. Miriel smiled, satisfied to hear her thoughts from my mouth.

"Exactly." She sobered at once. "We have to stay, there's nowhere to go, and anyway, no way to leave. Which means we stay in a court that hates us."

"Then our goal is to stay alive," I said. It was a poor jest, in part because it was no jest at all. Miriel's mouth only twitched, half-heartedly.

"Garad is our only ally. Him, and Wilhelm." She took a deep breath, and I saw her fighting to tell herself that what she felt for Wilhelm was nothing more than a girlish fancy, and in any case could cause her nothing but pain. "But, Wilhelm is powerless, and that leaves Garad."

"Not a poor ally," I said. *But a fickle one.* She nodded at the unspoken.

"And then our enemies. We know some of them, but not all, and they're powerful. Which means we need Garad's favor, yes?" I nodded, and she nodded back. "Yes. And I said we should wait for a chance, something that would set us free..."

"The throne," I guessed, and she nodded.

"It's the only way to survive at Court. I must make Garad make me Queen. My uncle should help us. And when I am Queen, then we have power in our own right. But until then, nothing is more important. I mean it, Catwin." Her gaze sharpened. "Not Roine. Not Temar." I swallowed, as I always did when I thought of him; I hesitated when I thought of Roine's steady faith in me. But I nodded.

"Not the rebellion," I rejoined. "Not Wilhelm." After a pause, she nodded.

"You know, I wanted to make Heddred whole," she said. "Above all, I want to help this rebellion. And once, I wanted Wilhelm. But I can never have Wilhelm...and I cannot help the rebellion without first having enough power to do so. I can't see any other way. So I must forsake it for a time, so that one day I can come back and help it..." I had no response, and so we sat in silence, thinking of what we would give up: for Miriel, her dream of happily ever after, and her sense of justice; for me, my loyalty to my family, and my childish love of Temar.

"You know, if we do this, we will be without honor," Miriel said. I frowned, questioning, unable to follow the sideways slant of her thoughts, and she looked back at me, meeting my gaze openly. "We will be liars, every day, to everyone but each other, won't we?" I nodded, uncertainly, and she smiled suddenly, feral and dark. "Then perhaps we should not fear other sins. We will make our enemies live to regret that they ever went against us. And then, when they are gone, we will shape Heddred to what it must be."

I shivered. Was this only the angry words of the scorned and powerless? I could agree if I believed that we would never be able to exact our revenge; what I feared was that we might be able to. I could imagine it only too well. I knew that at this very moment, I could make my way into any noble's rooms and kill them as they slept. Sometimes, I wondered why I did not do so. I shuddered.

"It is not all dark," Miriel said, understanding. "Catwin, this is a dark path, but the end is good. And think—do we have any choice? I've wondered, sometimes, if the Gods mean us to tread this path. That is our fate together—to lose everything we have held dear until now, so that we may heal our Kingdom." I looked at her, and saw a woman whose fierce idealism was warped into ambition; I feared for her, and yet—

She was right. There was no other path. My dream came back to me, and there was the feeling of a net closing around me, fate drawing me into a pattern too big for my eyes to see. I shook my head involuntarily.

"Let's worry about surviving, first," I said softly, to distract myself. "I don't think that part is going to be easy."

"That's your task," Miriel reminded me. "To keep us both alive. And mine is to enchant the King." Unconsciously, she straightened her shoulders, turned her head to show the line of her jaw. Her uncle had bidden her to learn how to stir a man's desire with only the set of her head, and she had learned it well. He might regret that, now that her talents would be set to the task of enchanting the court for her own purposes, and not his. He had always used us for his own ends; now he was our enemy, even if he did not know it.

"What are you thinking?" Miriel asked me.

"Fooling your uncle is the first thing we need to do," I said softly. "There are only two ways to survive having him as an enemy. One, make him think we're friends again. Two, be stronger than he is." I looked over at her, and she nodded.

"Or both," she said promptly, and I thought that the Duke would indeed be sorry that he had forged her into such a woman. He should not have had her taught military history. She was quite good at it.

"Or both," I agreed. "So for now, we have to make him believe we're all friends again, so he can help you become Queen." Miriel nodded decisively.

"You keep us alive, and I will become Queen." It was a poor jest, in part because it was no jest at all.

"You're not afraid he'll lose interest before you can get a treaty signed?" I asked curiously. It was the other question that had been worrying me. Garad had flaunted her to the court, he had taken great joy in defying his guardian. What if that wore thin, and reality intruded, before Miriel got a crown on her head? But she only grinned at my fears, a knowing smile.

"I can do it," she whispered back. "You'll see. I'll do it. One way or another." She smiled. "I'm the best, the very best."

There was the sound of a door opening, and both of us sank back against the chairs without another word. The maidservant came into the room and glared at us. I smiled blandly back, but for once she had the grim smile of a gambler with a trump card.

"The Duke is coming to see you this morning," she announced. "So look sharp."

Miriel rose gracefully from her chair. "Of course we will make his Grace, my uncle, welcome," she said smoothly. "Come help me get dressed, Anna. Catwin, stoke up the fire and send a page for refreshments. Fresh fruit, and chilled wine."

It was indeed a gracious welcome—and an extravagance, of the sort the Duke abhorred. It was the gesture of a Queen, such as the Duke had wished Miriel to become—and a reminder that she had come closer to the goal on her own account than he would like. I quirked my mouth, and hastened to do her bidding.

Chapter 2

We were waiting when they arrived. Miriel stood serenely with her hands clasped behind her back, and I stood next to her in the same pose, my stomach flip-flopping in terror. I wondered if she felt the same, and after a glance at her decided that she did not. Now was her time to perform, to enchant, to weave the illusions she was so skilled at making. She would be focused only on the words she had practiced, the expressions and postures she thought would be most useful to her.

I had no such distraction. Resolutely, I had not thought of Temar since the night of the murder attempt. He had been the one to pin me against the bedpost, an arm across my throat, while the Duke swept into the room, observing myself and Miriel with pitiless blue eyes. And it had been Temar who had breathed in my ear, "I told you I would not intervene for you again. Do you want to get yourself killed?" When the Duke had told us, Miriel and me, that we would be confined together, Temar had released me and left without another word.

I was terrified of seeing him, terrified of the jumble of emotions in my chest. His question had felt like a warning, and one did not warn enemies in such a way. In the long days that had passed since the revelation of the King's love, had Temar meditated on my lies and turned from my ally to my enemy? Beyond even that, I wondered now—at the worst time, waiting to see him again—if it had been he who sent the poisoned food? What if he was leading me away from the truth, as I had led him away from the truth of Miriel and the King? Was this his revenge, was he laying a trap for me? I did not want to think that, and yet no wishing could deny that he was as good a suspect as any. I felt as if I would be sick.

As the guards took up their positions at the walls, I noted their layout and their weapons. Temar had once told me to do so, and Donnett had agreed: "Every armed man who didn't come in with ye is yer enemy," he had said. "Remember that, and ye might survive." And he had snorted, for he still believed that I would be useless in a fight. I wondered if anyone had told Donnett where I had gone. With another twist of my stomach, I wondered what Roine had been told.

The guards were spaced evenly about the room, effective enough that I wondered if the Duke truly expected us to try to escape while he was speaking to us. I had a moment of real fear, wondering if he was going to kill us—at length, I decided that if he had wanted to do so, he would have chosen a less public place. A cellar, perhaps, or the hidden tunnels. The Winter Castle. The thought did not fully set me at ease. The Duke would take his revenge for our ploy at this meeting.

I took a last look around myself, and when I looked back, Temar was watching me. I swallowed as I stared back at him, hoping that he could not see my fear and yet knowing that he could. For a moment, I wished that he could see deeper, and know how my heart twisted to lie to him; I did not want him to think me a cold-hearted traitor. I studied his impassive face, the way he quietly radiated anger, and wondered what lay in his mind. It was strange to stare into a man's face, and wonder if he had planned my death.

I supposed that I was going to have to get used to that.

As I bowed to the Duke, Miriel swept him a curtsy. "Good morning, my Lord uncle." He did not waste words. He never wasted words.

"Have you considered yet how you wish to live at court?" He eyed her narrowly, hoping for a misstep, but she spotted the trap at once. She had been on her guard.

"My Lord uncle, as my guardian, it is yours to say if and how I shall live at court." Her voice was clear, but her eyes were on the ground. He took a long look at her, and then nodded.

"And if I choose to keep you at court, and weather the scandal you have created?" Very economical, was the Duke. Not one to let an opportunity through his fingers, especially when that opportunity was to shame his enemies.

I tried to look nowhere and betray nothing. We were being watched by the two most cunning and observant people I knew, their senses heightened by the fight. Miriel must play this well, and I must not betray her by showing my own emotions.

She wavered visibly, and even knowing that she would have prepared each gesture, I feared for her. Watching Miriel was like watching a play—only there could be no saying how this would end, no way to know what secrets the other actors held. I could only hope that at the end of this, we would have the Duke's agreement to

---

make Miriel Queen.

"My Lord uncle..."

"Speak up, girl, I don't have all day." I snuck a glance, and saw his grim, victorious smile. A wave of derision swept over me. He truly believed that he had caught her.

"My Lord, if you were to forgive me..." She swallowed, as if the words hurt her pride to say. His derision, his belief in his victory, would grate on her. She would long to tell him the truth of it. But she had the goal in her sights and she would bear it all, knowing that it was to betray him someday.

"If you will accept me back, I will be obedient to you." Miriel enunciated each word clearly. She was fairly quivering with the effort of saying it out loud. I let myself swallow at last, and I dropped my eyes to the floor. I struggled to keep my face blank as the Duke gave a great crow of laughter.

"You will? Ah, and what makes you say that?" I hated him at that moment, and Miriel hated him. He knew that she would. She walked a fine line: knowing that her defiance stoked the fire of his anger, and yet knowing that he expected it, that he would suspect her of playing him false if she was too calm.

Ever surprising, Miriel looked up. She looked directly at him, her face open and set grimly. "I don't want you as my enemy," she said honestly. "You would destroy me." He nodded. "And it is in our interests, each to see the other rise, if only we are allies."

"Ambition?" His face flickered. He did not want her having her own ends to achieve.

"I want to be Queen," Miriel stated simply. "Isn't that what you wanted?" It was the most subtle of jabs: I know you would use me and discard me, and now I have trapped you into saying it, or lying about it. The Duke raised his eyebrows, considering his response, but Miriel was already shifting, hoping to set the Duke off balance. Her jaw was set, her eyes narrowed.

"I want her place," she said flatly, and his eyes flickered. He was not sure what to make of this. "You saw her as well as me. She thinks I'm nothing. She thinks I'm not fit to give her son advice. She thinks she can turn him away from me and destroy me once his favor is gone. But she would not even be on her throne still if it weren't for the battle at Voltur. Who is she to think we're nothing?"

The Duke's face had gone strained, taut. He did not trust Miriel. He did not want to trust her. But something awoke in his eyes: memories of countless Council meetings, his words disregarded, his achievements forgotten, all for the accident of his birth. And it was a good thing to believe that Miriel would want revenge on another enemy.

"But together, we can undo her. So." Miriel bit her lip. "If I am obedient to you...we could rise together."

"Interesting." His face had returned to its usual impassive expression. "You know, I doubt that you can do it. I don't think you can hold him that way, for that long." He smiled, and I saw that he was using the same ploy, setting her off balance. He let his smile stretch, then waved his hand and his eyes hardened. "But there are more important matters. How do I know you are not trying to play me for a fool, Miriel?"

"I would not dare." Miriel ignored his slight to her abilities. Her voice was muted with real fear. "If you wanted, you could have executed me. I am your ward, it is the law. And I have learned now that I cannot deceive you. You can know that I am not trying, for I cannot risk your displeasure, my Lord uncle. And..." She closed her eyes. "I have learned my lesson."

"It will not take another lesson?" His voice was wintry.

"My Lord uncle, I only barely survived this one. This is the court. I cannot afford to make mistakes."

"Sufficient." He walked over to her and tilted her chin up with his fingers. "You will obey me, Miriel. I will expect it." I did not like the sound of his voice when he won, and I knew without looking that Miriel disliked it as well. The surprise was Temar; ahead of me, his face had gone as blank as I had ever seen it. There was something here that he did not like, and it was not mistrust of Miriel. I filed that away.

"Be aware, however, that I will not be made a fool of. I will be watching you, and watching the King. I have ways of learning what you do, learning what you say, learning what you think. If you play me false, I will know, and I will make you beg for me to kill you to put an end to your pain."

"I will not play you false," Miriel said, a quaver in her voice. "I swear it." Gone were the days of her clever turns of phrase, her prevarications. She had made her choice of course, and she lied without hesitation.

"Good." The Duke released her. "Now. News from Ismir." He strolled over to the table and took a seat. He looked for a moment at the refreshments. "Wine?" It had been his intention to make Miriel serve him, but she was not to be trapped in that way. Her pride had a breaking point.

"Catwin," she said simply, and so I went to the table and poured a glass of wine for the Duke, and handed it to him. Miriel watched him as he took a sip, her face unreadable.

"The King, no doubt bereft in the loss of your steadying influence—" he looked at her coldly "—has been less...welcoming...to the Ismiri envoy. Tempers are fraying. He reminds the envoy daily that House Warden will not take accusations of murder lightly."

"What do you want me to do?" Miriel asked, no hint of insolence in her voice, and the Duke took another sip of wine.

"I want to have this out," he said. "Kill them all, break their army on the mountains, and take their capital. But the King will never do that. He does not have the stomach for it. So. I want you to remind him of his dignity. Remind him that he must not tolerate such statements. Remind him that Dusan should silence Kasimir's accusations. And tell him, for the Gods' sake, to mind Kasimir's threats to invade." He drummed his fingers along the side of his glass. "If anyone else asks you, you will be shocked and hurt that anyone should accuse the King of such an act. Look foolish if you must: play the young girl in the first flush of love. The King is your idol, he can do no wrong in your eyes." Miriel considered, and then nodded.

"Anything else?"

"The rebellion." His eyes narrowed. "It's quiet, but not gone. They're waiting for something. The King must not be persuaded to let Jacces go, just because the violence has died away. He will turn the southern lords against him; they want vengeance."

"Indeed." Miriel did not betray, for a moment, that she would help the rebellion when she was Queen. She had made her choice: for now, the rebellion must wait. She considered. "And if *she* talks to me?" she asked. We all knew who She was.

"Sweet. Sweet and deferential. And if anyone asks you about her, she is a magnificent Queen, one you are proud to serve. She'll get nothing from us that way. If she insults you outright...say only that you are honored by the King's regard, but do not dream of anything beyond his wishes."

"Yes, my Lord. What have you told the court, as to why I have not been seen for a week?"

"I told them that you were ill," the Duke said. "There were rumors of poison, did you know?" I was on high alert at once, every muscle quivering. "Ridiculous," the Duke said, too easily. "Foolish to think that anyone would poison a child. I told them so."

I could not help myself—in that moment, I had to know if it had been the two of them. I cast a look at Temar and, to my surprise, he was watching me as well. But I got nothing for my indiscretion; his face was unreadable. If it had been he who slipped the poison into our food, there was no guilt showing in his eyes. I shivered; there was a reckoning coming, but I did not know how, and I did not know when.

Unlike me, Miriel had been braced for the reference to poison. Her smile did not slip even a fraction. "Foolish indeed," she concurred sweetly. "Am I to be well enough to attend dinner tonight, then, my Lord?"

"I expect it. And I expect you to be charming, and sweet, and remind all who see you that the King has chosen you because you are the finest of the maidens at court. Do not put on any airs, or be familiar with him: a curtsy to the throne, nothing more. Let him seek you out.

"I will let you prepare yourself for your return to court. Oh, and another thing—if the King arranges to meet you, you will send Catwin with a message. I expect to know where, and when. And allow him no liberties."

"He has never asked anything dishonorable of me," Miriel said. There was a note of pride in her voice, and her uncle's eyes gleamed. He was quick to cut her down.

"If you are not incompetent, he will. Within a year, at most, I should think. You will tell me when he does."

"But hold him off." Miriel's voice was expressionless.

"No one has ever found a better way to keep a man." The Duke sounded amused. "Deny him what he most wants, and he will give you what you most want." He smiled. "Perhaps, at any rate. If you can do it."

Miriel's eyebrow quirked, and then she shrugged one shoulder. "Yes, my Lord uncle."

"You don't intend to disobey?"

"And be ruined and cast aside?" Miriel countered. "No. I do not." He laughed, and left the room, and Temar left with him, without a backward glance. When I looked back to Miriel, she was watching me.

"Watch where your loyalties lie," she said sharply. "I'll not tolerate you mooning after him." I did not retort that this was not mooning, this was not infatuation. I had adored Temar from the first, it was true, but with the easy worship of a child. Temar might be handsome, but he was like a living, breathing work of art—better, he seemed half a legend, like a character from a storybook. When I watched him, it was not because I pursued him as a maid will, with her mind on marriage—the thought was laughable, we were Shadows. I watched him because he had been my friend once, and I did not know what he was to me now, or what I was to him.

What was the most jarring was the sense, in the evenness of his gaze, in the way he watched me, that I was his equal in a way I had not been before. Just as Temar had lifted me from orphan child to something more, something special, my deception had lifted me from student to adversary. Now, for the first time, I was not the lesser of the two of us. It was so strange a thought that it had not occurred to me until now, seeing him here.

And—my heart twisted—I did not think anything could make me forget the guilt that I had lied to him; after so many months wondering when fate and the Duke would set us against each other, I had been the one to move first. He might have tried to kill me, but I had expected nothing less—we were Shadows.

But I had no words to explain that to Miriel, any more than she could explain to me how it was that she glittered so brightly, enchanted the court so wholly. I only bowed my head in acquiescence.

"Yes, my Lady."

Chapter 3

Whatever Miriel thought of her uncle's instruction, she prepared that night as carefully as if she had been going to a private dinner with the Dowager Queen. She was a vision of purity: a dress of a rich cream silk trimmed with dark blue, pearls and sapphires embroidered onto the cuffs and sapphires set in silver for her ears. Her maid brushed her hair until it shone, and then Miriel sat for a long time in front of her looking glass, turning her head this way and that, biting her lips to bring color to them.

I watched her for a time, feeling the wonder I always felt when I watched Miriel spin her illusions out of nothing. I could feel my heart beginning to beat faster as I contemplated going once more into the glare of the Court. My mind was a jumble; this was a dark path, I knew, and something in me shrank from it. But Miriel was right—what other choice did we have? At Court, we must fight first for security, or we would not live to fight for the things we held dear.

I shook my head to clear it of foolish fancies, and craned to see myself in the looking glass. I was feeling well-dressed myself, wearing clean clothes for the first time in days. Miriel had had the maid braid my hair finely, and in the looking glass, I could see that it fell like honey, strands of different colors glinting in the light. I had taken a moment to study the wide cheekbones, the pointed little chin—

I could have been a pretty girl, even, and I would have faded next to Miriel. I did not want that to bother me, I felt as if it should not matter. Tonight, even as I wished with all my heart for her to be a success, I saw her at her most charming, her most well-dressed, and it did matter. I knew that half the murmurs that arose at her passing were rumor and intrigue. "She's the one who..." And yet, I could hear the longing in their voices, all of them. A longing that no one had ever felt for my attention, my smile. No one ever would. I smiled at her as I held the door open for her to leave, and hoped that she could not see the envy in my eyes.

Miriel walked through the halls as if they were her own, as

if she were already Queen, but with her usual gracious smiles to servants and lower gentry, even when they gawped at her; every person in the palace knew of her now. It seemed incredible that the world had continued on, as if nothing had happened, but such was the case. I felt truly alien, an outsider moving through the constant stream of people in the halls. Our lives had nearly been ended, and the world moved on without pause...

Miriel slowed her pace as we approached the maidens' chambers, and gestured me forward to her side. I saw only the faintest glimmer of herself in her eyes—she had pushed her soul back, far away, and she wore her mask now.

"Watch Her for me," was all she said to me, and I knew she meant Marie, and later, Isra. Marie might be nothing more than a puppet, but she was, just as Miriel was, well-trained. To watch her, one would think that perhaps Guy de la Marque had played as long a game as the Duke had. I knew that she would not easily be pushed into the background. Whatever advantage Miriel seemed to have now, Guy de la Marque would not let his daughter leave the field until the game was over and done with.

In the maidens' chamber, all were assembled and waiting for their invitation to the hall. Each night, the King would arrive for dinner with the men of the Council, and the Dowager Queen would arrive with the highest of her ladies in waiting. Then, the King would send invitations to each of the chambers: the unmarried men, the boys, the unmarried women, the girls. Each would arrive, and pay their respects to the throne, and then be seated.

As we entered the room, I saw that the maidens in the chamber were all circled around Marie. There was a new girl, with fair hair and eyes near as blue as Miriel's, waiting hesitantly at the outer edge of the group; I resolved to ask one of the servants who she might be. As Miriel entered, the girls looked up and a hush fell over the room. She smiled, warmly, affecting not to notice, gliding over to speak to one of the minor nobles who had always been kind to her. Many of the girls wavered, but Marie de la Marque broke the silence without hesitation.

"So she deigns to join us once more." Her voice was sweet. She was a vision in palest rose pink, her golden hair falling over her shoulders, her sky blue eyes dancing with malice. She smiled. "Perhaps the one who detained her all this time has grown tired of her presence?"

So she had been primed to make a scandal of this, then. I

swallowed as I heard the murmur of surprise at her boldness, and a laugh from her friends. Miriel turned, as if surprised to find that Marie was speaking of her.

"Mistress de la Marque," she said, and she curtsied. "I beg your pardon. I am afraid that I do not understand the jest. I have been away from court due to my illness." It did her little good to appear dense, but it was the best she could have managed.

"Playing the innocent?" Elizabeth Cessor asked sharply. Her gaze was filled with spite; she had thought that only the other well-born girls could be true competition for the King, and she resented the fact that a common-born girl might take her place in the running. "You fool no one."

There was no response to make. Miriel curtsied again, a confused half-smile on her face, and turned back to speak to the women who crowded around her. I could hear her explaining again that she had been ill, she had not seen anyone—no, no one save her uncle, of course. No, of course not the King. The King! Coming to her rooms! What an idea.

I knew that she gritted her teeth against such banalities. Tonight, she was surrounded by enemies and sycophants, and she hated both; death had come for her, and those who crowded around her would never know. She ached to curl her shoulders dismissively, she wanted to form witty retorts to the young women who had tried to shame her, to the girls who asked her for news of the King. But she was to be sweet. She was to be charming. She was to win as many as she could to her side, so that when the King moved to choose her for a bride, her way would be clear.

While Miriel laughed and talked with the women who gathered around her, introducing herself to the newest of the young women, and Marie held court a few yards away, the rest of the girls swirled awkwardly. The smooth yearning towards Marie had been disrupted by Miriel's return, and I watched, wearily amused by the predictable uncertainty of the maidens. By now, the gossip had made it clear even to the least observant girl that the Dowager Queen did not approve of her son's choice, and there was a divide: those who backed Miriel, either for love of her or in a calculated bet that the King would win out, and those who backed Marie, certain that the will of the regent and her chosen protector would triumph against an untried boy.

Not one of the girls was sure of her choice. In the absence of orders from their parents, the girls looked over their shoulders, even those at the center of each flock looked across the room. Those who had chosen Marie had been sure that she was the more suitable bride for a King, but now they were perhaps remembering that the King had surprised his mother with his preference for Miriel—what was to say that he would not surprise the Dowager Queen once more? Who could be sure that he would obey her orders? Those who had chosen Miriel, however, betting on her charm and her intelligence, were reminded that Marie was a fine choice for the wife of a King. The King must marry for advantage, everyone knew that—and Marie wore the crests of de la Marque and Warden, cleverly embroidered onto her gown. Miriel and Marie affected not to notice, but I knew that Miriel would see everything. She would be marking the loyalty of each girl.

When the crier had appeared, to summon the maidens to dinner, I found that the confusion at Miriel's return was just as prevalent in the main hall. The maidens were silent as they approached the banquet, but their appearance caused a stir, and I could see all of them color, self consciously, under the scrutiny of the Court. Even the lowliest gentry and servants now knew Miriel's face, by description if not by sight, and so as the maidens processed up the long aisle to their table, whispers arose in their wake like the stirring of wind through a forest. No one could help but notice the two girls, both beautiful, both proud, both attired as richly as queens, and no one could help but look up at the thrones, to see the faces of the royal family.

To be sure, those at the high table tried to remain impassive. But there was no mistaking the leap of joy on the King's face when he caught sight of Miriel, and none could have missed the sharp glance his mother threw, and the frown at her son's happiness. At the right hand of the Dowager Queen, Guy de la Marque watched the scene as if he were surveying a battlefield, and his wife gazed at Miriel with undisguised dislike.

The two whose emotions I could not name were the Ismiri envoy and the Head Priest. To judge by their contemplative stares, Miriel was a puzzle to them, and a key. But what they, themselves, thought of her, I could not have said. The Head Priest, in particular, watched Miriel as if she were a particularly worthy opponent, but one for whom he held no enmity; he did not seem to share Isra's furious dislike. And then, to my horror: his gaze swept about the edges of the room, and came to rest on me. Did I see him nod? To me? I shivered and moved away, so that he could not see me behind one of the columns. How did the Head Priest know to look for me? I must find out.

The maidens were nervous, their laughter too loud, their witticisms strained in the face of the court's scrutiny. Every face in the hall was turned towards them, and then back to the throne; back and forth went the looks, and round and round went the whispers. Money changed hands, sometimes discreetly, and every once in a while a shout of laughter was hurriedly silenced. The hall descended into the awkward chatter of those who are straining to hear others speak.

Everyone spoke of Her. Some murmured under their breaths that she was a real beauty, a girl with wit and fire, a perfect match for a young man. Others muttered that she was no fit match for King—Gods, there had to be ten women with better connections than she had. As I listened in on the conversations, I noticed the lack of two things over all others: the hint of true scandal, and a preference for Marie. A very few of the courtiers, of the oldest and purest blood, objected openly to the rise of the merchants. These were the men of the council and their families, whose wealth stemmed from the royal coffers. The rest had, inevitably, fallen on hard times and married their sons and daughters to merchants: money for nobility. They could not object to the Duke's leap upwards, they could not argue loudly for the right of blood to triumph.

Many of them, indeed, had no objection to the Duke at all. He was a hero of the war, and whatever his ruthlessness against the Ismiri, he was known to rule his lands fairly. He was the protector of the western front. His niece was known to be intelligent and kind, and she was a beauty, graceful on her feet and sure to sit well on a throne. And while Marie had been primed to drag Miriel's name through the mud, no one in the hall was mentioning any scandal at all. I was intrigued; I filed it away for later thought.

But—I was forced to admit—however little the courtiers seemed to prefer Marie, there could be no serious objection to her at all. She was lovely, noble, well-educated, and prettily-behaved. Those who objected did so because they misliked Guy de la Marque—and no one would voice an objection of the King's guardian too loudly.

"My money's on the Marque girl," one of the servants said indiscreetly, as a group lugged a large platter past me.

"He's mad for t'other one," a companion objected.

"So he'll take her as a mistress," the first said, his shrug tipping the tray dangerously; an apple rolled to the edge and was crushed underfoot in the rushes. "He's no fool, this one. Why have one, when he can have both? You'll see."

My blood turned to ice. I had not thought of that. I turned back to look at the King. He was thoughtful now, withdrawn. After looking at Miriel when she arrived, he had not looked again. Were the servants correct? Would he do such a thing to secure peace? If Miriel's draw faded before he were to marry her, we would be lost.

I gritted my teeth, and returned to my perusal of the room. "Worry after," Temar had told me once. "When you observe, your mind must be clear. No expectations, no distractions." And so I watched, carefully. I watched the young women, I watched the bitterness of their elder sisters, reckoned too old to be a good match for the King. I watched the young men, neglected and trying to hide their surliness. I watched Wilhelm, trying not to stare at Miriel and yet yearning for her. I saw how he closed his eyes when he heard her laughter.

After I had strayed a little ways down the hall to listen in on the nobles, I returned to my post, waiting to see what the Dowager Queen might do. If I had been Isra, I thought, I would have let the King show his colors. I would have forced him to make a decision before the whole court, to let him stumble diplomatically. A chance to see what he might do if left to his own devices, and an opportunity to come to his rescue. But then, I had been raised in the household of the Duke, and trained by an assassin—and the Dowager Queen was an aging noblewoman, trained in needlepoint and dancing, and clinging desperately to her fading power.

Towards the end of the dinner, she dismissed the musicians, and whispered to de la Marque, who smoothly announced that the Council must meet at once at the conclusion of the meal. With this move, there would be no entertainments after dinner, no chances to dance or converse. No one would have the chance to see what the King might do, with Miriel returned to court, and there was no chance for the King to visit the maidens' rooms at the conclusion of the meal.

As if the danger was the King's opportunity to speak to Miriel with the eyes of the court on both of them. As if he had been lured away by dancing, and could be kept from her with such a simple ruse. Did Isra truly believe that if she only kept the King away for an hour, he would forget his infatuation and turn meekly to Marie with a proposal on his lips? The corner of my mouth quirked; I sobered at once as I realized that I was wearing the Duke's predatory smile on my face.

As the King left the hall without a backward glance, I thought I might be the only one who saw him murmur a few words to a page. Certainly, neither Isra nor de la Marque watched as the boy set off around the room, but I traced him as he walked towards the boys. He waited until each group began to withdraw, and then he detained Wilhelm. A word only, and Wilhelm nodded. I watched him leave, wondering if I might have been mistaken in what I saw, but as I waited for Miriel's table to be dismissed, another page crept up beside me.

"A message for you," he said awkwardly, unsure how to address me. "The lord says he'd be pleased to see you at the usual place." He was wide-eyed, sure that he was speaking to a lordling's mistress, unsure as to what the lordling might see in a girl who wore breeches. I was not minded to disillusion him; I nodded.

"Of course." I sent him away with a bow, and then I looked about for Temar. As I gazed about, I caught Miriel's eye. Just the slightest quirk of an eyebrow from her, just the tiniest nod in return from me. I escorted her back to her rooms, and went to find Temar.

I found him outside the Council chamber; he looked far from pleased to see me when he saw me standing in the hallway.

"Yes?" he asked. His usual ready smile for me was nowhere to be seen. His arms were crossed across his chest, his face set in a frown. His stance was unwelcoming, but there were too many people who might hear; I went close and stood on tiptoe to murmur in his ear.

"We're to meet the King. Midnight, the wine cellar, our building."

"Report to me afterwards." Temar's face had not changed in the slightest. At a loss for words, the gulf between us too wide for me even to think what to say, I bowed and left.

Chapter 4

"Check the hallway," Miriel ordered. She had set aside her fine jewelry, and exchanged her gown for her nightgown and robe, beautiful and modest, tied to the neck. She had twisted and turned in front of the mirror, getting ready, but there was little to be done with such a simple tableau. In the end, she had only dabbed rosewater on her wrists and her neck, and told me that it was time to go.

I opened her door as quietly as I could and peered down the hallway, both directions. I saw one pair of guards on their rounds, but no one else.

"We're going a different way tonight," I said.

"Why?" A note of mistrust appeared in her voice. She wondered what Temar might have instructed me, and I tried to swallow down the resentment that she should doubt me already, on the very first day we had the chance to act as allies. In truth, I could not have said that I trusted her, either. Words whispered in the darkness were one thing, but outside of the confines of her rooms were a dozen or more who would use us for their own ends. I tried to tell myself that neither of us would be able to look at the other without doubt yet, that such a thing would take time. When my silent admonishments to myself did not work, I resolutely turned my thoughts away; I had to trust, or I was lost. What else was there for me?

"If anyone sees us, we can say we were called to the Duke's rooms," I explained. Knowing she would be more carefully watched, and without Temar's advice, I had done the best I could to guarantee that her reputation would not be irrevocably damaged if we were seen. Miriel nodded at this idea, biting her lip, and we set off with Anna glaring after us.

Donnett had once told me how the Palace Guard would patrol a building, and so I was able to lead us out of their way with little trouble. We walked quickly, and I hoped desperately that no one would see us. I knew we would make a noteworthy pair if anyone caught a glimpse of us down a hallway: Miriel with her dark hair and her striking looks, dressed all in white like an angel; and myself, fair hair drawn back, dressed severely in black.

We made it to the Duke's rooms without being followed; I had lingered, each time we turned, to see if anyone would poke their head around a corner to watch us. Then we dashed down most of a long corridor and Miriel took a moment to slow her breathing before nodding to me to open the door to the cellars. I preceded her, as I always did, my left hand close to one of my little razor-sharp daggers, where it lay concealed in a pocked of my shirt. But I need not have worried: as usual, only the King awaited us—and, in a corner, Wilhelm. I bowed deeply, and gestured Miriel down the stairs.

The King held out his arms to her, but she hesitated, instead holding out her hands. Even in this moment of reunion, of triumph that he wanted her still, she would not be led into indiscretion; even with the Duke's assurance that drawing back would only lure the King on, I marveled at Miriel's daring. Who denied a king?

Miriel did, and he did not reproach her for it. He understood at once what she meant by holding back from him, and he cupped her small hands in his own, the overlarge hands of a growing boy. He even knelt at her feet.

"Forgive me," he said warmly. "I was so glad to see you. But, never—I shall never ask anything dishonorable of you." All of the passion of youthful love and honesty was in his face. I thought of the Duke's words, half promise and half threat, that the King would do precisely that before the year was out. "I shall protect you from the gossips," the King assured Miriel. "And so I must ask you to forgive me once more." I blinked at the sight of an anointed King, on his knees before a merchant girl's daughter, and begging her pardon.

"Forgive you? Why so, your Grace?" Miriel stared down at him in pretty confusion. I marveled at her ability to be so many different women, a dozen Miriels, who might know anything the King wanted her to know, and be ignorant of whatever he wished her not to know, who might never have been poisoned, who could be completely unaware that she was the target of intense hatred. To see her, I would never have known she had faced an assassination attempt.

"For neglecting you at dinner this evening. I could see the gossip at your arrival and I knew—" He broke off and squeezed her hands. "Ah, I would shield you from all of it, if I could."

"When you marry, all of this will be forgotten," Miriel said sweetly. She smiled a sad smile, but her tone was like milk. I, who had been waiting all evening to see how she would play this meeting, realized now what she meant to do. I raised my eyebrows. "Which is why you must do as you have done, your Grace. I do not reproach you, for I know why you must—believe me when I say that I know what must be. Do not speak of shielding me. We must shield *you*."

"To what purpose?" He could not fathom what she meant.

"For the sake of your marriage," Miriel said, her brow furrowing. "You must marry soon, your Grace. You and I know that our friendship is honorable. But if I were to speak with you at dinner, dance with you—it would give grist to the gossips, and I would never do that. I cannot stand between you and your duty. Your Queen must feel secure on her throne." It was masterfully done. At last he saw what she meant, and he shook his head violently.

"No, no—I swear to you, my Lady, *you* will be my Queen." It was a moment of victory, but Miriel did not revel in it. It was too fleeting: promises of the young, given in the dark of the night. She smiled sadly and, seeing that her point had hit home, twisted the knife.

"Oh, your Grace, I wish so much—" She broke off and blinked away tears. "But they will never allow it."

"The Council?" His voice grew dangerous. "It is *I* who am King, my Lady."

"Your Grace—"

"Call me by my name," he pleaded.

"I cannot!" The words were ripped from her. "I cannot do such a thing. It is to break my heart when you marry— and you *must* marry for advantage."

"What advantage would be greater than to have a Queen at my side who could advise me?" he asked persuasively. "Whose counsel I could trust?" She paused, as if struck by this—as if there were no counter to his logic.

"I..."

"Just think on it," he begged her. "If you would not wish to be my Queen, I...but I would rather have you than any woman the Council would suggest."

There was no safe answer. Careful of talking herself into a corner, Miriel only gazed at him, wide-eyed, her lips slightly parted;

to look at her, one would think no words could be sweeter to her ears.

"Now," he said tenderly. "I have been sorely in need of your counsel." He led her over to the great wine barrel where she always sat, and lifted her up, smiled up at her face. "Did your uncle pass along my regards? I did not wish to send a message to you, for I knew my pages would be watched, but I told him—" Miriel never wavered. She pretended that we had not been held, fearful, in seclusion, wondering what lies the King had been told, wondering if he cared for her still.

"Of course. Your words were a great comfort to me. I thank you, your Grace." He smiled and squeezed her hand.

"Good. Have you heard the news from Ismir?" I marveled at how quickly he cast aside love talk for statecraft, but Miriel was quick to match him. If only she loved him, I thought sadly, they would have made quite a pair. We could throw her towards the throne without the artful lies we needed now. But then I might as well wish for Miriel to have royal blood. There was no time to mourn what could not be.

Don't be soft, I told myself, and I shook my head to clear it.

"The slander that Duke Kasimir repeats?" Miriel frowned. "I try not to listen. It is beyond belief."

"They say he grieves deeply for his cousin," Garad said, fair to a fault.

"He may," Miriel said, unimpressed. "A man in grief may say anything. It is not Kasimir that I blame."

"It is not?" He blinked at her.

"No." Miriel shook her head. "I blame Dusan. He must grieve as well, but he does not spread such slander—and so he must know that to do so is wrong. And if he knows that, is it not his duty to be clear that the accusations are Kasimir's alone? Is it not his duty to be just to a fellow King?"

"I had not thought..." Garad blinked. "Ah, my Lady, you should be on the Council!" He laughed. "Why do they not see as clearly as you? You are correct, of course." He was grave now. "I must write to Dusan, and ask him why he does not put a stop to these accusations. How quickly it is solved! Can you dissolve the rebellion so easily?"

His amusement was mixed with genuine hope. He did not see Miriel's face flicker into blankness for a moment, and then back; when she smiled, he basked in the glow of it. At my side, Wilhelm shifted slightly, as if he would speak. I looked over, but he said nothing. I looked back to see the King clasping Miriel's hands in his own.

"Ah, I cannot tell you—the Council is useless, they hem and haw, they told me I should send troops, and then when I finally would, they say I cannot—the violence has died down. I must bring this Jacces to justice, and they say that I cannot. But what else is there?"

"Do they say why?" Miriel asked. I could almost hear her, cursing her uncle for a fool for not telling her what to say about this. Then, she realized the fact just as I did—I saw the flash in her face—that the Duke had left her way clear to say whatever she would. If he were angry, she could always protest later, wide-eyed, that he had given her no instructions.

"Yes, they say that to quarter troops among the people would cause wider unrest." His face twisted. "But there's no other way! His mob killed a man, hung him from the rafters of a cathedral! It cannot be allowed to rest. They must be brought to justice, and the people must see the leaders of this madness crushed utterly." Miriel tilted her head to the side, her face as relaxed as if she cared nothing for the people her King planned to kill.

"Have you sent another proclamation to them?" She was coming at it sideways, as she always did, and I sighed quietly. Miriel might say that she would put her quest for the throne ahead of the rebellion, but if there was a chance to avoid violence, she would play for it. She would be indirect, she would be sly—she would never let it come to open conflict—but Miriel would not stop trying to turn the King's mind to tolerance. I would have been a fool to expect otherwise, and from my weary amusement, I knew that I had never truly expected her to hold to that. Her life had been threatened time and again, and it was no longer enough for her to sit quietly by as she was used as a pawn; I knew myself enough to know that I envied her that conviction.

The King did not understand this; how could he? He frowned at her.

"What do you mean?"

"You could send a messenger, to read a proclamation in each town. Explain that you have been a just King, a kind King. Remind them that they have prospered under your rule. Ask them to cease their..." She searched for the word. "...continued unrest.

Tell them that now that they have ended the violence, they should give up Jacces, so that the matter of the murder may be closed. Remind them of the man's wife and child, who were robbed of their family. Remind them that it is a matter of honor." The people of the Norstrung Provinces would never give Jacces up; Miriel knew this. But she knew, also, that she might persuade the King to hold off on sending her uncle, and that was the most important thing. Her uncle would crush the rebellion with whatever weapons came to hand.

"I should not have to remind them of anything," the King said sulkily.

"Indeed not," Miriel concurred without hesitation; her smile was bland, her tone sweet. "But this way, if you are kind and gentle with them, and they do not cease their rebellion, none could complain if you were to send soldiers later."

He was struck by this. "You think this could work?"

I could see that Miriel yearned to say, *of course not.* She knew, as a child of common blood, that commoners yearned for their rights as much as did nobles. She knew that these men, educated and wealthy, would not simply go back to their homes and be content to have other men rule their lives.

"Who can say how they think?" she asked instead. "But it should remind them that they can have no complaint of you." She blushed at Garad's smile.

"You are a wonder," he said warmly. "You have solved these problems in minutes, when it takes the Council hours even to decide what to argue about." Miriel gave a peal of laughter, and I saw his face light up.

It was strange to watch, I thought. He had refused to listen to her pleas, exposed her to unthinkable danger. He was so blind that he truly thought he sought honest advice from her, and not the blind agreement that had surrounded him his whole life. I, who knew how bitterly Miriel had been disappointed by him, could not help but think poorly of him, but I also could not help but think that he was pressed upon by forces no ordinary man endured. He did not seek advice to rule his country harshly, or levy taxes on his people to fill his own coffers. His view of a golden age was not evil, only childish. Beyond his blindness, he was growing into a kind man.

I watched them as they spoke, their heads bent together, her finishing the lines of poetry he quoted, him offering her books from the royal library. I saw him as Temar had once encouraged me to do so: as a man. I watched the man and tried to see where he ended, and the Boy King began. And I watched my new ally, wondering which of her smiles were artifice, and which were borne of her genuine affection for the man he wished to be, but could never be.

When Wilhelm said, sounding pained, that it was time to go, the King kissed Miriel's hand and lifted her down from her seat. He said something for her ears only, and her face warmed.

"I know I should wish it," she said, and then she took a step back and curtsied formally, as she always did when she left him. At the bottom of the stairs, she cast a look over her shoulder, and blushed when she saw him watching her still. She bit her lip and turned back to climb the stairs, a vision of modesty, holding her robe closed at her neck.

"What did he say?" I asked, low-voiced, as we half-ran down the corridor to her rooms.

"That every time he lifted me to sit there, he wished he was lifting me to the throne." Her smile was serene. She might have been speaking the most beautiful of love poetry.

"That's..." I could not find the words.

"I believe you want to say, very promising. Yes?"

"Of course, yes. My Lady."

The next morning, dutifully, I brought my report to the Duke.

"She speaks the truth," Temar said, when I had finished. He had been watching me as I gave my report, while I tried to ignore his sullen presence. My temper was not improved by the feeling that they had tricked me: that they would not have known what had happened in the cellar if I had not told them. I wondered if there was any way to find out that would not end with me being beaten.

The Duke gave a grim nod at his assassin. In the early morning light, I could see his age in the shadows under his eyes, the glint of grey in his beard. He stared off into the distance with eyes as cold and black as jet.

"She is right, it is promising," he said at length. He let his tone show that it was not quite promising enough. I, who would need to report this to Miriel, wondered just how I would convey that.

"Her words on the rebellion were passable. Tell her to remind him that such ideas are dangerous. He cannot become complacent."

"Yes, my Lord." I had the suicidal urge to point out that the King had always thought as much, and it had been Miriel who tried to make him think otherwise. As any liar, I was amazed that the Duke could not see my subterfuge, plain as day. I was especially nervous when he added, "Someone has told him to be lenient. Not the fools on the Council. Find out for me." I saw my opening.

"He said that the High Priest spoke to him of it, my Lord."

"He did?" The same question could have been asked with the lift of an eyebrow, but the Duke could not seem to believe his ears.

"Yes, my Lord."

"What did he say exactly?" the Duke demanded, as relentless as ever in the search for knowledge of his enemies. I thought back.

"That the earliest scriptures were quite populist." I began to frown. Something was coming together, close to the surface. I tried to keep my face straight, but the Duke had not even noticed. His snort told me what he thought of the High Priest's theology.

"Does Isra know?"

"The King thinks not. He said that the High Priest came to see him alone."

"Huh." The Duke looked across the room, as if he were seeing across leagues, across decades. "Is the King pious?" I frowned, trying to think of our meetings.

"He has never spoken of the Gods in our presence. He swears by them sometimes. I don't think so."

"Tell Miriel not to collude with that. She is not to nag him, but she should be able to disclaim that she is devout herself."

"Yes, my Lord." Useless to ask him what his reasons were. "Do you have any further instructions for Miriel?"

"She is to continue to eat only what Marie eats. I will take no chances with her in the confusion of a banquet. You, however, may resume your lessons. She will be with her tutors during the day, and the other maidens. It should be safe enough. As to your lessons..." He gave me a hard look. "Tell me what you have learned so far."

"Fighting with dagger, shortsword, shield, and spear. Tumbling, wrestling, throwing. Pressure points. Spying techniques. Basic medicines." I paused. "Poisons."

"Ah."

We had never spoken of the assassination attempt. The

Duke had not allowed us to speak any defense of ourselves on the night that he found me in her rooms, and he had not given us an opening to speak of it since then. But from the gleam in his eyes, I knew now that he knew of it. And, unexpectedly, anger rose up so strongly that I nearly choked with it. He might know because Temar had known the signs of it, or Anna had reported our words to him, and he might know of it because he had been the one who gave us poison, himself.

"You know of it, don't you, my Lord?" I challenged him.

"Know of what?" I clenched my fists at the useless question. If he wanted to drag this out, well, then I would say it outright.

"Someone tried to poison her."

"Yes. And you." His face gave away nothing. He watched me like a basilisk, his gaze half paralyzing me with fear.

"We don't know who," I said, suddenly awkward. In the face of his stare, I repented of my challenge.

"Indeed. Many people had cause to do so." He was enjoying this, I realized, and so I gave up the pretense of subtlety.

"Was it you?" He smiled. My rudeness was private, and so he found it amusing. He enjoyed blunt speech, so long as it did not reflect poorly on him.

"I, too, had cause to do so." That was no answer, and he knew that I would see it at once. He smiled as he saw me struggling to find words. "So, think on it, Catwin—" it was terrifying that he remembered my name "—with that clever little mind of yours. You set yourself up to be my enemy. Think on it, and decide if you wish to remain as such. I want you to go back to Miriel and tell her what we have spoken of. Bid her think on it."

"You wouldn't ever truly forgive me," I said, testing.

"I am not wasteful. Think on that as well, but that thought is for you alone. You may go."

As I walked back to Miriel's rooms, I found myself frowning. The Duke would not say if he had tried to kill her or not, and I could not decide what I thought. Was he only trying to benefit from another's actions, making sure that Miriel feared him? Or had he thought her too unbiddable, had he seen an opportunity be rid of her and pin the crime on one of his rivals, all in one move? Had he known that she would be used against him by his enemies, and then—when he could not even control her himself—he decided that he would no longer be bothered with her?

And why would he ask not only her, but also me, if I wished

to be his enemy? I wondered if that was why Temar had glowered so; he would not forgive me, but the Duke would. Beyond my own apprehension that the Duke watched me, I found a glimmer of hope. A crack between Temar and the Duke. If only we played our cards right, Miriel and I might do well from that.

Chapter 5

The next morning, my training resumed, and I approached it with as much intensity as I could muster. The first attack had been poison, by a named enemy—more intended to frighten Miriel than to take her life. It had not even been sh who had been the true target, but instead the Duke. And the second attack, for all it had been a clear attack at Miriel herself, had been poison as well. We were targets for our own sake now, and I feared that I was not prepared. Poison was one thing, but who could say what the next attempt might be: a knife in a dark hallway? A bribed palace guardsman? I insisted that Donnett dress in his full gear, with all of his weapons, and then we sparred as close as I dared to a real fight, every clash filled with the desperate fear that if I could not do this, I could not protect Miriel and myself.

"What's burning you?" Donnett asked when we finally broke away. He wiped sweat away from his brow. "I've never seen ye fight like that."

"Something happened," I said grimly. "I need to keep training. I need to be better."

"Aye? What happened, then?"

I looked over at his easy, honest face and felt the first glimmer of doubt. I knew this man's life story, I knew the names of his sister's children and the one whore he saw in the city, always the same girl. I knew what he thought of nobles and their fights, and I knew he was loyal to the Duke. All of a sudden, that felt like nothing. I wondered what he might be hiding.

He saw it. "Someone betrayed you. And now you're wondering who you can trust."

"Yes," I said shortly. To avoid meeting his eyes, I began stretching.

"I'd hope you'd know better than to think I had a part it in, lad. Think on it if you don't believe me. You know I'm not a one for sneaking around doing nobles' dirty work for them. You shouldn't think I'd be workin' with whoever it was."

I sighed. "It could have been anyone. Not just nobles. That's the thing."

He did not respond at once. Instead, he joined me in stretching. We ran through the stretches he had taught me, and then he watched me run through the stretches Temar had taught me. Only when I had run out of things to do, and was sitting silently on the ground, did Donnett speak again.

"Was it the little lady, too?" I nodded silently. "And somethin' as we'd all have known about if they'd succeeded?" I nodded again. "I thought as much. Then you're in a pickle, little one."

"What d'you mean?"

"Think on it," he said. "If the little lady had died, who would've been the first ones everyone suspected?"

"Guy de la Marque, the Dowager Queen...maybe the rebellion, if they were clever." I did not say the Duke, I only held up a fourth finger, and Donnett, to my surprise, nodded.

"He doesn't like surprises, that one. And I hear she gave him one. And you would've been part of it." He gave me the knowing look of a parent. "Never ye mind that now, I don't want t'know. What ye should be doing, though, is askin' yourself—would any of them risk everyone thinkin' it was them? Say what you will about the King's guardian, he's not a dim one."

"Well, what do you mean by that, then?" But I knew what he meant, even before he said it.

"My money says the one who betrayed you is someone you wouldn't suspect."

We never spoke of that again, but we began to spar harder, and for longer. Donnett no longer laughed at me and told me to hit once and run away quickly. He knew that I would not have that chance in a true fight; a lady in a tight gown and silk slippers could not run away fast.

From somewhere, I was not sure where, Donnett procured a dressmaker's dummy, and the two of us began to spar to protect it. I started next to it, or far away, but whatever the case, it was my job to keep him from reaching it. Donnett had no clever line, as Temar did: *now you're dead, and Miriel is dead.* Whenever he tapped the mannequin with his sword, he only looked over at me, and then raised an eyebrow. If I did not understand the maneuver he had used, he would explain it. When I did understand it, we went again.

Every day, without fail, I arrived for my lessons with Roine soaked in sweat and exhausted beyond belief. At first, she complained of it. Then, seeing that I was not going to stop, she simply allotted me the same amount of work and said only that I was expected to finish it by the next day. She did not answer my questions for help, saying that I must learn to apply myself to all of my lessons.

She was very short with me in those weeks. We spoke very little—Roine feared for me, and my stubborn insistence on staying at court had turned her fear to anger. The first time I had been allowed to see her, she had held me close, embracing me and crying, and when I had at last come for lessons, she had taken my hands in hers and begged me once again to run away.

"Do you believe me now?" She had demanded. "I told you that you would be a target, and it isn't worth it," she said urgently. "It isn't, Catwin. You are only a child, and no child should need to look over her shoulder as you do."

"I have to stay," I had replied. "Did you not once say that fate lay heavy on me?" It was childish, to throw her words back at her, and I was sorry when she paled at once. She had no response to that, and I added, "How could I leave Miriel now?"

Irritation had flashed across Roine's face. "Do you think she has the slightest loyalty to you?" she demanded. "Do you think she cares at all for your welfare?"

I only shrugged; I did not want to admit that I was never sure of Miriel's friendship. When we met in the evenings, huddled together over the table and speaking in whispers, it was to share more information than we ever had together. We planned together for our meetings with the Duke now. I always told Miriel the secrets I had learned from the servants, and she told me what her fellow maidens had said and done at lessons and at dinner.

We build up our own theories of who might be making a power play in the Council. We waited, we listened, we watched to see who spoke to whom; I told Miriel which lords were at odds with each other, and she told me which of the maidens were friends, and the gossip of the ladies. We pored over histories and lineages and found the fault lines that ran, spidery, through the court, the long-buried resentments that Miriel could one day exploit, just as her uncle did now. We made no move to upset her uncle's plans, but every day we became less powerless, less isolated and ignorant.

And yet, sometimes it was as if those days of forced seclusion had never been. Our silent camaraderie had been as a dream: not only fleeting but forgotten. Temar's suspicion grated on me every day, and I could not refute it, only hope to wait out his anger and the Duke's condescension. In the constant glare of the court, Miriel was given a dozen slights and insults each day, raising her temper; and she could never let it out there. And so Miriel was as quick to criticize me as she had ever been at the start, and I was quick to rise to it.

Now she had a new theme: beauty and ladylike behavior. I was wanting in both, and she was quick to remind me of it, taunting me about my britches and my daggers, reminding me that no proper girl went about without skirts, that I would never find a husband... With others, I had always been able to shake off such words, but Miriel possessed the innate ability to find the very sorest point, to twist her words so that they slid under my skin.

Soon, I found I was hotly defending myself against her taunts, and not long after that, I started hissing back insults of my own: Miriel was too short, she'd never been good with numbers, that gown made her look sallow. I was outmatched, and I knew it, but I would not back down. Since our pact of friendship, we had been either in collusion, or at each other's throats. We fought like stable cats, the only check on our behavior being that the Duke would punish us both if he knew.

And yet, I clung to the belief that Miriel held to our alliance, as I did. We had never openly fought before, and it was almost as if we were equals now—and the moments of cooperation could not be ignored. Sometimes I wondered if we didn't fight so much because we were each other's only ally, the only one to whom we could show our resentment, our fear, our anger—and our talents. To do so with anyone else would be death.

And Miriel was quick to smile at me now. She had noticed when I was injured after bad bouts with Temar or Donnett, and had once sent for a balm from Roine, presenting it with a curious half-smile, as if she were still uncertain on how to give gifts; I thought of her presents of new clothes and knives, and how she always brushed away my thanks. Miriel was kind, and she had never been taught how to be—she was learning on her own. I never knew what might be behind her eyes, I could not always see when she wore her court mask and when she did not—and often, it took her hours to lower her guard. But I liked to think that Miriel had some loyalty to me.

I could not admit any of this to Roine, there were too many secrets behind it. More, I was almost ashamed to speak of it to her, whose hard eyes showed how little she thought of Miriel's loyalty. Only months ago, I had been the one complaining of Miriel, while Roine told me not to be so hard on her. Now, in the face of Roine's anger, I was too embarrassed by my own change of heart to disillusion her. I only shrugged, uncomfortably aware that this was the first time I was keeping a secret from her.

"I can't leave her," I said simply. "You of all people know that she's in real danger. I can't leave her."

Roine had pleaded with me. She had cajoled, she had begged, she had even taken me by the shoulders and shaken me, and told me not to be so stubborn. In the end, she had sunk into unhappy silence and now would barely speak to me at all. I tried to lure her out of her bad humor, but to no avail.

"Did you hear the news from Ismir?" I asked her one day.

"More noblemen puffing themselves up like cocks in a stable yard?" she asked acerbically, not looking up. I suppressed a sigh.

"Duke Kasimir says that he has proof that Heddred was behind Vaclav's death," I said. I cast a look over her, and saw that she was shredding leaves, her hands moving delicately. "What do you think of that?" I asked her.

"I think it changes nothing," she responded. "Kasimir wants war, he'll say anything to get it, and enough here want it that he'll get it, too."

"The King wants peace," I said, and Roine shook her head.

"He's only a boy. He'll fold soon enough. The best he can do is pray."

I said nothing. Roine's sudden turn to faith perplexed me. She had raised me with her own strict adherence to the scriptures, but all of her scorn towards the priests and their rituals. Roine had worked to heal others, to help the poor and the sick, and disdained the church with its ornaments and jewels. She prayed in her own rooms only, saying that she preferred to revere the Gods than their priests.

And yet, since we had come to the palace, she had prayed more often, and now she sometimes said to me, "I am going to pray," and I knew she was going to the cathedrals themselves. I had once seen her kneeling alone in one of the Palace chapels, staring up at the altar, and I had crept away so that I would not disturb her in her prayer. What she found there now, I could not say.

Temar also haunted the chapels now, but I knew what he

43

was watching for: the High Priest, and the Dowager Queen. The Duke had viewed Isra's reliance on the High Priest's advice only as a key to her, until I had told him of the High Priest's thoughts on the rebellion. The Duke was now frankly at a loss, suspicious of the Dowager Queen and her advisor, wondering if it was possible that Isra plotted to unseat her own son.

There was little chance that she would be so indiscreet, and so blasphemous, as to plot in a chapel, but Temar wished to observe the comings and goings from the High Priest's apartments and offices. Often enough, I knew, he would leave the Duke in Council meetings and creep across the palace to the royal chapel, where he would lurk quietly in the shadows and wait for what he might see.

I knew this, because I followed him; Temar no longer told me where he spent his time when he was not training me. Before, Temar would have told me about his spying as a lesson illustration, asking me where I would hide in a given room, or from where I might observe a specific event. He shared information with me, if not entirely freely, at least as between friends. Then, I had thought shyly that perhaps he was proud to have me as his protégé, and yet I had doubted that it could be so. Temar was a master of his craft, and I was little more than a street urchin: sneaky, yes, but without the same eternal watchfulness. I was growing dangerous, but Temar had been honed until everything about him was a weapon.

I had thought that I could hardly be a credit to him, and I had always striven to overcome that. Now, I could see that he had been proud, and that he had taught me well enough for me to deceive him. The truth was bitter indeed—Temar's pride in me had made the sting of my betrayal far worse for him. It did not matter that Temar had been lying to me on the Duke's orders, trying to limit my training in case he should need to best me; he had not truly expected that I could deceive him, outwit him.

It was Temar who must look the Duke in the face and tell him that I had learned my sneaking and my deception from the Duke's own Shadow, and that Temar, consummate spy that he was, had not seen to the heart of what I was hiding. It was a blow to his pride that he had misjudged my character, that he had not been able to see my deception at once—but it was more than that alone: he must also accept that I, who adored him, had lied to him without a flicker. In his anger, he could not see that I was torn apart with remorse; he thought my betrayal cold blooded.

Even in the midst of my guilt, I knew it to be ridiculous.

Temar was an enemy. I had always suspected as much, and I repeated Miriel's words over and over to myself: *it doesn't much matter who did it.* I had always hoped, and still hoped, that Temar might not be the one who had set out to kill me—but, I told myself, it did not matter. He aligned himself with the Duke, who would have killed me. He was an enemy.

My guilt was meaningless, misplaced, and worse than that, it was dangerous. There was no sense in mourning a friendship that had been doomed from the start. I told myself that, very sternly, trying to mimic Roine's voice, or Miriel's. They would chide me for my soft feelings, and I chided myself. But it did not help. I had lied to a man who was my friend, and that had hurt him, and it did not matter that this was a game of intrigue—it still hurt. I still felt guilty when I watched him, and saw the wall behind his eyes.

It would not be until much later that I could look back and realize that Temar had been a shrewder judge of character than he realized. He had sought a tiny copy of himself, a child he could mold into an assassin as he was, and he had found one. His error lay in seeking a child with the same fierce loyalty that made him so valuable to the Duke. He had asked me to shape myself to Miriel, to be her shadow and her servant in all things, and yet neither Temar nor the Duke had thought far enough to realize that I would be loyal to Miriel and not to them.

I wonder, now, if Temar ever understood that fact.

So, denied his friendship, I followed him about the palace, and I had the chance to see his genius in action. It turned out, in the wake of the King's revelation and the firestorm of near-scandal, that Temar was a courtier without match—only he pandered to servants, who then whispered to their masters. I heard some of the wild rumors that had swept the castle, each more lurid than the last, but by now those had been dismissed as wild fancy; it took determination to pry them out of my paid informant in the stables.

No, by now Miriel was no longer a whore in the making, but instead the tragic love of the King, an icon of virginity, his only friend. I heard detailed stories of how she had sworn that she loved him more than life itself, and would rather die than cast a shadow onto the name of the shining prince who would bring a Golden Age to Heddred. She had been his councilor, an advocate for peace, a clear-eyed advisor, a defender of his ideals.

Everywhere—everywhere—I walked, Temar had gone before me, with a whisper here, a shocked denial there. His network of informants was now turned outwards, and I marveled at it, and sighed that his chilly demeanor forbade questions on just how he had accomplished such a marvel. Far from sharing delighted secrets as to how he had protected the Duke's interest, our lessons were a great show of stilted awkwardness. For days, Temar barely looked at me. He lectured me on throws and holds until I was fairly yawning, and only practiced them with me when he could find nothing more to say. We moved together like dancers, politely avoiding each other's eyes.

He could not be cold to me forever, but the thaw was very slow. First, he forgot himself and helped me up from the floor after a throw. Then it was an absent-minded greeting when I came into the room, and later a careless laugh when we saw a lordling trip over his absurd shoes. I did all I could to hasten the return to normalcy, one day bringing him a roll when I knew he had not been able to have his dinner, another day arriving early to set out the gear so he would not have to, and sometimes he smiled at me before remembering his mistrust.

We spoke as little as possible on the matter of Miriel and the King, and we never once mentioned the matter of the poison in my food. We both knew what I had done, from the lies to the evasions, and I saw how much that hurt him. I knew better than to ask Temar outright, as I had asked the Duke, if he had put the poison in my food. I did not know what I would do if the answer was yes, and Temar, for all his secretive qualities, was not a commander and a politician—where the Duke had only stared, Temar's face would flicker. I knew that I would see the truth, and I feared it even more than I feared another assassination attempt.

Miriel saw it. Indeed, she saw more than I wished she would, and our alliance was young enough still that she doubted me. We were always circling each other, clinging together for comfort and sharing secrets, and still fearing whenever we saw a hint of betrayal. It had been simmering beneath the surface for weeks, and it came to head one day. Temar had brought us a message from the Duke and then withdrawn, and I looked after him down the hall.

"Don't look at him like that," Miriel hissed at me, and I turned to her with a ready scowl. I was bad-tempered, aching from my lessons, and was baited into a fight easily enough.

"Like what?" I demanded.

"You love him," she said flatly. "You're besotted with him."

"With the man who might have put poison in our food," I said, trying to make a joke of it. She did not smile.

"I know," she said coldly. "I would have thought that you would learn your lesson from that. But you have not. So, now I am ordering you: put aside your feelings for him."

"He trained me..." My voice trailed off as I struggled to put words to it. Miriel was surrounded by her own kind, young women seeking advantageous marriages, nobles brokering power. Temar was the only other one like me in the world. He was my rival and my friend, in a way that no one else could be, not even Miriel. He was the only one like me in the world.

Miriel did not care. She stared at me with such hard eyes that I wondered if I had been mistaken in my assessment of her. I wondered if she had no heart at all, like a clockwork doll.

"The day will come when you and he will be declared enemies," she said brutally. "So you forget your feelings for him now. Because otherwise we're both dead, and I won't die for your folly."

"Like your folly?" Wilhelm. It was the only weapon I had, and even my shame at pressing her on her very sorest point did not keep me from doing so. She clenched her hands and swallowed, and I attacked on another front. "Or the rebellion?"

"That's different. They could be our allies one day, I have a plan for it. Temar will always be your enemy."

I hated her for that. I could have reminded her that I watched her all the time, and that I knew she wanted to dislike the King more than she did. I could have reminded her that she slipped sometimes, and started to tell him what she really thought about one topic or another. I wanted to tell her that I was not just a Shadow.

I had made my vow, however. I had told her that I was on her side, only hers. I had forsworn the complicated loyalties of a human. And for some reason, whenever I opened my mouth to tell her that she could take her vow back, for I was done with it, I could never make the words come out. Even as I told myself that I was a fool, even as I waited to be proven wrong, I could not help but hope that Miriel had meant her vow just as I had meant mine.

The last days of winter were not a time of joy. They were a time of gathering war, of learning to navigate the snake pit of the court, and Miriel and I did so in a strange isolation. We could only half-trust each other, and we had sworn not to trust anyone else at all; I, at least, knew now that this was more difficult than I had reckoned by far, and I tried to hold my resentment close. I would never have said it out loud, but in the darkness of the night sometimes I thought that Roine had been right: no good came of courts. I should just leave.

Chapter 6

In the torrential downpour that marked the end of winter, a messenger arrived from Dusan of Ismir, demanding to see the King alone. The pageboys had huddled inside, out of the rain, and so it was only the Royal Guard, fiercely loyal to the King, who saw the man. It was the Royal Guard, who, now accustomed to the avidly inquisitive nature of the court and Council, and the increasingly secretive nature of the King himself, escorted the messenger directly to the King's chambers.

Thus, there was no one to remark on the fact that the King had received a messenger, and no one to call a meeting of the Council. No one knew to be listening at the door when the messenger announced very simply that King Dusan now held proof that his former heir had been assassinated by an agent of none other than a member of the King's Council. Holding proof, Dusan required that Garad bring the man to justice.

The King, ever unpredictable and more than slightly unsure of himself, ordered the messenger held in the royal presence chambers, and instructed the man to speak to no one else, not any of the Council, not even the Dowager Queen, on pain of death. Then he sent a messenger, at a dead run, to find me and bid that Miriel come to the King at once, discreetly, for reasons he could not name.

Donnett let me go early, with a glower at the messenger, and I toweled off, trying not to wonder what this strange summons might mean. I wondered if we should tell the Duke, and at length decided only to send a message—with no thoughts on what the summons might mean, how could the Duke tell Miriel what to say? And so the only remaining puzzle was how to get Miriel away from her tutors and to the royal chambers themselves without being seen. Now was not the time to go exploring in the tunnels below the buildings.

In the end, the best I could do was bid her change her gown and put on a cloak. I told Anna to send a message to the Duke, and then I led Miriel on a circuitous path, through kitchens and servants' corridors, finally coming into the main hallway near the entrance to the King's rooms. It was a back corridor, ostensibly blocked off from the throng of people who waited near the main doors for a glimpse of him, and two guards looked round sharply at the sound. I checked that no one else was about, and then beckoned Miriel out of the servants' corridor.

For a moment, the two of us only stared around ourselves in shock. We came to the Palace proper for dinner and services, but we had never been allowed to roam around. Even I, who sneaked to the library every few weeks, had never spared a glance for my surroundings. In daylight, the Palace, even this back hallway, was so beautiful that I could hardly believe my eyes. The columns that flanked the windows were carved in the shape of birds, fish, leaping deer, each different and perfect. The windows themselves were set with panes of colored glass, so that light of scarlet, sapphire, and royal purple was cast on the rich marble floors. Up on the vaulted ceilings were painted tableaux of the saints: Saint Eral with his sheaf of wheat, Saint Nerian with her quill and parchment.

The Royal Guard cared little for our amazement. "Who are you?" one of the two demanded. "You—are you carrying weapons?"

I froze, but Miriel drew back the hood of her gown and smiled her seductive smile, and the guards relaxed at once. None of them, I was sure, could be unaware of the King's infatuation, and they had been told to admit her. With another suspicious glare at me, they opened the doors and ushered us inside, from one richly-appointed chamber into another, and another. We passed through an antechamber, hung with velvets and silks and with a throne for the King to receive guests, through a reading room with brocade couches and hanging lamps, and into the King's own privy chamber itself.

I had never seen the King so distraught. When we entered the room, he was prowling around like a caged lion, and his eyes looked haunted. Miriel let her cloak slip off her shoulders, and as I caught it and looked for somewhere to hang it, she went to him at once, her hands held out.

"Your Grace," she said tenderly. "What can have happened?"

"The worst thing," he said. "I can't think what to do." He cast his eyes around the room, as if planning an escape, then sighed heavily and looked back to her. His shoulders slumped. "Kasimir was right. I cannot believe it, but it was so. Vaclav was assassinated, there was poison in his food."

"But by whom?" Miriel asked. I could hear worry in her

voice. Had it been her uncle? The King dropped into a chair and sank his head into his hands. His voice was muffled, but we heard him clearly in the empty room.

"Gerald Conradine." In the stunned silence that followed, Miriel cast me a glance, and then, tentatively, reached out to touch the King's shoulder.

"Your Grace…"

"It is the worst thing that could have happened," he whispered. "The father of my friend. I had thought the problems behind us, that the bad blood between Conradine and Warden was gone. But what can I do, but bring him to justice?"

I saw Miriel's mind working furiously. "Do you believe, your Grace, truly, that it was him? To what purpose would he do such a thing?"

I could see the path, circuitous and dark: Gerald Conradine, having disposed of the peaceful heir to Ismir, would wait for Heddred to go to war, the Duke and Guy de la Marque leading the charge while he waited behind. And then, with a scattering of bribes, the two leaders would fall, the army might turn against them. Old loyalties ran deep, who could say but that the soldiers might remember the last Conradine king? And with a few assassinations, it would be done, the kingdom back under the warlords.

I had never trusted the man's bland, smooth smile. And—I realized with a start—might he not have aimed to kill more than one person with poison? Few enough people knew who I was, but Wilhelm might have told his father of me. And Gerald fit with Donnett's theory: he was a man many would never have suspected, had Miriel been killed.

No, if she had been found murdered, Guy de la Marque would have borne the brunt of the suspicion, and Marie would be deemed unsuitable for marriage to the King. With Miriel gone, and Marie discredited, Gerald might well have a clearer path to the throne: Cintia. Cintia, well-placed to admit assassins to the King's chambers; Cintia, who could be trusted to step aside for her father and mother when Garad was dead, or simply rule as a puppet queen.

I did not like the fact that the list of our enemies only grew longer, the more I thought about it.

"Yes, I can believe he would do it," the King whispered. "He told me that the peace with Ismir would never hold. Before the assassination, he urged the Council to invade. He did not like that I would not do so. I only wanted peace..."

"You cannot think of what could have been. There are only two paths to peace now," Miriel said simply. "Your Grace, you must either prove that Gerald Conradine did not have Duke Vaclav assassinated, or you must hold him up to justice. If you admit it, but shelter him, there will be bad blood indeed—between Heddred and Ismir."

"How could I prove that he did not do it?" the King asked.

"What is the evidence against him?" Miriel countered.

"A man who came forward, saying he had information for the King. He said that he had been paid to bring poison to a man in the Duke's household, but had not known why. The servant was long gone, but they found the man who paid him, and he said under torture that it had been the Conradines who sent him." Miriel did not even flinch at the mention of torture; sentiment was far from her. She knelt gracefully on the floor of the room, at his side, her skirts pooling around her.

"Who tortured him?" she asked.

"I don't know who." The King shook his head. "But what does it—"

"Was it Kasimir's men?" she asked, delicately. "For we know that a man will say anything, under torture." From her knowing smile, she expected the King to understand her, but he only frowned.

"We can discredit him, but that gives us nothing," he said, frustration rising in his voice. To her credit, no irritation showed in Miriel's eyes.

"Perhaps not. But Kasimir is power-hungry, and he has been outspoken about many things. One of them: Voltur. We know that Vaclav desired only peace, he would not have regained Voltur to avenge Kasimir's father. Say..." Miriel paused, and looked off into the distance. "Say that Kasimir approached Gerald Conradine: in return for Gerald's help in assassinating Vaclav, so that there should be no trace leading to Kasimir, and in return for Voltur, Kasimir would help the Conradines reclaim the throne. Gerald refused, and Kasimir vowed revenge."

"Is that true?" the King asked, astounded. I tried not to sigh at his ready belief, but Miriel was more controlled. She only shrugged her slim shoulders and smiled up at him.

"It could be," she said, with a cunning smile. "That is all. It is highly plausible, is it not? Who benefitted most from Vaclav's assassination? It was not Gerald Conradine, it was Kasimir. If you tell Dusan of this, he will be unable to name you as wrong. And—" she held up one finger "—were you to convince him, Dusan would choose another heir. A more peaceful heir."

The King gnawed at his lip, and I remembered how quick his mind was, when he was not staring into Miriel's eyes. I saw, too, that he was not above this lie. He did not have the look of a man who objects on moral ground, but instead the look of a man who fears only that his lie might be found out.

"How could I explain why I did not warn him of Kasimir's treachery?" he asked, at last. I turned to look at Miriel; I could not have answered it myself. But she was equal to the challenge.

"You were ill," Miriel said simply. "*You* were never told. Gerald Conradine took the offer directly to Guy de la Marque, who did not wish to trouble you with it."

"That would cast Guy in a poor light," the King observed, and for a moment, I thought Miriel had gone too far in her uncle's interests. The King would see that she was undermining every other powerful player in the Court.

"Truly?" Miriel asked, as if surprised; she had anticipated this. "Think a moment—Guy de la Marque and Dusan fought against each other in battle. De la Marque has no reason to love Dusan, nor protect him, and would Dusan have believed such a warning from the mouth of his enemy? Would he not have seen it merely as an attempt to sow discord? I think many on the Council would believe that he had done the right thing. Even Dusan should understand that."

"Ah." The King settled back in his chair, and Miriel gave a little smile to herself. She was correct, of course—such an action would be understandable. And yet, with the littlest change of inflection as she told the story in the maidens' chamber, with the most casual comment dropped at just the right place in a conversation, Guy de la Marque would come to be known as the guardian who embroiled his King in a political fiasco, and exposed his rival to shame and suspicion.

"I would have to take this to the Council," the King said, finally. I marveled at his ability to discard the notion that a councilor of his might have assassinated a future head of state. The fact no longer mattered to Garad at all; did the Court warp all it touched? "Gerald would agree, of course, but Guy..."

"I am sure that he would understand that Heddred and Ismir need peace," Miriel said sweetly.

"Yes," the King said, but he spoke uncertainly. "Here, help me prepare what I should say..."

As we left a half an hour later, creeping once more into the servants' corridor, I stole a look over at Miriel. She had a little half-smile on her lips, as satisfied as the cat that got the cream. We walked in silence for most of the way back to her rooms, my disquiet growing ever greater.

"You realize he might well have done it," I said, finally.

"It's likely enough," she said with a shrug. "But it can only be good for us. Now the King will always believe that Gerald owes him a debt, and whether or not Gerald did it, he will also be at the King's mercy."

"Are we not even going to ponder who might have done it? You think it's wise to leave a murderer in our midst?" I asked sharply. We paused as we emerged into the kitchens and crossed to the stairs, a few of the cooks taking sidelong glances at Miriel.

When we were safe in her rooms, Miriel turned to me with her arms crossed.

"All of them are murderers," she said. "Any of them would have done it if they thought they could get away with it."

"Yes," I said. "But only one of them *did* do it." I thought of the Council and frowned. "Probably. It was probably not all of them."

"Oh, what does it matter?" Miriel threw her hands up. "Why do you care? So we know to watch him now. But why worry?"

"What if he's the one who tried to kill *us*?" I demanded, and she froze in the act of taking off her cloak. I pressed the point home. "Poison used to kill Vaclav, and then poison used to try to kill us. And who benefits if you die? Not Guy de la Marque, everyone will suspect him. The Council might even block the King from choosing Marie. But suppose you were gone, the King would grieve, and who would he turn to for comfort?"

"Wilhelm, I suppose." She did not understand me.

"Yes, exactly. Wilhelm. And *he* could suggest that perhaps there was another woman suitable for the throne." I could not believe that Wilhelm would be party to a plot to kill Miriel, but if he did not know...

"Cintia," Miriel said, her lips hardly moving. She pressed her face into her hands, and then raised her face again, looking stricken.

"Wilhelm would have…" She shook her head, and whether she was denying the thought, or telling herself to set aside her feelings, I could not know. Then she sighed and straightened her shoulders. "We must speak to my uncle."

"And what if *he's* the one who tried to kill us?" I asked bluntly. "Then we gain nothing. We're in this just the two of us. We shouldn't tell him yet."

"We gain nothing anyway," Miriel said. "Except that now he'll have a tool to destroy another rival. So you choose, Catwin. You can mistrust him, and make nothing of it, or you can mistrust him, and use his power to destroy those who could harm us." She saw me hesitate. "You knew what you were getting into when you swore to be my ally," she reminded me. "You knew that we would have to side with anyone we could. You knew then that my uncle might have been the one who ordered us killed, and you still agreed to be on my side. Don't you turn coward now."

"It's not cowardly to think about what we should share with him and what we should not," I protested. "*You* agreed that we were our own side, not his. I think you just don't want to believe that he could have done it."

"Oh, I don't know," Miriel said. She tilted her head to the side. "It would be convenient. It would make so many of our enemies the same person, don't you think?" She frowned at the look on my face. "What *are* you thinking? You look peculiar." She wrinkled her nose at me, and sighed when I did not respond at once.

I thought on the way she had looked on the day that she first realized that the King would not hear her advice. I remembered talking to her in the aftermath of the attempt on our lives, and the passionate intensity in her voice when she had spoken to Roine of the populist movement in the south. Miriel was quick to anger, and for a few short days, she had been quick to laugh, too; after, she had sunk deep into her misery. Her blood ran hot, not icy. Miriel was not this strange, cold woman who cared only for ambition, who made a joke of this attempt on her life.

"I think that you're casting away everything of you," I said slowly. "You *should* feel betrayed that your blood kin would try to kill you, you're only pretending that you don't. You're playing a part, and sometimes you forget what's you and what's the other Miriel. You said you would be forsworn if you needed to be, my Lady, but you deny yourself every day for no reason at all."

"Now you're just talking nonsense," she said. But she said it uncertainly, and when I caught a glimpse of her eyes, I could see her fear.

She was very quiet that night, and the next, and the next after that. I was pleased to have found words for the strangeness in Miriel's eyes, but I was no less disturbed by it than she was. For, to tell the truth, I was no longer sure of myself, either—weeks of silence with Temar, careful lies to the Duke, secrets from Roine. I was no longer sure where I ended, and my training began.

Chapter 7

The Duke was well pleased with Miriel's strategy, and he used it readily enough, but he did not thank her for it. Back from the emergency meeting of the Council, he presented her with the changes he had made to the story, the line she was to take with Garad, and the sentiments she should espouse to the court, all without a word of appreciation for her quick thinking, or his new weapons against Guy de la Marque and Gerald Conradine. The only satisfaction in his voice was at the fact that he had seen Guy de la Marque humbled by his own ward; he did not even look at Miriel as he dismissed the two of us.

I realized then that he was not pleased, because he had expected no less. He would have been quick to rail at her if she had failed, but in success, Miriel was no more than a tool. She only attracted his notice when she disobeyed, and otherwise, she was as necessary but as soulless to the Duke as his sword, or his armor. He would curse a weapon that broke in his hand, but would never thank it for its aid.

I was more offended by this than she was. Miriel bore it without a word of complaint, as if she, too, expected no less from her uncle. As our sixteenth birthdays approached, she became quieter and more thoughtful. She was less quick to anger; when we returned to her rooms after a day of lessons and an evening of dancing in the maidens' rooms, she would sink at once into a reverie and would respond little to my queries. She studied and practiced as much as she ever had, if not more, but it only seemed to occupy part of her mind.

I would find her staring out at the night sky, saying nothing. Although she did not seem particularly melancholy, nor angry, I could see trouble in her eyes. My comment to her had hit its mark, and she had not stopped thinking about it since.

I did not chide her, for I thought that I might understand, a little, the turmoil she was in. Miriel's true self and her mask self were close enough that it was difficult to separate the aims of the two. Miriel, speaking earnestly with the King about the necessity of preserving peace, might forget for a moment that her mask self only agreed with Garad's beliefs on how to achieve peace; she might begin to offer an opinion that commoners be given a voice in the government. She might, when plotting our strategy with me in an evening, forget that she was not only pretending to trust and work with the Duke.

We lay awake together at night, her in her great four-poster bed and me in my little cot, and I, at least, thought on what I had expected when we came to court almost two years past. I had been so deeply afraid of being trained to kill, so determined that I could not be an assassin, that I had not thought to guard my mind from the subtle, ceaseless lies of the Court. I had hated Miriel for being the cause of my half-imprisonment here, and I had trusted Temar completely.

I had thought that I knew who and what I was. But I was learning now that I had become a shadow in my heart, obeying Miriel without knowing what drove me to do so, and lying to the only two people I would have said I loved. And Miriel had come to court despising me, she had thought me nothing more than an instrument of her uncle's will. What she thought of that now, when she would ask my advice and take it, listen to me and plot with me, and even offer me her arm to lean on when I was hurt from my lessons...that, I did not know. I could only hope that she was as confused by our unlikely alliance as I was.

Tentatively, we came to behave as if we might be friends. We celebrated our birthdays together in the darkened receiving room once Anna had drifted off to sleep. I had begged a little fruit tart from one of the pastry chefs, and Miriel had filched a bottle of wine from the cellars after one of her late-night meetings with the King. Sitting together on the floor by the dying fire, we giggled at the memory of her brazen thievery, the wine making everything funnier.

"Happy birthday," she said, finally, raising the bottle to me and then taking a sip. She passed it over.

"Happy birthday," I repeated, and took a mouthful, making a face at the taste. Miriel, who drank fine wines with every dinner, gave a giggle at me, and I wrinkled my nose at her.

I had the thought, unwelcome, that by this time next year she might be a Queen. I knew not to mention it; this night was too simple to mention plots and schemes, too happy to mention her disappointment in Garad. When she curled her knees up to her chest and rested her chin on them, though, I knew she was thinking of the same thing.

"I hope this year is happier," she said simply. It was as fanciful as wishing for a fairy godmother, but I lifted the bottle to her and drank, then passed it back. We finished the bottle in quiet contentment, knowing that the world waited outside, in all its malice, but that tonight, just tonight, it was not here to hurt us. Then we hid the wine bottle behind some books and crept back to bed.

Dimly, before I drifted off to sleep, I remembered my dream of my birth. My mother had spoken of betrayal, but not after the first assassination attempt—only after the second. Betrayal was a funny word, I thought. Not enemies, not disasters, not danger. At the edge of consciousness, my mind loosened with wine, it did not seem so fantastical a thought anymore, I could even accept that the poison had been the first of many. And, with the merciful absence of foreknowledge, I slipped into sleep.

In the morning, we woke to pounding headaches and a small pile of gifts. Squinting my eyes against the light, I carefully examined each package, but saw nothing to make me too suspicious. Miriel opened each carefully, and exclaimed at the beautiful leather gloves she had received from the King, monogrammed in golden thread. From her uncle, she received a bolt of silk the exact color of her eyes, and from one of the maidens, a slim volume of poems.

"Nothing from Isra," she whispered to me with a mischievous grin.

The surprise was a gift from the Ismiri envoy: a delicate bracelet of gold with a single golden pearl. I snatched it from her at once, twisting it this way and that in the light, but I could see no residue on the metal, could smell nothing beyond the familiar tang of gold. At last, perplexed, I gave it back.

"He knows my birthday?" Miriel asked. She cast me a look as confused as my own. Was it an offer of friendship to a future queen, a calculated bet that Miriel would win out, or was it a warning? A strange warning, but a stranger gesture of friendship. Even the Duke, turning it over in his fingers later that day, only shook his head and told her to be cautious.

But there was no being cautious for Miriel: she could not afford to change a single facet of herself, with the eyes of the court on her. She danced and rode and sang as if she had not a care in world. She watched what she could, she caught sight of the looks in the courtiers' eyes, but it was I who must watch courtiers, and note their sidelong glances, and sneak along corridors to follow them.

I watched, scared, knowing that something must happen, that—as Temar had said—there was too much unresolved in the Kingdoms. I could not say how the dice would fall. The mood of the court shifted with baffling frequency, and it was Miriel who excelled at tailoring her actions to the tiny flicker of another's smile. I watched for long-laid plans, and the court was the distraction, the mask of those who schemed and waited.

King Dusan's accusation, and the King's measured response, had created a veritable storm in the court. Gerald Conradine had been loyal all this time, and none of them had known, ladies whispered to each other. How fascinating, and how unfortunate that they had all been so unkind to him. Why, he had even been more loyal than some others on the Council—they had planned for succession with the King still living, after all, and all the while Gerald had been offered the throne and had refused to plot against his rightful monarch.

It was chivalry embodied, it was dreadfully romantic: the Conradines became the focus of the court. For the first time in months, Anne wore the Conradine crest proudly, embroidered intertwined with the Warden crest. Gerald accepted the newfound admiration of the court with a satisfied smile that put me more on edge than ever before. Wilhelm was no longer the most shunned of the boys, his prowess in hunting and weaponry was mentioned often, as well as his quick mind. And Cintia, pretty Cintia, became a rival to Marie and even to Miriel. Miriel's influence over the King might be undimmed, but Cintia was the court's darling, the girl who had been a nobody, utterly overlooked. Now, everyone remembered how charming she was, how beautiful, how well-behaved. She was praised and feted until I thought that perhaps we had made a grave miscalculation.

The Dowager Queen watched this changing landscape with narrowed eyes. She was not an unintelligent woman, she had survived the long years since her husband's death, looking out on the sea of insincere faces, smiling at all and trusting no one. She had not faded into the background when Guy de la Marque had been chosen as Guardian of the King, but instead held equal power. She knew better than to try to advise a boy outright against his desires, and she knew better than to trust anyone who might benefit from her son's youth—indeed, anyone at all.

In this unpredictable time, she allowed herself to be eclipsed. She told her son that she prayed for peace with Ismir, and she was unfailingly courteous to the Ismiri envoy. She did not mention Marie's name, but instead praised Cintia unsparingly, smiling on the girl as if she were the favorite of all the Queen's kin. It was next to nothing to send the maidens and the boys away, and then have the ladies and their eldest daughters dance, detain the King so that he should think of Miriel but see Cintia dancing before him.

Seeing the Dowager Queen watch, and wait, I felt a flicker of unease. Better when she had been our declared enemy, when she had been foolish enough to go against the King, when Cintia had been a nobody. Too many were rising too fast for my liking.

My solace was that Guy de la Marque's favor fell in opposition to that of the Conradines. The Court turned on him in an eyeblink. If only he had thought to tell the King sooner about Kasimir's plot, the courtiers whispered, think how many months of tension could have been avoided! We had come so close to war, and for what purpose? Of course, the courtiers were willing to concede, de la Marque had owned up to the event so as not to ruin Gerald Conradine's reputation—but his perpetual narrow-eyed expression suggested that he had been far from pleased to do so.

For the first time, I felt sympathy for this ambitious enemy of ours. He would see Miriel dead at his feet before he would lift a finger to save her, but then, the same could be said of the Duke and Marie. I knew that de la Marque had made his bid for power, knowing full well the capricious nature of the Court—but it was something else again to see their spite in action, and watch him bite his tongue against the very truth that the King forbade him to speak. Truly, the King was a difficult master to serve.

Even in the Council meetings, where the truth was known, Guy de la Marque had lost his glamour. Gerald Conradine's successful command in the war made for much discussion, while the accusations about Vaclav's assassination were set aside; like the King, the Council seemed to think that the truth was a trifling matter. Unlike the King, however, the Council was spoiling for a fight, and it was more convenient by far to believe that Dusan had lied, attempting to rip apart Heddred by sowing unrest.

So focused were they on the West that they failed to pay heed to the spreading unrest in the South. Lord Nilson, having returned to his lands, sent desperate pleas for another royal proclamation, for Arman Dulgurokov to return to his provinces as well and control his people, for the King to send troops, money, anything. While Garad fretted and the council hemmed and hawed, while Miriel sweetly advised patience with the rebellion, Nilson was becoming more and more desperate. He knew that the relative silence of the rebellion was no true peace, only an army lying in wait.

Temar told me, in a whisper, that Nilson reported that his coffers were running dry with the cost of keeping his soldiers on patrol for so long, that he feared for his own safety, even in his castle among his own servants. What, he had demanded, should come of this if the unrest were to spread into the Bone Wastes? What then? But the Council ignored him, too busy with their reminiscences of the last war, and the war they seemed to hope for. The rebellion was only peasants, they said. One mob, but that had been an isolated event. What could come of farmers, armed not even with pitchforks, but only with words?

Chapter 8

"It would help me to know what the Council advised the King about Ismir," Miriel said calmly. "The envoy bowed to me the other night; am I to acknowledge him, or no?"

"The Council does not know what to advise," the Duke said bluntly. "They want war like little children would, for the excitement. They have no stomach for war, and no head for peace. They wish to invade only to spite the King, but they know it would be to no purpose."

"You do not think we could win?" Miriel asked curiously. We had never heard the Duke seem wary of this war; I, too, was perplexed.

"Not a full-scale invasion, no. Let them invade; let them fail. We held Voltur once, we can do so again." I saw Miriel's smile falter briefly at the thought of the Winter Castle under attack, but she pressed on.

"And what am I to tell the King, then?" She tilted her head. "Or convince him of. And what about the envoy?" She sat straight in her chair like a princess, her gown not touching the padded back, her arms resting only lightly on the arms of the chair, carved to look like hunting lions. In the months since she had sworn obedience to the Duke, and his favor had risen, he had granted her such liberties as sitting in his presence. I stood behind her chair, my hands clasped behind my back, and watched the Duke.

"Be polite to the envoy, no more. Do not speak with him for longer than necessary, but give no offense. And do not advise the King of anything for now. Just tell me his thoughts. Direct him to speak about the rebellion; I would know more about what he thinks on that. He only looks unhappy when we discuss it."

"What does the Council advise him on that?" Miriel queried, and the Duke frowned.

"They see it as no threat. They say that it is only peasants. They tell him that it will die down if he ignores it, they tell him to let Nilson handle it alone."

"It's been nearly a year," Miriel observed neutrally. She

---

played her uncle as if he were Garad, she was too clever to ask outright what he thought. I saw Temar watching her closely, but the Duke did not notice.

"I don't trust this silence," he said finally. "There are no letters, but the spies report the same whispers in different villages. We have a dozen spies there and not one can find a trace of Jacces. They're getting money from somewhere—they must be, to hide him. Mavlon, maybe. The news is moving too quickly for it to be only rumor. They have supporters, and I *will* find out who they are." He frowned. "Has the King mentioned anything else regarding the High Priest?"

"No." Miriel shook her head and bit her lip. "I will ask."

"Subtly," the Duke cautioned her, and Miriel's eyes flickered. She nodded her head. "And send Catwin to spy on the King's chambers, have her observe who comes and who goes." I tensed, as I always did when the Duke mentioned me by name. Miriel only nodded.

I went, at her command, that night, and the next, and the next. I darted into the long hallways and crouched, a shadow among shadows, to see who might go to see the King. I watched and I waited for anything that would help us destroy our enemies, and in the meantime, my other lessons suffered for it.

"Stop yawning," Roine said sharply. "It's disrespectful."

I closed my mouth and sighed, and then caught a glare for that piece of rudeness. While Temar had been unable to stay cold to me, Roine seemed to grow more irritated with me by the day. Her irritation had been piqued by my present practice of spying on the King's chambers in the dead of night. Every day, I was more and more tired, and Roine was displeased.

"I apologize," I said meekly, and her face softened.

"I wish you wouldn't sneak around for him," she said. "He has Temar for that, you could remind him of it."

"You'll get me in trouble," I protested. "Besides…" I trailed off. I enjoyed this new task. The palace was beautiful, and when I walked through it at night, it felt like some deserted fairytale castle that was my own, like I was the long-lost princess who had found her way through the forest and would lay claim to the place. It made for a better story than the web of lies that was my life, always looking over my shoulder and waiting to be caught out.

I had to admit to myself, however, that I liked the sneaking about, just for the sake of it. I was good at hiding, finding a shadow and nestling into it; I always had been. There was enough satisfaction in sneaking successfully down a hallway that I could push away the twinge of guilt that I was spying—and spying on my King, at that.

Even as I became more of a shadow in those weeks that I watched, I learned to pity the man I spied upon. I told the Duke that there were no interesting visitors to the King's rooms, and it was almost true. The Dowager Queen arrived once or twice to bid him good night, but she was not a favored guest, she did not stay long; the guards did not even close the doors behind her. Guy de la Marque would come to pay his respects, but for moments only. The envoy was never summoned, the High Priest never snuck down the long hallway to see his King. The King was, most nights, alone.

One night, I heard Wilhelm's voice in the hallway, laughing. He knew the guards by name, and they—unlike almost any other person in the castle—were neither sycophantic friends to the Conradines, nor particularly suspicious of the boy. Just as the Royal Guard knew of Miriel, they knew that Wilhelm was Garad's one friend. I peeked out, and saw him holding a little pie and a bottle of wine, and frowned at the strangeness.

I saw him one or two times more, both times with something small: a chunk of cheese and some bread, a couple of apples, fruit wine. When I realized what I was seeing, my heart ached. Wilhelm was going to Garad to sit and talk, bringing enough for a little feast, as I might have done for Miriel. The King and his friend would sneak about and steal sweetmeats and bread so that they could sit and talk together, so that Garad might pretend that he was not a King, who might command the pastry chefs and the sommeliers to bring him the best of anything.

I did not tell the Duke of this, and I did not tell Miriel, or Roine, or Temar, or even Donnett—who might have been one who could understand my pity. I kept it to myself, as closely-guarded as a state secret. I thought of it sometimes when I saw Wilhelm appear up the tunnels to summon the King back to his rooms from a late night debate with Miriel, I thought of it when I saw the King sitting at dinner with the servants holding huge platters of roast boar and duck and stewed venison in front of him.

And I thought of it when I saw Wilhelm swallow and look down, as his King spoke of crushing the rebellion in the south. I thought of it when Wilhelm forgot me, like the shadow I was, and watched Miriel with longing in his eyes. The King's only friend, and,

I thought, a true friend indeed, and yet pushing away his anger at the King's politics, pushing down his desire for the King's mistress. Wilhelm had been despised since he was born, and now he walked the hard road of a royal cousin and heir; I did not envy him.

In those times, I had the misguided notion that my life was simpler: my friends were not the great powers of the nation, nobles who might shape the lay of the land for generations. I was not caught between love and duty, I thought. Those I loved were my Lady, a palace healer, a palace guard, and an assassin I knew better than to trust. I watched them all, at nights and in their meetings with each other, and thought myself beyond their machinations.

"I am sending a messenger to Mavlon," the King announced one night. He was looking at Miriel, his eyes warm at the sight of her, sleep-tousled and sitting on a great wine barrel. Still, he was half-occupied with his discontent. "They are the ones behind this Jacces, I know they must be...but we cannot find a trace from here. The spy will be able to learn more, embedded in the court. Someone will talk."

"What if Jacces really is only a peasant from Norstrung?" Miriel queried. She needled him on this, undermined him; it was her only defiance that he could see, and even though he could not understand it, it was a dangerous game. I frowned at her, over the King's head, and I saw him frown as well.

"He cannot be. He is an educated man, he is well read. We have sent men to watch and ask questions, and none there know of this man, none could name who he might be. No commoner is so subtle. He holds to their cause, but he writes like..." The King frowned. "He writes like a priest, he writes like a philosopher. Like one of the men at the academies, perhaps. I told the envoy to seek out the academics in Mavlon."

Miriel had stopped attending, she had gone very still; a change had come over her face. Garad, turned from her, did not see it, and in a moment she had composed herself. She settled her shoulders and regained the adoring half-smile she practiced and practiced. She drew a breath and said, lightly, "Your spy will be able to learn this man's true identity, your Grace. It was clever to send him. But do you not need to return now? Wilhelm, what is the time?"

As we walked back to her rooms, she was fairly quivering with excitement. I waited patiently in silence, but she said nothing.

She walked with her head up, and she smiled to herself, but she did not speak to me. She was cherishing a secret and when I could not bear wondering anymore, I said,

"So?" She looked towards her bedroom, and I waited until we could hear one of Anna's predictable snores. "She's asleep." I said. "Tell me."

She shook her head. "Tomorrow. I need to think first."

But she did not tell me. As I slept, her excitement had turned to a melancholy such as I had never seen from her. The days passed and she spoke little, she hardly took the time to brush her hair or preen in the mirror, the life went out of her as soon as she returned to her rooms. I helped Anna undress her, and when we had gotten her into her nightgown and robe, she would go sit in a chair by the fire, holding a book but seeing nothing.

"Please tell me what has happened," I said finally. She shook her head.

"It is nothing to us," she said, and I felt a flicker of hope. She was not forgetting our alliance.

"You could use my help," I said persuasively.

"No." She shook her head again. "You'd ruin it." She cut off my retort with a sad smile. "Not like that. You would learn the truth of it. And I can't know the truth, Catwin, I really can't."

"It's always better to know," I said, quoting Roine. Miriel was as curious as I was, I could not think what she might not want to know.

"You don't understand." She closed her book and looked at me unsmiling. "You know as well as I do that Garad won't hear me, he won't listen, he wouldn't ever favor the rebels. Yet, anyway. Am I right?"

"Yes," I agreed cautiously.

"And we need his favor to survive, don't we?" She waited for my acknowledgement.

"Yes."

"So, until I am safe, I cannot speak to him of it. I cannot plead for them as I would wish to. Every day I swallow down my words and my thoughts, and I do nothing for the rebels and their cause, and it sickens me to my very heart, Catwin." I would have jested at her melodramatic language, but she looked so sad that I did not dare. Unable to find words, I nodded.

"Every day at services, I pray for the rebellion. I pray and I pray, and that is all that I can do. I try not to hear of it, I can't know anything about it—because if I know of it, I will want to speak for them. Do you understand? Yes. And so I can't know this, I cannot know of this thing I suspect. What if I'm right?"

"You think you know who Jacces is," I said slowly, and Miriel gave a little cry, a breathy sort of scream. I blinked at her.

"*That's* all you heard?" she demanded. "I tell you all of that, and all you can say is that you think I know something?" I stared at her in surprise, and she picked up a china ornament and hurled it at the wall; I flinched as it shattered. She had barely moved for days, now she was violent in her anger, she threw herself out of her chair to stand before me.

"Do you not hear me?" she cried. "I am close to breaking, and what then?"

"You said you wanted to survive." I was pressed up against the back of my chair. "You said we would have our revenge later, but we needed to survive. You said it was all we could do."

"I didn't know how it would be! So don't throw that in my face."

"Don't—" I snapped. I pushed myself out of the chair to stare her in the eyes. "You throw my vows in my face every day! You're quick enough to remind me of *my* duty!"

"It's not the same," she hissed at me. "You don't give up what you are for your duty. You don't know what it's like to wear a mask every day."

"I don't know?" I plucked at my black tunic. "What d'you think this is? Why do you think I'm here? Do you remember when we first came here, and the Duke told me what I was to be? Do you remember what he said? He said I wasn't a person anymore, he said I had no soul any longer."

"Oh, you didn't believe that," she said scornfully.

"I didn't then," I retorted, "but I do now. Now I know he was right. If it were just me, I wouldn't be here. I wouldn't walk around this place and know half the people wanted to knife me for the sigil on my chest. But you're here, and I can't run away anymore. So every day I walk back into the court, and every day I watch for your enemies and I make them my enemies."

"The King?" she challenged, and I nodded.

"He's not my ally. He doesn't have my loyalty, you do. Or the Duke," I added in a whisper. "I watch him, even when you don't. I remember he's our enemy."

"It's all about enemies with you," she accused me. "You only

———

68

care about who we can trust and who we can't."

"We can't trust anyone," I said fiercely. "Except each other. That's the most important thing."

"No! It's to live so we can do important things, because there *are* more important things! Things like the rebellion, that shape the whole world. Catwin, there's a world beyond the court, and who said what, and who danced with whom!"

"Not for me." I clenched my hands to stop myself from grabbing her and pulling her close, as she did when she wanted to hiss something in my face. "I took my vow to keep you safe, and so that's what I do. I protect you. There's nothing more important, and you can't say it doesn't matter—who's rescued you a dozen times so you could whine about philosophy and sympathize with rebels? Me. You wouldn't even *be* here if it wasn't for me watching your back." She stared at me, wide eyed. "So you decide, because you're the oath-breaker. Not me. You decide what you want. Until then, I'll keep faith."

I did not wait for her response, for I knew she would have none. I turned around and went to bed, not bowing, not waiting for her. I left her staring after me, and I lay in the dark and thought myself a fool to have trusted her.

Chapter 9

The next morning, not speaking to me, Miriel woke early and sent Anna to order hot water for a bath. She shed her clothes—I was glad to see that there were no longer any bruises on her skin—and she bathed silently. She would smooth her hands over her skin, covering it with the rose-scented soap she used, and then she would scrub at it until her skin was nearly raw, so pink that once or twice I nearly moved to stop her. I sat in the room with her, ostensibly studying, but watching her and wondering what change my words had wrought this time. She did not acknowledge my presence even once.

I sat and snuck glances over at her, a book open on my lap. I could not think what to say to her. I could not find the words to apologize.

At last, she sluiced clean water over herself and wrapped a bath sheet around her body as she wandered around to each of her wardrobes, looking at the priceless gowns inside. She selected one of a pale pink trimmed in white and had Anna lace her into it, tightly. She slid a cuff of pearls over her wrist, and twisted tendrils of her hair back, to be pinned.

"How are you?" I asked her, tentatively. I saw her consider an angry retort, a witty disclaimer; she only shrugged her shoulders and continued to look in the mirror.

"You were right," she said, after such a long pause that I had forgotten the question. "We need to survive." I knew that tone in her voice, and I knew there was a reason she had waited for Anna to leave the room. I only waited, and her next words came in a rush. "But I can't just let the rebels go without aid. I have to try to help them."

Even expecting it, I felt my shoulders slump. "Don't."

"It isn't a choice, Catwin."

"Yes, it is!" My voice rose, and I went over to her, knelt at her side and took her hands in mine. Once, she would have slapped me for such a thing; now, her eyes flared but she did not pull away. I tried to find words that would explain to her, a girl who had never

70

known hunger or cold or homelessness, what it was that she risked. "My Lady, this is to step into danger. Can you not see that?"

"Catwin." Miriel smiled, and I made the mistake of looking into her eyes. They were very warm. She squeezed her fingers around mine. "Don't you want something to believe in?" I blinked, then shook my head and tried to pull my fingers away. She tightened hers.

"This is believing something that could get us killed. It's dangerous to believe it." I heard Anna's tread on the floorboards in the privy chamber, and I lowered my voice. "To help them would be treason."

"It's not treason," Miriel whispered back passionately, and as Anna entered the room, Miriel picked up her hand and twisted her wrist about to look at the bracelet. "Yes, thank you, it's clasped now." She smiled at me, then over at Anna, who only glowered; it was her usual method of dealing with the two of us, now.

I left for my lessons, but I found that in the coming weeks, I could not banish her words from my mind. Something to believe in, she had said. I did not think I had ever believed in anything. Certainly not something so dangerous as an uprising against the monarchy itself, but when I thought on it, I was not even sure what I thought of the Gods, or the saints, or the old myths.

At the Winter Castle, I had never thought further than the next day. First, I had been a child, considering my next meal or my next escape into the tunnels in the rock. My life had been stolen rolls and skinned knees; the noblest thing I had done was help Roine with her patients. I had had a gift for that, but no call such as Roine felt, to heal the ill, set bones, and cut away disease. When I had been chosen to be taught by Miriel's tutors, my world had narrowed simply to avoiding the Lady's anger as much as I could.

We had traveled to Penekket and I had learned just how big the world was, and what could be found at every corner of the land. I knew more than I had ever dreamed existed, and yet I was still a child: I had seen no farther than my next meal, my next training lesson, my next encounter with the Duke. I watched what happened, and I pondered on what it might all mean in the future, and yet...

Something to believe in. I did not have anything to believe in. It had never occurred to me to find something to believe in. I did not even know how to believe in anything, beyond staying alive.

I watched Miriel, as if I could learn the secret of it from her.

After her melancholy, and her excitement, she had returned to her studies with fierce intensity. She sent me to the library for more books, and I had more than a few close scrapes with the Royal Guard, when I was weighed down with heavy volumes and could not have run fast enough to evade them. Miriel read the books voraciously, and I saw that she was beginning to write her own tract on the subject, hiding the pages behind books on the shelf. I asked her to tell me her suspicions, but in response I received only a mischievous smile, and the assurance that it was right in front of my face.

"Is it Wilhelm, that you think is Jacces?" I asked her. "The Duke? Garad? Who?"

"Oh, figure it out yourself," she said. "The sooner you do, the sooner you can go spy on them."

When she was not writing or studying, she seemed to be learning all over again how to be the most enchanting and desirable of women. She practiced her dancing until the tapping of her shoes drove me to take my books and barricade myself in the bedroom. She practiced walking back and forth until I thought she would wear a path in the floor. She was learning to walk with the tiniest sway in her hips, and she now greeted everyone with an enchanting flicker of the eyes: down modestly, and then up through her lashes.

She had been perfectly accomplished at being enchanting before, and so I was bemused at this new obsession. Garad seemed no less enchanted with her now, and almost every one of the maidens had taken to dressing their hair in curls, and wearing the colors that Miriel wore. I watched her, waiting for a clue, and one day I found the key to all of it.

"Tighter," Miriel said, over her shoulder. "In at the waist."

"My Lady is perfectly slim," Anna panted. "The dress looks beautiful."

Miriel frowned, she put her hands flat on the front of the gown and pressed, looking down, and at last I understood. I gave a snort of laughter that I tried to turn into a cough, but it was too late. Miriel shot a glare at me and turned pink with embarrassment, and I saw her mouth turn down at the corners.

In the past months, I had grown until I looked like a gangly colt, turning unexpectedly awkward, losing the balance I had so carefully cultivated. I felt as if I must train twice as hard just to keep the same control of my muscles. I was awkward in my own body, and I hated it—and, hating it, self-conscious, I had noticed only that

Miriel, on the other hand, had stayed as perfectly tiny as she had been when we arrived before our twelfth birthdays. I had envied her the lack of strangeness. She did not need to go back to the Quartermaster, week after week, begging for new clothes and being frowned at.

Now I saw that this was a problem for her as well. Being small was not a problem in itself—the Dowager Queen's short stature had created somewhat of a fashion for tiny women. No, the problem was that Miriel continued to be as slim and shapeless as a child. Where the other girls were growing into new gowns, Miriel's gowns fit as well as they ever had. The drop-waist gowns that were coming into fashion only accentuated Miriel's lack of figure.

It had been one thing to be the smartest of the girls when all of them were children. Then, a merry laugh and a brilliant smile would do to attract the notice of those seeking a bride for their son. "She'll grow," I had heard more than once, one father to another as they haggled over dowry. "And four children in as many years—her mother was fertile." But now, as the other girls did grow, matching the awkward coltishness of the growing boys, Miriel remained small. A liability.

So she worked without ceasing to be the most interesting, the wittiest, the most vivacious of the girls. She sparkled as never before, the graceful turn of her head and the cheerful peal of her laughter were copied not only by the other maidens, but by the Queen's ladies. Miriel outshone Marie, who had faded into the background with her father's disgrace, and she outshone Cintia, who had been so ignored for so long that she seemed almost to prefer to be overlooked.

The Duke noticed, and one night he summoned me to his study alone. I went, wondering what strange trouble we had gotten into now. Had Anna heard more than we thought? I resolved to speak to Miriel about that, and to tell her to hide the philosophical treatise she was writing. If I got out of this alive, of course. I breathed deeply and tried to calm my nerves.

"My Lord?" I asked as I entered, and I bowed deeply. I always tried to act with all the respect the Duke wished of me. I took a deep breath, and remembered one of the things I had learned from Miriel almost at once: clever prevarication was no better than a lie. A lie was a lie, and a lie required commitment. If I needed to lie in this meeting, I must do so freely, without hesitation. There would be no mincing words with the Duke so that he might look back and see that I had never truly *lied*. I just wished that I knew what this meeting was about, so that I might have had time to come up with a good lie first.

The Duke looked up from his work with his customary indifference, and at his lack of rage, I felt a flood of relief so great that I thought I might lose my balance. Then I looked at his eyes again and wondered for a moment what it was that he saw when he looked at me, at anyone. It was one of the puzzles of our meetings.

He did not tell me that he had a task for me, for both of us knew that I was only summoned when he wanted something from me. He did not ask how I fared, because he did not care, and he did not ask how Miriel fared, or if any crises had arisen. He assumed that I would tell him if anything important had happened. And so the Duke wasted no time with trivialities; in his presence, I became aware how many unnecessary words other people used.

"You are to ensure that Miriel remains a virgin," he said bluntly. He looked back to his work and made a mark on one of the documents he was reviewing. The conversation, such as it was, had finished. He expected me to go now.

"My Lord..." I tried to find some way to phrase my question delicately. "Is there some specific...threat?"

He cast an annoyed look at me, and then his eyes narrowed. "You tell me, Shadow. Is there? She takes more care with her appearance now. Is there a man? Is there a threat?" I stared at him mutely, thinking of the men who stopped to stare at Miriel in the hallways, of the priests who stole glances at her during services. I thought of the noblemen who put their sons in her way, and then wondered if they were too old for her themselves.

I did not consider telling him the truth: that Miriel was worried that she was too small and, to be truthful, skinny as a boy. The Duke would have little sympathy for her plight, and only be angry to find a fault with her. So I shook my head. "Nothing specific, no, my Lord."

"She does not encourage any man?" he pressed me, and I almost smiled. He should know that everything about Miriel spoke of desire, spoke of subtle yearning; he had ordered it to be so. Miriel could encourage a man with nothing more than a word of greeting. At the ripple of her laughter, I saw unslaked longing in men's eyes. Every gesture was an invitation, every word was a whispered promise.

But the Duke's instructions to her long ago had been

———

followed to the letter: whatever her promise, Miriel never gave anything of herself. She stood out of reach, a veritable goddess, flesh and blood and yet as unattainable as a woman made of snow and ice; she melted out of reach of a man's fingers, and she walked so that the hem of her gown might barely brush a man's boots.

"No," I said. "She does not encourage any man. Beyond the King, of course. And she never does anything improper with him," I hastened to add. He stared at me in silence, until I felt compelled to say something more. "So I do not think there is a threat, my Lord."

The Duke looked as if he did not entirely believe me. "There is always a threat," he said. "Miriel is beautiful." If he felt anything for his niece, be it love or pride, none of it was evident in his voice. He might have been speaking of the weather conditions for a siege. He might have been discussing a horse.

"Even if she were not beautiful, young men delight in seduction. And there are many who would be glad to have my heir dishonored and unfit for marriage." The look in his eye indicated that I had best be content with this explanation, but I did not bow and withdraw. I was sifting through evidence in my head.

"How am I to ensure this?" I asked, finally.

"With force, if necessary." The Duke did not seem to understand the question.

"If you have further questions, you may ask me," Temar said smoothly. I let him draw me out of the Duke's study, into the public room, and then I shook my head at him.

"I don't understand. Why would he call me here unless he suspected her, and if he suspects her, why isn't he angry? She really hasn't done anything," I assured him.

"I know," Temar said, so blandly that I wondered what else he knew. He saw me thinking it over, and smiled a smile with a lot of teeth. "He doesn't suspect her," he assured me. "But the Council has made...a suggestion."

I raised my eyebrows and waited, and Temar smiled. I saw the anticipation in his eyes; he wanted to tell me what he had heard. He wanted to share the information he had gleaned at keyholes. Sometimes when I saw the conspiratorial gleam in his eye, things seemed as they had always been: the two of us quick to notice the same details, able to share a joke with only the flicker of an eyebrow.

"Someone mentioned the other day that it was not uncommon for a King to have mistresses. That it was not so uncommon for a King to marry for duty, but take his pleasure where he pleased." I closed my eyes briefly. A political marriage, and a mistress. In one fell swoop, the King would have ruined Miriel, and would himself be free to marry another daughter of the court.

"Was it Gerald Conradine who asked?" My voice was bitter.

"Efan of Lapland. But you're not far off. He has..."

"...a daughter?" I guessed, and Temar nodded. "Again, close enough. They align themselves behind the Torstenssons, even though it was the other way around long ago—before the Conradines, Efan's family ruled a portion of land. Without the Conradines holding the West, the old allegiance is slipping away. Could be, the King would see a chance to unite the West while he faces the east."

"And so I am to keep Miriel from being compromised by the King, so that she remains fit for marriage."

"Exactly." Temar's eyes gleamed. "More than that—she must be beyond even his reach. Only one thing keeps a smart man from recognizing what's to his advantage, and that's the chase. So you keep Miriel out of his grasp."

Chapter 10

Not a few nights later, I was summoned into the Duke's presence once more. The outcome of the last meeting gave me no comfort—coupled with the Duke's relative kindness since our attempted murder, it added up to too many odd things. I feared that this meeting would be the end of such civilized behavior. I was tempted to meet with Temar, and demand that he tell me if I was in danger, ask what the Duke suspected.

Then I realized that my paranoia was due in part to my deception; how obvious would such a thing be the man who had taught me everything I knew about lying? And—I must face this—I no longer trusted Temar to take my side. Every time I remembered that, I wondered if it had been worth it to use up his trust in the way we had.

So I was on my own. I used a breathing technique that Roine taught some of her patients to use when in pain, and I felt my heart stop racing quite so quickly. At the door of the Duke's rooms, I unclenched my hands and tried to ignore the fact that my dinner seemed about to escape. Then I squared my shoulders and went in. As his guards closed the doors behind me, I bit my lip.

"Welcome, Catwin. Please, have a seat." The Duke waved to the chair that Miriel was now permitted to use. He was smiling at me, and clearly attempting not to terrify me by doing so; that put me on edge, even as it gave me the disrespectful urge to laugh. Given how uncomfortable the Duke looked, it must have been years since he had tried to smile like this.

Half-fearing some sort of death trap, I walked over to the chair and sat down gingerly. No blades dropped from the ceiling, no trapdoors opened below my feet, and I exhaled as softly as I could. I looked around myself. The room seemed to be empty but for the two of us, and I wondered if Temar was hiding somewhere, watching me.

"Temar tells me that you are progressing well in your studies," the Duke said, with a trace of his usual brusqueness.

"Yes, my Lord." Certainly, my dedication to my craft had

been honed by my brush with death. Temar might not speak to me with kindness any longer, but I knew that I was doing well. He could not stop taking pride in his training, and when I excelled, I marked the approving gleam in his eyes; I marked, too, the flicker of apprehension when I outmatched him in sparring. There was the dark sense between the two of us now, that any fight could be to the death. I wondered if Temar's fighting was improving even as mine did; I saw him using the techniques on me that I had used to win against him.

He watched me. He watched me as if I could become an open adversary, and when I saw that look, I sometimes felt that I could see farther into his soul than I ever had before. At such times, I wondered who Temar was, and where he had come from. I had studied his features, but I could not match them to anyone else I saw, even at the Palace. Someday, I thought I might venture out into the city and examine the traders and travelers to see if I could find dark eyes like Temar's, curly black hair. I could ask that person who they were and where they were from, and I could begin to unravel the puzzle of Temar. I could have a fighting chance of knowing what lay behind his eyes, and what desperation drove him to—

The Duke's voice called me back.

"You are to be commended. I had my doubts that a—well, never mind." He heaved a breath, and I had a moment of amusement; it was taking him much effort indeed to beat around the bush. "You have acquitted yourself well."

"Thank you, my Lord." The assassination attempt hung, unmentioned, in the air. I could not think what he wanted to ask me.

"I once asked you to consider your loyalties," the Duke said to me. He steepled his fingers together and stared piercingly at me. "It has occurred to me that, although you once hid the actions you used to do so, you have always worked in my interests. My niece is safe, and her reputation is unstained. You have done well."

"Thank you, my Lord." I was growing more wary with each compliment.

"You have also prospered from my patronage, have you not?" He gestured to my fine clothes, to the well-crafted weapons I carried. I was sure, now, that he was having me watched. He was within one quick lunge, and only one man in the world knew me well enough, and moved quickly enough himself, to stop such a thing.

It was a dizzying thought. I could kill the Duke—

"I have prospered, my Lord," I said, steadying myself. He smiled again and spread his hands out.

"And so," he said smoothly, "what profit to us being enemies?"

"Were we enemies, my Lord?" Always, when speaking with him, some piece of bluntness rose in me to match his own. He smiled now, as he always smiled. The fact that he found my rudeness amusing was one of his most terrifying qualities.

"I think you know," he said. Then he must have remembered that he was trying to be nice to me. "I was…displeased…that you had hidden knowledge from me. I was not your friend. But we are practical people, we do not need to carry grudges. You will agree that there is no reason we should be at odds with one another."

"Yes, my Lord." No reason, beyond the fact that Miriel planned to destroy him one day. No reason beyond the fact that I would never trust him, and I knew from Temar that the first rule of surviving was remembering that an untrustworthy person was an enemy. That list now included Temar, and the Duke.

"You are a clever child, Catwin. You know that I can make a good friend."

It came clear in a flash: he was not trying to convince me to guide Miriel's loyalty, he was trying to lure me away from her. He knew now that Miriel had her own ambitions. Alone, her ambition was no match for him, but she had me now, and he had seen what the two of us together might do. The only way the Duke could convince himself that he had not made a terrible mistake would be to convince himself that I was loyal to him.

Tell me the truth, Catwin—you've always been good at seeing people and knowing what they're thinking, haven't you? Temar's voice echoed in my head.

Following quick on the heels of the first thought came another. I was the tool that Miriel could use to achieve her own ends, and Miriel could be the Duke's enemy. Logic dictated one thing: if I was not the Duke's servant, I should be destroyed. One did not arm one's enemy. The Duke was a seasoned commander, he would know this; it was by his patronage that I had learned it.

These thoughts went through my head in a moment; there was no room for hesitation.

"I know it, my Lord. I did not think you could forgive my

error in judgment. But if you are saying that you can..." I took a moment to stroke my fingers appreciatively over the arm of the chair. Let him think that he could buy me away from Miriel with such a sop as this.

"It is forgiven," he assured me.

"Thank you, my Lord." I added, with heartfelt honesty, "I do not want to be your enemy." *Your open enemy, your declared enemy.*

"And so?" His eyes glittered. I made a private vow that one day, I would tell him that he would have had a chance to win my loyalty if he had only asked for it.

I shrugged, as if at a loss for words. "I will be a friend to you," I said. "Although my friendship is not..." He raised his eyebrows. "...much to brag of, for a Duke." He laughed in careless agreement. He did not think I knew how much I was worth to him.

"I am glad we had this talk," he told me. "I will make sure that you stay well informed. You will do the same for me."

"Of course, my Lord."

"And, Catwin—"

"Yes, my Lord?"

"Tell Miriel to find out from the King where he is searching for Jacces. Tell her to plant the idea that it may not only be Jacces' funding that comes from Mavol. The more we search, the more I think he is not in the Norstrung Provinces at all."

It was all I could do to keep my face straight—that last sentence had given me the missing piece of the puzzle: Jacces was not in Norstrung. There was a reason there were no printing presses to be found in the peasants' houses, no stashes of books, no troves of learning. Nilson's men had looked everywhere, the Royal soldiers had questioned anyone they could lay their hands on, and no one had known. Of course, of course.

No one had seen what was right in front of our eyes. And that information had laid the other clues bare for me to see; Miriel was correct, it had been in front of my face the whole time. And so, trembling with relief and new knowledge, I bowed to the Duke, and went to find Miriel and tell her of this new development.

"It's the High Priest," I hissed to her, as I came into the room. She looked up from her studying with a ready grin, and I began to laugh. I could not even be angry at her for a moment; we reveled in the knowledge together.

"Just so," she said, simply. "And so, now that you know...I have a letter for you to take to him."

"*What?*" Her ready jumps from information to action had always baffled me.

"It's not signed," Miriel said. "Just letting him know that someone at court has figured it out...and is an ally."

"You idiot, what if he has you killed?"

"It's not signed," Miriel repeated. "And I would think I could trust you to deliver a letter without him seeing you." Her voice was sharp, and I threw up my hands.

"Think about it—he's been smuggling his letters out of the Capital without even Temar seeing. He's got a spy network, he's been planning a rebellion for years. And," I added pettishly, "he tried to kill you once."

"For leverage against an enemy," Miriel countered. "Catwin...I am still leverage against his enemy, and after that meeting in court, he knows that I have the ear of the King. We know he's willing to kill to further his ends. Is it not wise to show him that we are his allies?"

"Oh." I sat down and pondered. "I hadn't thought of that."

"I thought not. And I'm glad you've figured it out at last. We couldn't have waited much longer." She drew a letter out of a purse at her waist, and held it out to me. I pocketed it, reluctantly.

"I have news, too," I told her. A plan had formed in my mind: give the Duke some useless tidbit. Not something that would get her in trouble, but something that she would not have told him herself, something that would prove my loyalty and gain me a small portion of his trust. I had not been able to think of something, but I was sure that between the two of us, we could contrive to come up with an idea. Miriel proved, to my surprise, intractable. She refused absolutely. At this inopportune moment, Miriel was suddenly unwilling to deceive.

"We have to tell him *something*," I said, frustrated. The conversation had wound on for an hour. I was hungry, and tired, and beginning to be genuinely angry.

"Oh? Why? Why can you not let it rest?"

"I've explained three times." My voice grew sharp, to match hers.

"Yes—that you throw me on his anger to make yourself look good!" Miriel glared at me. "Well, I don't agree to it."

"You know as well as I do that he's waiting for something. He suspects you, he thinks you will defy him again. You've played on that before, yourself! If I hadn't suggested this, you would have."

That thought made me particularly bitter. "You would have thought it a clever plan if you had come up with it."

"But you suggested it," she pointed out, agreeing without hesitation. "It benefits *you*."

"It benefits both of us."

"You would doubt me, if it were the other way around." She justified herself without looking at me, but I saw from the stubborn set of her jaw that she felt her position was growing precarious.

"Give him this," I said, trying to be patient, "and he won't go looking for something else. Just this one thing." She did not calm down, she flared up.

"What did he offer you?" she demanded fiercely. "Tell me the truth."

"I told you, he only said—" I broke off, unable to look into her eyes, and then I hopped down from my perch on the sill and pushed my way past her, out of her bedroom. How many times would it take me to learn this lesson? First Jacces, now this. Miriel trusted no one, and while I had learned to trust her, she would never let herself trust me. She demanded my trust, she would not rest until she had my secrets, but she made games of what she knew. She had never wanted us to be a side together, only to have me on her side—and she would always be waiting for me to betray her. In the rising tide of my anger, I conveniently forgot the dreams she had shared without hesitation, the secrets she gave me, the theories we came up with together. She had given me enough to ruin her a dozen times over, but I could not remember that with fury beating its rhythm in my temples.

"What are you going to tell him, then?" she asked nervously. She was hovering in the doorway, nervous and yet, as always, framed perfectly by her surroundings. I opened my mouth to tell her that I had no second plan, not having anticipated her anger.

"I haven't decided yet," I said. It was an attempt at the prevarication she did so well. "I'll go deliver your letter now," I added, as insolently as I dared. And, as I would never be able to spar away my anger with her, herself, I went off to find Donnett.

"Ye can't be too hard on her," Donnett said, sometime later, as I poured water on a scrape. He snorted when I looked at him. "Lad, ye may be able t'sneak well enough, but yer as subtle as a boar when yer angry."

"And *you* want me to be understanding of nobles?" I asked, skeptical.

"Aye," he said cheerfully, with a twinkle in his eye. "It's hard on 'em, lad. They're not all there in the head. It's from marryin' their cousins all those years," he added, in a whisper. I gave a watery laugh and he clapped me on the shoulder. "Cheer up," he advised me. "It'll blow past."

But it did not. As the weeks wound on, I waited for my own anger to fade, as it usually did. I waited for Miriel to forgive me, as she usually did. But instead, we watched each other like polite adversaries. We never came to open opposition; we still shared bits of information, we still worked with the tiny signals and unspoken commands we had developed. But I found myself wondering if she might indeed be hiding more than I knew, and she watched me with quiet suspicion; whenever she saw me with Temar, her eyes flicked back and forth between us, and she did not care that I saw.

She knew that I had not told the Duke of Jacces, or her letter—indeed, I had not told anyone of the many letters I had passed back and forth between the two of them, my routes between the palace proper and Miriel's chambers becoming ever more complex, to evade the spies I was sure Jacces had set to find his supposed ally. Miriel needed me; she left the letters for me, and waited for me to retrieve the responses. But she knew that I could tell her uncle, and she hid her thoughts from me now. She did not share the content of the letters she exchanged with the High Priest, and I did not ask.

I had thought at the time that the Duke's offer had failed, but now I wondered if he had planned this. Perhaps he had known that I would take the offer to Miriel, and that she would be suspicious. He might have known, with some deep cunning, that our tenuous friendship needed only a nudge, and then: a widening gulf, silence where there had been laughter, an edge in our voices. Or perhaps that had been a plan of Temar's devising.

In my hopeful moments, I tried to believe that Miriel and I were simply outgrowing our squabbling. In my exhausted, resentful moments, I thought that it had been foolish of us even to try to build our own alliance, never mind a friendship; we had learned one secret, oh, the greatest secret—but that success could only be followed by failure. A half-breed noble girl raised in seclusion, romancing a King: that was fanciful, and dreadfully romantic, a fairy tale in the making. The bedtime stories never mentioned friendship between a future Queen and her little orphan bodyguard, and now I knew why.

We might share quick minds and have grown up together in the same nowhere corner of the world, only to be thrown together under the harsh rule of the Duke, but Miriel and I were far apart in station, in glamour, in skills. How could the King's mistress share her view of the world with a shadow half-soldier? And without such an understanding, how could they share dreams? And from there: plans, a side of their own. It was impossible.

Worse, we had compounded the bad luck of being part of the Duke's faction with the foolishness of plotting against him. I asked myself if I had run mad. Two girls, choosing for their target a war hero, with an army of a retinue—and the army of Heddred—in his camp. While we had begun a correspondence with the leader of the rebellion, that had led to no open alliance—and was our lack of progress not good? Shameful, how pathetic our rebellion was: a few words, a few secrets. But better that we abandon such an ill-starred alliance before it led us too far into danger. We could still walk away; the High Priest would never know that his correspondence had been with us.

What Miriel thought, I still do not know. We slipped away from each other, in evenings of silence, too-polite exchanges, smiles that did not reach our eyes. I was as lonely as I ever had been. It was worse than when I had come to the palace, knowing no one at all. Then, I had had Roine's friendship and Temar's guidance. I had not had any secrets to keep. Now, I lived two lives, my teacher mistrusted me, my surrogate mother would not speak to me. And I had lost even Miriel's friendship.

I waited each night for the slow, deep breathing of Miriel and Anna, and then I curled into a ball and wept onto my pillow. I was so alone, and I was so afraid. I had never faced the world alone. I did not know how to survive alone. However symbolic Miriel's support had been, it had been all that stood between me, and my fear.

I made sure that my eyes were dry and my face clean each morning, and I felt myself become very quiet. I made my face a mask, as Miriel once had, and wondered if the tight knot of fear in my belly would ever go away. The days seemed ceaseless and unchanging, I opened my eyes each morning with weariness.

And then, as we moved into the thaw of the year, the King came to Miriel with an incredible plan.

"Why should monarchs pretend to be allies while all they share are cold words?" he demanded. "Do you know, I have never met King Dusan. We have never met, and yet—and yet!—we write to each other as if I am my father, or as if we are our grandfathers, back and back. And why?" He was too excited to wait for Miriel's response. "Think how many insults and how much anger we carry on and on from those generations. It is not our anger, it does not need to be this way. It should not be this way."

He was flushed with conviction, and I had two thoughts at once. First, that he was almost unbearably naïve, and that the Council must be at a loss to find ways to advise such a boy. Second, that I could see why Miriel had begun to fall in love with him, all those fateful months past. Even now, made bitter by disappointment, I saw a warmth in her smile that was not only deception. Garad shared her same hopeful heart; I had the fleeting idea that life had warped them both, and it was sad that they could never now be truly happy together—whatever Garad might think.

"So tell me!" Miriel was flushed and laughing at his passionate speech. "What was your idea?"

"Oh, my love—" Miriel's smile never faltered at the endearment "—my love, you must be my champion in this—"

"*Tell* me!"

"—for I know the Council will be ranged against me, and I could not bear to have you against me as well. They will tell me it is impossible," he finished in a breathless rush. Miriel wrapped her fingers around his and smiled, so warmly that I myself wanted to confide in her.

"You must tell me this idea that makes you so happy," she said, and a smile broke across his face like dawn.

"We will travel to meet Dusan," he said. "We will all meet together on the plains, the whole of the Courts, all the great nobles of the world, and discuss the future of Heddred and Ismir like men, not squabbling boys. It will be a great event, the most historic moment of our nations! It will be the true beginning of the golden age."

As we walked back to our rooms, I said to Miriel, "You did very well."

"I didn't know what to say," she confessed, with a laugh. "Such an idea! What do we do now?" I sobered, and checked the hallway. It was empty, and so I put a hand on her arm to slow her. I did not have to say anything; she knew what I meant without me speaking a single word. I saw her bite her lip.

"You're not betraying him," I assured her, my voice low.

"He'll tell them all tomorrow," I assured her.

She nodded. "I know. And you're right. And it's a good plan."

"And you've been very good about not getting us into trouble," I conceded. It was not everything, but it was enough, after our laughter, to open the door. She inclined her head, like a Queen.

"Then let us go tell my uncle," she said.

"This is a bad idea," I said, out loud, before I thought. A bad idea to begin working against the Duke once more, a bad idea to renew our alliance. It was dangerous. Miriel only tilted her head to the side, and smiled. She did not have to ask what I was talking about, she always understood me.

"Don't leave me, Catwin," she said. "You're all I have."

Chapter 11

Garad had been correct: the Council swore that it could not be done. The Duke, having gone white with fury at the thought of ushering the Ismiri army through Voltur Pass, had raged at me and at Miriel when we brought him the news. Miriel sat, pale and trembling, and I knew that she hoped only to escape this meeting without her uncle's anger turning to violence. Finally, his fury had burned away, and he dropped into his great, carved chair and stared at the wall.

"Do not encourage him," he told us, and we nodded, frightened into silence. "Let us try to bring him around."

And so he had gone to the Council meeting the next day, where Gerald Conradine predicted betrayal on the open plains, and Guy de la Marque told the King that he overreached himself; this time, none on the Council spoke against him for raging at the King. They, too, were terrified. Half of their time was spent assuring Garad that Dusan would never agree to such a thing, and the other half was filled with desperate pleading to abandon the idea. Every member of the council had lived through the last war, most of them had fought in it, all of them had lost family—Ismir had been beaten back, Heddred had won, could the King not leave well enough alone?

Their pleas fell on deaf ears. Garad sat silent on his throne while the men of the Council spoke earnestly. He listened to their words, he marked who spoke and who did not. He nodded in response to some comments. He let the Council beg him until their voices failed, and then he said simply that his mind had been made up, and he would send the invitation shortly by courier.

The Duke, forewarned by us, had regained his composure enough to sit quietly in the Council meetings, biting his tongue against what he saw as willful stupidity. While the other Council members left, only to join together in knots and mutter fearful predictions in the banquet hall, the Duke would retire early to his rooms each night, unnoticed.

Only those of us in his faction knew that he was working to

create a plan that would both win him the adoration of the King, and soothe his own troubled mind. When Miriel and I were called in for urgent meetings with the Duke, we could see maps strewn about on all the tables, little figurines set up to show Voltur guardsmen, Kleist troops, the Royal Army.

Temar, in a rare moment of friendship, showed me the Duke's most recent plans. He brought a map to our lesson, rolled up carefully in a leather tube, and he had me brush off a table in the corner so that we could spread the map out on a clean surface.

As we smoothed the map out and laid little weights at the corners, I could not help but marvel at my life, that priceless objects were everywhere now. I had become so inured to gold, jewels and silks, books and maps, that I rarely thought of it anymore. And then sometimes, Temar would show me a book or a map, and I would remember that I was wearing warm clothes, that braziers burned in my bedroom, and that my belly was full and had been every day that week.

"Miriel cannot speak of this to the King," Temar cautioned me, and his voice brought me back to the moment. I nodded, in agreement with the principle, but Temar still felt the need to explain. "We cannot let the King think that the Duke discusses his plans with Miriel. The King cannot think that they are a united group."

"Yes," I said simply. It was not worth the argument to tell him that I knew as much; when Temar thought of me as a child in need of instruction, he did not think of me as a woman who had betrayed him. I fought the uncomfortable thought that I did not want him to think of me as a child at all, and poured the little figurines out of their bag. I held them out to Temar, one by one, and he began to place them on the map.

"Here is where the King would meet, yes? And this is a portion the Royal Army." He tapped to the north of the King's proposed meeting place. A blue figurine went there. "Another here." East of the meeting place, equally ready to meet the King if he were in need, or stand against an advancing force.

"Now." Temar placed three green figurines on the board to the south, behind a mountain. "These forces can sweep west and north, or east and north, to flank the Ismiri. Retreat can be stopped by a detachment of Voltur guardsmen—" blue figurines, placed in the foothills "—or enabled by sweeping the guardsmen along the north flank, to funnel the Ismiri back through the passes. What do you think?"

I did not know what to think. Although I was the one who studied combat, Miriel was the one with a head for army maneuvers. As young ladies were not taught such things, she had read of them in my books, and now I went to her when I had questions about something Donnett or Temar had taught me. I was memorizing the layout of the map, so that I could ask Miriel about it later.

But Temar was waiting for a response now. I pointed to the green figurines.

"Green is the Kleist army?" I asked, and he nodded. "Is the rest of the Royal Army at Penekket?" He nodded once again. I was running out of questions. "Who commands the Kleist army?"

"Edward DeVere," Temar said, surprising me. "Guy de la Marque will need to be with the King, of course, and DeVere knows the land." I nodded. My surprise had been foolish. The DeVere family did indeed own that land, stretching from the Western road at the north, almost to the Bone Wastes in the south. It had been their proximity in the West that had first allowed the Duke to seek them out as potential kinsmen. They had been happy enough to sell a second son to him, and ignore the fact later.

Temar noticed neither my wandering thoughts, nor my lack of skill in deciphering the map. He had been tense all the time we were speaking, and now he said, worriedly,

"The guardsmen will hold Voltur, and a detachment will wait to make sure there's no sweep behind Dusan's party." I heard real fear in his voice, an echo of the Duke's own. The Duke had raged at the stupidity of allowing the Ismiri army—even a detachment—across the border, and he planned for the possibility of the King's assassination, but his one true fear was that of Voltur falling back to the Ismiri. Temar, in his strange, almost symbiotic bond with the Duke, had taken on the fear as his own. It was a danger from which he, in all his skill, could not shield his lord.

"But the Duke likes this plan," I said, cautiously. It was an attempt to comfort him, and I felt foolish when Temar snorted, his fear forgotten.

"Of course not. He looked to Voltur and the Royal Army to keep the Ismiri at bay, he always feared an invasion. Now we've let them over the pass ourselves and stretched the armies out. No, he doesn't like the plan. But it's the best that can be done if the King keeps insisting on this." He looked over at me, and I realized that the last portion was a question.

"He does," I said. "Unchanging."

"And Miriel says?" I tried to keep my shoulders from stiffening at his habitual suspicion.

"The usual. That peace is to be desired, she supports his plan for a golden age."

"Huh." He did not ask more, and I did not offer it, and neither did we mention the suspicion that ran between us. That was the rule now. We lived in a half-truce, bought by determined silence. It was more bearable to behave as if nothing had changed save the greater cooperation between Miriel and the Duke. It was certainly better to pretend that such cooperation was real.

Accordingly, neither of us mentioned that one of the two had nearly overset the plans of the other, that both of them would gladly see the other dead at their feet, and that there was a strong possibility that one had tried to kill the other and pin the death on his political rivals. By denying the enmity between Miriel and the Duke, we denied the root of our own.

If we were two other people, perhaps, we might have believed that this truce could last forever. Perhaps it truly would have lasted. Yet we faced the truth that it could not work for us. We might be human, no more and no less than the thousands that crowded into the palace walls, but we were also Shadows. Both of us were accustomed to watching for danger, and laying traps to seek enemies out and kill them in their lairs, before they followed us to our own. Neither of us would be able to let such an accomplished enemy lie in wait indefinitely.

Both Temar and I knew that a reckoning was coming between the two of us, and that it would happen when one of our masters turned on the other. We also forgot this fact, half out of convenience and helplessness, and half because our illusion of friendship was so convincing that we had begun to believe it. The most painful times were when the inevitability of it broke through the illusion we had built up, when I remembered that one day he would be a sworn and declared enemy. We were making it worse, pretending to this friendship, but I do not think that either of us knew what else we could do. Certainly, I did not.

It had been a dark and lonely winter. Temar's anger had been expected, nearly a relief after the months of waiting for him to discover the secrets I held. I had borne it without complaint, telling myself that it was no more than I could expect. But when Roine's

---

pleading and tears had turned, also, into cold silence, and my tenuous alliance with Miriel had crumbled, I had felt very alone indeed.

Now, with Miriel's distrust less sharp, I could bear Temar's suspicion. She would be glad when I brought her back a portion of the Duke's plans, and asked for her help in deciphering them. But when I returned to Miriel's rooms that day, I was greeted by a sharp glare from Anna, and Miriel pacing around the room in her best gown, looking panicked.

"He's sent for us," she said bluntly. "Put on your good suit, quickly." She prowled around the bedroom while I changed, looking in the mirror frequently, and I could hear her murmuring her prettiest phrases to herself. She liked to practice before she went to see the King; this unexpected summons had panicked her.

"He said we were to be very discreet," Miriel said, and I could hear the distaste in her voice. It was a matter of contention between the two of them that he insisted on discretion. Miriel never said a word against it; indeed, her words said the very opposite: that discretion was wise, that he must keep himself above the reproach of low people and filthy minds. But she wondered what it might mean, that the King—having gone to the trouble of announcing his infatuation to the court—still took care to keep his meetings with her secret.

Now, like Miriel was doing herself—I could see the fear in her eyes—I wondered if the King was planning to tell Miriel that he could see her no longer. He might well be entertaining offers of marriage from powerful groups within the Council. I racked my brain, and then I remembered Temar's words to keep Miriel out of the King's reach. I pointed to her gown.

"That's too demure."

"What?" She looked down, and then shook her head. "I look beautiful." There was no narcissism in her voice; she was only stating a fact.

"Yes," I said impatiently, "but you look...untouchable." She was dressed in the softest spring green, a heavy winter gown with elaborate brocade at the cuffs of the long sleeves, and a chain of crystals around her waist.

"I'm supposed to be untouchable," she reminded me. "My uncle even reminded you of that. I only put myself forward and flirt when we're in the eyes of the court. Then I'm out of reach." I thought of the subtlety of her flirting, the delicate flutter of her eyelashes, the tiny sway of her hips. She was masterful in her flirtation, entirely above reproach and yet with allure in every word, every gesture. But it was no longer enough, and most especially not enough if her suspicions about this meeting were true. I shook my head.

"That won't work anymore. You need to be proper, but you need to be within his reach."

"What if he's going to tell me—" she broke off, white-faced. "I'll look a fool, if I display myself like a whore and he doesn't want me anymore." But she moved as I touched her shoulder, and I set to unlacing her bodice.

"You won't look like a whore," I said. "And even if he is summoning you to say that, it's not because he doesn't want you. *You're* to dress so that he knows what a mistake he's making. Then be demure. You'll get him back."

"Which dress, then?" she was intrigued.

"The new deep blue, for summer."

"It's too thin," she demurred, but I shook my head.

"That's the point. You'll be shivering when you arrive. It looks vulnerable." I helped her into the gown and laced it as quickly as I could. She looked in the mirror and nodded, noticing—with a professional eye—how the color made her hair gleam, how it set off her eyes. It was a deep, rich color, the silk so soft that one could hardly look at it without wanting to reach out and stroke it. Her skin was creamy, and she shone with youth. Freed of the heavy folds of the green dress, the sway of her hips could be seen. She nodded at her reflection, and then I helped her put a cloak around her shoulders and we set off.

"My Love," the King said, as she came into the room. As she did with him, Miriel gave a little shrug and the cloak slithered from her shoulders. I saw the King's eyes take in every inch of her, and he swallowed. As I knelt to pick up the cloak, I commended myself on a job well done, and hoped beyond hope that he had not set his stubborn mind to giving her up.

"My love, I have the most wonderful news for you," he said, "but...also a most delicate question." I melted away to the side of the room, laid Miriel's cloak over a chair, and tried to become invisible.

"Dusan has accepted your proposal!" Miriel guessed, breathless, and the King laughed, nodded, and grasped her hands. He was relieved to see her looking happy; I knew that she had put his cautionary words out of her mind in an instant. She must be seen to celebrate his good fortune. She sobered, however, as his face fell.

"Please, your Grace, do not look so sad. This is the most wonderful news, surely nothing can be so bad as to cause you to frown."

"Oh, my love..." The King dropped into his chair and sank his head into his hands. "I must ask something of you, and it pains me—and it pains me that you might mistrust my motives."

"I could never mistrust your motives, your Grace," Miriel said. "I am your loyal subject, you have only to command."

"I would never command you," he said. He leaned forward to her, his eyes pleading. "The Council besieges me with proposals of marriage, and I must persuade them that I am open to reason, that my mind is not clouded by love." From the distaste in his voice, I knew that he was quoting one member or another. "They have become quite obsessed with you, my dearest. They wish to know how often I see you, where we meet, what we speak of. I thought...I mean to say..."

"You must put me aside, your Grace," Miriel said sweetly. She spread her hands. "If I am the cause of mistrust, if the council commands you—"

"The Council does not command me!" he burst out, and I marveled at her courage. She twisted the knife at the risk of his displeasure.

"Of course not," Miriel soothed. "But I would not be the cause of unrest. If you and I must part..." her voice broke, and she squared her shoulders. "Oh, your Grace. I will not cause you any difficulty. You will hear not one word of complaint from me. It will be as if we had never met."

"No, no!" He reached out and clasped her hands. "No, never say that we should part. Oh, dearest, I could never bear such a thing. Look at the tears in your eyes! No, it would be too painful for us."

"Then what?" She looked bewildered, hopeful.

"I meant only that it might *seem* that I entertained other offers of marriage. I never would! Never," he said emphatically. "I could not bear to marry another. But it would seem as if I could, as if I no longer watched you at dinner. I would speak nothing of you to the Council. I would meet you only when I was sure no one followed me—perhaps, sometimes, Wilhelm could carry messages to you. Would that be acceptable to you?"

I marveled at a King, asking forgiveness of a girl such as Miriel. She had him in her thrall as deeply as ever, and I knew she was itching to throw a triumphant smirk in my direction. I wondered if I would always be able to see beneath the mask. Certainly, Garad did not; he was flushed with worry. He could see only a woman who might be upset with him.

"Oh! Oh, yes." Miriel smiled up at him. She took a deep, shuddering breath. "Of course, your Grace. Only tell me what I must do. I will do anything I can to help." She blinked back the tears she had so conveniently conjured, and smiled once more. "And then, please," she begged him, "tell me more of the meeting with Dusan?"

While we walked the twisting corridors back to our rooms, I stole a glance over at her and saw that her face was set not in triumph, but in frustration and fear.

"Why are you worried?" I asked, curiously. "He could not bear the thought of parting with you."

"He thinks he cannot," she said grimly. "But, right now— every decision he makes, he discusses with me. *That* is why he cannot bear the thought of parting. He thinks he cannot live without me by his side every moment."

"But this is only a false separation," I said, determined not to understand.

"No, he *thinks* it is false," she said, trying to be patient. "He will think: I will not look over and smile at her, so that no one knows I am thinking of her, but I will still hold her in my heart and smile to think of her. And then the next night, he will think the same thing. And the next night, and the next night—and then one night, he won't think it at all. And it will be the same with advice: first he will wonder what I would think, and write to me, and then one day that will be too much trouble. He will think nothing of it at all, but one day he will realize that he has been living without me at his side and he has not even missed me."

Her voice had dropped as she spoke, and now it was only a trembling whisper. Her hands were clenched, and I saw that her frustration had been a refuge against real fear. Her eyes were wide, and I reached out to touch her shoulder.

"Don't worry," I said. "I don't think he could ever forget you that way. And it won't last so long—you'll have him back at your side before there's even a chance for him to forget you." Miriel took a deep breath, unclenching her hands and straightening her shoulders. She nodded.

"I hope you're right," she said, but I knew she did not believe me at all.

Chapter 12

For a time, I truly thought that Miriel had been mistaken. The King sent whole sheaves of love letters, it seemed, pages upon pages of ardent prose—and, to my silent amusement, poetry—and Miriel sent back letters fully as lengthy. Despite herself, she was becoming caught up in his excitement for the upcoming event, and even I was impressed by the sheer spectacle of it. Garad was eager to tell Miriel every detail of his plans, and she was pleased enough to help him plan it all.

It would have been difficult to remain indifferent. The meeting of the Kings was to be an event to end all events. A call had gone out in the city, in the outlying towns, and craftsman came by the hundreds, clambering into carts to be taken out to the plains east of the mountains. With them were sent long wagon trains of lumber, stone, and plaster dust, for there, on the plains, a veritable town was to be built just for this: the Meeting of the Peacemakers. Miriel and I giggled over the self-importance of the name, and even the Duke's mouth twitched when we told him of it.

Garad spared no expense; indeed, he was relishing the chance to show Heddred's prosperity. Fields were bought from farmers and plowed under to make way for miniature palaces and elegant houses, stands of trees cut down to make way for inns, and then exquisite gardens built up around them. Royal servants were sent to be innkeepers, hostlers, pages, bakers. There was going to be a plaza paved with marble and inlaid with the crests of the two royal houses. Artisans set to work carving the sheaf of wheat, the symbol of House Warden, and the leaping fish, the symbol of King Dusan, into the woodwork of the mansions, adorning the lintels of the doors, the backs of the chairs. Everywhere one turned, there would be a gilded sign, a carving, a rich carpet, each with the two crests intertwined.

Royal servants were sent out of the palace to inspect the wares of the merchants who had flocked to the city. One could barely move out in the streets, so thickly did they line the roadsides. Furniture, lamps, cloth, rugs, and baubles of all kinds were hawked from the street corners, everything carved with the sheaf of wheat and the leaping fish. The servants went proudly, the royal crest on their tunics, to search out the finest wares; they were also sent, more quietly, to search out the finest of the whores, and offer them passage to the village as well.

The best goods were bought by order of the King and loaded into carts, an endless wagon train that now raised a cloud of dust one could see stretching on for miles. At the end of the train came wagons full of cured meats, whole wagons of onions or potatoes, casks of wine and dried fruits, sugar and oil. With them rode the royal cooks, looking put-upon and surly.

In the bustle, I heard many of the servants sighing and shaking their heads, making grand statements about the vanities of the rich and how nobles never thought of the trouble for the common folk when they made such farfetched schemes. They did not bother to lower their voices to me. Temar and I might be considered strange, secretive, unusually close to the nobles, and potential killers, but we were also servants, and that counted for something—enough, at any rate, that servants did not always stop their chatter when we approached.

Every day the complaints grew more prevalent, and the rumors grew more and more preposterous. In any given day, I was likely to hear a story or two on the fanciful side of plausible, and ten or more that could never have been true at all, at least one of which usually involved sorcerers or assassins. A few servants had even asked me to my face if I'd been told to kill any of the Ismiri nobles. Even as I rebuffed these, stories of the King's tyranny spread unchecked.

"—and said that any plasterer as *didn't* report for duty would be killed!" one servant hissed to his companion.

"Yer being crazy," the other man said, heaving a bag of flour into the wagon. "How'd they know, then?"

Or: "And who's to stay with the little ones, then, if we're all to go? They're leaving a palace of children, I tell you, and it'll be burned to the ground when we're back."

And another woman: "All his Majesty's furniture! I ask you, will he be needing all four presence chambers? And a piano? What will he be using that for?"

Not all of it was fairytale and complaint, of course. From the gossips, I learned that the King's uncle Arman Dulgurokov would be smuggling his mistress along, disguised as a washer-woman, that no less than three of the council members had come to inquire about the availability of whores in the plains city, and that several of the young ladies of the court were atwitter about a masquerade ball that might allow them to slip away unnoticed with handsome men from Ismir. When I heard that last, I shook my head and resolved to speak to Miriel about it at once.

When I arrived in her chambers, the place was a riot of color, swatches and bolts of fabric strewn across the couches and her bed. Miriel herself was being fitted for a gown, a deep red— permitted, as it was the color of House Warden—and choosing swatches of fabric for another dozen gowns. Netting and ribbons trailed all over the room, and a veritable army of seamstresses rushed back and forth, offering different colors and cloths for Miriel's perusal.

She shot me a look as I came into the room.

"Where have you been?" she demanded.

"Arranging your lodging with the stewards." I leaned against the wall and folded my arms. I had wanted to advise her that half the ladies of the court would be trying to sneak into noblemen's beds, and she had best be careful not to be accused of the same, but I was not about to do so with the seamstresses here. Seamstresses heard the best of the gossip, and they would be keeping an ear cocked to hear what the King's reported mistress and her servant spoke of.

Miriel made a show of ignoring me. Her excitement had bled away in the past few days, and now she was half-crazed with worry about this event, having been called to her uncle's rooms nearly a dozen times in the past few days. There were lectures on propriety, and the fine line between reminding the King where his heart lay, and playing the whore. First, the Duke had thought it best that Miriel should appear the most accomplished of the Queen's maidens, so that the Ismiri might think her a natural next Queen— but then he had called us back the same day to say that perhaps it was better if Miriel were hardly noticed at all. We had enough enemies here. The day after, he called us back to tell us that Miriel *should* be noteworthy, but not when she danced—

On and on it went, and Miriel grew more and more frenzied and snappish. The King never failed to send messages to her, carried by Wilhelm Conradine, or passed to me by a Royal Guardsman. Still, in the flurry of preparations, the King was making good on his plan to appear finished with Miriel. He no longer looked at her at dinner, he did not stop to speak to her if he visited the maidens' chambers after dinner, he no longer even met with her in the nights in case they should be watched. Instead, he danced with Linnea Torstensson and Maeve of Orleans, Elizabeth Cessor and Marie de la Marque, and from amongst the older girls he singled out Cintia Conradine.

Miriel had to bear her own fear of his growing independence, and also the gleeful rumor-mongering of the Court; she was always surrounded by whispered comments and hidden smiles. The Duke's suspicion of the plan—he had worried aloud that it might be a sop, only to avoid a scene with Miriel as he cast her off—only worsened her fears.

She had started to take her frustrations out on me, snapping criticisms of every little thing I did, and our constant spats had only gotten worse. Every piece of spite and malice to which she could not respond at dinner was marked, totted up, and dealt back to me. It reminded me of the old days, her veiled insults and her anger, and no matter if she sighed and apologized, I was beginning to grow tired of it.

So now I strolled over to one of her upholstered seats, pulled the expensive bolts of fabric off of it, and plopped down, propping my boots on the table. At once she turned to glare at me.

"Get up." She tossed her hair as she turned back to admire herself in the mirror.

"Why?" I stayed where I was.

"Because you need to be fitted for new clothes." Her voice sharpened. "And because I told you to."

"I don't need new clothes." I looked at her gown and shrugged. "No one will pay any attention to me anyway, not if you're doing your job correctly." Her eyelids flickered at the blow.

"You're in my train, remember," she warned. "People see you. We're to be perfect. You can't wear those britches and that tunic. And not those boots."

I had a moment of pure horror. "You don't mean to put me in dresses?"

"Don't be ridiculous. You'd look a fool in a dress." Only Miriel could take your words and slide them back under your skin without seeming to try. She smiled, sweet as poison. "But you could at least wear something better than that baggy old thing."

This argument again. I froze. Since our last birthday, I had grown like a beanstalk, shedding the baby fat Miriel had so mercilessly teased me for. At first, I had become so thin that my ribs had showed. No matter how much I ate—and all the cooks' threats could not keep a growing child out of a kitchen—I never gained back the roundness in my cheeks or the childish pudginess on my frame. Even with stick-thin arms and sticking-out ribs, I had grown enough the fine suit of clothes that had been commissioned for me had strained across my body, and in the past few weeks especially, I had noticed things happening that I wished would stop.

I had been terrified that Miriel would notice, and so I went to the armorer who, fed up with trying to clothe my still-growing frame, had agreed to give me a tunic far too big for me. Miriel had teased me about it for weeks, alternately exclaiming delightedly about how provincial I looked, and hissing that I made her look like a minor noble, one who couldn't afford to dress her servants properly. Once, fed up with her taunts, I had hissed back that she was really just a merchant girl, her father a poor noble and her mother a new one, and I had earned a ringing slap across the face for my trouble. But she had let the issue of the clothing go, at least until now.

When she saw me hesitate, Miriel's eyes narrowed.

"What? What are you hiding, then?" In a flash, as fast as thought, she was across the room, her hands ripping at my tunic, pushing it aside from my stomach as I struggled to back away. The seamstresses were not even bothering to hide their interest. They watched, wide-eyes, as—unable to push Miriel off me, not permitted to grab her wrists or throw her as I would another attacker—I was pushed up against the wall, her shoulder jabbed up topress against my chest, her hands holding the tunic away from me. She stared at the bared flesh of my stomach, then back at me, her eyes narrowed. I was so wrapped up in my own embarrassment that it took me a moment to realize what she was looking for. When I did, I laughed in her face, I was so incredulous.

"You think I'm *pregnant*?"

"What else would you hide so?" she challenged me. "I expect it—you're disgraceful! Flaunting yourself in britches and boots like a man, showing your legs! You're out in the yards, wrestling with Temar, practicing with the men!" My face flamed, but I said nothing; I had heard the sharp note of jealousy in her voice, and she knew it. My freedom terrified Miriel, offended her, intrigued her. Her face colored, too, and she looked away, stepping back as I pulled the tunic straight.

"Well? Get down to your linen. Let the seamstress measure you."

There was no gainsaying her. After a silent moment, I pulled the tunic over my head, and heard her indrawn breath as she saw what I had been hiding. I felt a flash of spite; of course she had not seen beyond the tunic, of course she had not thought to ask why I was wearing it. Miriel never asked why, not where I was concerned. This was the basis of our relationship these days, more so than my britches or her beautiful face: Miriel did not trouble herself to watch the servants, and I did not trouble myself to tell her that she missed much useful information that way.

Now, she stared at the linen bindings I had wrapped, as tightly as I could, over my chest. "You're turning into a woman, then." Her voice was flat, and I heard the match to my own disappointment, which was so sharp that I could not even bring myself to respond.

I was not a fool. I knew that these things happened to other girls, that they grew bosoms and that their hips widened and their waists narrowed. That was a good figure, good for childbearing, good for catching a man's eye. But it was useless to me, who needed a clear draw on my bow, who needed a sword belt to lie flat at my waist, who needed not to catch any man's eye, but instead slip unseen through the palace.

So when I looked down one morning and saw the fabric straining against my chest, I had not felt the glow of satisfaction that I was turning into a woman. I had felt horror. I had felt betrayal. This could not be happening, I told myself. It happened to other women—but not to me. Not to me. I was not really a woman, after all, as Miriel was so fond of pointing out, but some strange thing, half girl and half boy. I did not want to be a woman. I had run to Roine and begged for linen to bind my breasts. Her lips had tightened, as they did when I asked for something that would help me continue in the Duke's service, but she had acquiesced.

Every morning since, I had risen early, snuck out of the bedroom, and wrapped the bandages as tightly as I could around my chest, one thought always in my mind: Temar could not see me that way. At the very thought of it, even weeks later, panic gripped me. Temar could *not* see me this way.

For some reason—and I hated this—my breath came short when I thought of that, and I knew it must be obvious, plain as day on my face. Things had changed. When I had sparred with Temar two years ago, it had been true play-fighting. I had adored him, but it had been the strange, clear love of a child; I had been consumed with his vision of the Shadow he wanted me to be. When we had sparred, I imagined I was protecting Miriel, I dreamed of using the throws against assassins, of winning a fight and laying my knife to an attacker's throat. Now, when we fought, I tried to focus on the necessity, remember the feeling of fighting for glory, and yet all I felt was a terrible self-consciousness.

I would lie awake at night with my pulse racing and my face burning as I thought of the day's lessons: Temar's cool, impersonal hands at my waist and his impassive voice as he lectured me for a throw, or his satisfaction at beating me in sparring. I knew well enough what lay between us: mistrust and lies, danger and anger. But it was all muddled, everything was strange in ways I would have died rather than confide in Miriel. Miriel, who was so quick to remind me that Temar was an enemy—as if I did not know, as if these feelings were not the worst possible thing that could have happened. I hid behind the truce that he and I had built up, and prayed that this all went away soon.

I tried to slow my breathing now, as Miriel looked me over. I knew that she did not see into my mind, that she could not see anything past the strange new shape of my body. I had hidden it not only because I was confused and ashamed, but because I had known instinctively that I should not let Miriel see these changes. Not Miriel, who was so stick-thin that she bought new gowns for vanity, and not necessity, who had to lace so tightly that she could barely breathe, just to try to get a hint of a waist, of a bosom.

How could I tell Miriel that this strange new body of mine was something that disappointed me? I knew that Roine would tell me not to be ashamed of myself, and I felt guilty for my thoughts. I knew that it was ridiculous. Every girl turned into a woman. There was no hiding what I was. But somehow I had thought I might, that my britches and my fighting and my unladylike studies might fool even my own self, and I would stay as I had always been—just me, just Catwin.

So I stood in complete silence while Miriel took one look at my burning face and then pretended to ignore me, and the seamstress moved about me with a measuring cord, remarking once on the smallness of my waist and then lapsing into awkward silence herself. I allowed myself a small inward smile at the fact that she did not know what to say. How did one compliment the Lady

Miriel's strange half-girl servant? No one knew. No one ever knew how to treat me. It was one of the few amusing things about my life.

I looked over once and saw Miriel staring into the fire, her arms folded over her chest, her face the very picture of scorn and spite. Miriel could care less that I wanted none of the odd shapes that seemed to be a part of my body now. She was the one who needed them, who was supposed to have the bosom and the womanly charms to go with her stunning face. She was the one who was supposed to enchant men, and there was she with her lack of figure—hard enough to bear—and here was I with all of the things her seamstresses sighed about.

When I was done, I dressed, silently, and left. She still would not look at me. She did not speak to me for the next week, in fact, through the fittings of my fine new tunics and britches, my new, soft, black leather boots. One morning, however, I found a package on my cot, wrapped in linen: Miriel had ordered me a tabard with the Celys crest, to drape over the tunic itself. Whether she had done it to ease my embarrassment or to avoid begging the comparison between our figures, I did not know—Miriel sometimes surprised me with her strange moments of kindness—but I knew better than to mention it.

So it was in polite silence that we set out from Penekket, sitting quietly together in the Duke's covered carriage as he and Temar rode outside in the sunshine. Miriel, desperate that this event should not mean the end of her influence over the King, forgot her sulkiness entirely and spent the entire journey murmuring pretty phrases to herself, practicing a clever toss of her head, or a witty jest. I, stuck in the jolting carriage, envied her the preoccupation.

Where I had first been awed by the procession of the nobles, marveling at the beautifully painted carriages, and fine horses, the jewels and the capes, the novelty had worn off quickly. The citizens of Penekket had turned out alongside the road to cheer our passage, throwing flowers and calling blessings, agape at the splendor, but they had seen it all only for a moment. Trapped in the slow-moving procession, watching the nobles as the days wore on and they drew closer to their Ismiri enemies, I knew that beneath all the finery, this procession radiated desperation and fear.

Chapter 13

"This is ridiculous," Miriel muttered. I shook my head and smiled brightly at her, a reminder to keep her own face pleasant.

"He wanted to show Dusan—and Kasimir— that Heddred is rich and powerful," I said. Miriel shot me a glare as her horse jibed at the crowd. She spread one hand along its neck, clucking at it a little to soothe it. We had spent most of the past two weeks in a carriage, and by rights should be glad to be out in the open air, but in truth, we were both overwhelmed. Garad had been determined that we should make a proper procession into the town, displaying our wealth to the Ismiri, and so we were wearing our best clothes in the summer heat, waving and smiling until our faces hurt. Thus it was that the crowd pressed around us, hoisting tankards of ale and throwing rose petals, and we struggled to control the horses that we plainly terrified at the noise.

"Could he not do it without taking all of us from the palace?" Miriel's irritation was clear despite the sweetness of her tone and the dazzling smile she was now keeping fixed firmly on her face. The servants and minor nobles of Ismir had turned out to see the King's procession ride into town, and we were all on show. On the other side of the city, the Heddrian servants would be crowding the road to see the procession of Ismiri nobles. I had heard endless speculation of what the Ismiri might look like, and some of the predictions were dire, indeed—I had even heard one or two whispers that they might have cloven hoofs, like devils.

Miriel was still muttering, but I barely heard her, I was so busy scanning the crowd for threats. The thought of this ride into town had given me nightmares; I had woken the night before drenched in sweat and terrified. The crowd pressed close, as it had done in my dream, and I could not help but scan it for the sight of a face I might recognize, any detail that would show me that the dream had been prescient, that a poison-edged blade waited here for the woman I was bound to protect.

I had made the mistake of asking Miriel if she was scared as well. She had been short with me when we left Penekket, but had grown increasingly withdrawn and silent as we progressed across the plains. When I had been in the throes of the nightmare the night before, it had been Miriel who woke me, shaking my shoulder and calling my name softly. When I had calmed myself and changed my clothes, I had taken notice of her white face, and how she lay sleepless on her little bed. I had asked her if she was well, or if she was afraid, too.

"Why, what have I to fear?" she asked sharply.

"I just thought—so many nobles. Tension." My voice trailed off. I could not say out loud that I feared another assassination attempt, but logic dictated that it was a very real danger. If our would-be murderer stood to benefit from tension between Ismir and Heddred, it would be easy enough to kill Miriel and fix the blame on some Ismiri noble or another—and be rid of her, for whatever reason they had chosen.

From Miriel's white face, I knew that she had been thinking the same thing. But these days were full of fear for her. It was very nearly worse to live in constant fear of the King's favor fading away. What was there for her if he dropped her? Favorites of the Kings could sometimes catch good marriages at court, but it was not likely. And it was equally likely that her uncle would simply kill her for her failure, and pass it off as an illness, a fall from her horse...

And, fearing this, she must hold her head high every day and ignore the whispers that she had lost him, knowing that a few thought less of her, others reveled in her apparent downfall, and the rest pitied her. Worse, she must watch the King laugh and dance with others, fearing that his subterfuge would become truth, and his heart would fix on one or another of them.

Worst of all, Miriel's prediction had come true: she was no longer his advisor in every little matter. They sent letters through Wilhelm, but such communications were limited, and so Miriel must hear of the King's decisions, knowing that he had undertaken them alone, and praying that he might not realize that her advice was unnecessary after all. Fear was with her always, and it wore on her.

"Well?" she challenged me, daring me to speak these thoughts aloud.

"I just thought—"

"Well, don't. Don't *pity* me." Her face was screwed up. "And don't you let anyone kill me." She had fairly thrown herself over on her side, facing away from me, the covers pulled up over her shoulders.

We had gone to sleep in an angry silence that barely concealed our fear, and now that fear rose higher as we rode into town, until I thought I might gag on it. The people threw rose petals, as they had been bid, and the nobles threw back gold from their purses, as was customary. The air was fragrant with blossom and loud with cheers and laughter, and yet behind it all was a dreadful curiosity, a hunger to know what might happen at such an unprecedented event.

With trepidation, I noticed the jaded expressions of the servants in the crowd. They did not expect a lasting peace from this. They were waiting for it all to go horribly wrong, and I felt so similarly that I nearly jumped in front of Miriel every time I saw a look, or a whisper, or a pointed finger. Her face was known, and not only by the servants of Heddrian courtiers. She was the niece of the man who had captured Voltur, she had been raised in what had once been Ismir's royal seat. They would have no love for her in Ismir.

We were too far back to hear the grand welcome from Garad to Dusan. Miriel sat at my side in the stopped procession, hardly minding that she did not have to smile prettily through the ridiculous speeches the two men were making, but grinding her teeth that it was Marie de la Marque who sat in the King's train, royal in her own right, daughter to the King's guardian, and once more a favored candidate for the King's bride.

We were told of the formal greeting later, while Roine braided my newly washed hair. She was traveling with us at the Duke's insistence, and I was hardly comforted at the thought that even he wondered if we would need the attentions of a healer. In true motherly fashion, she had insisted that I take a bath, even though I was glad enough to do so. On the road, there had been no such extravagances for a servant, but in this village we all had hot water, scented soaps, fine bath sheets. Newly clean, I felt like a noble myself, dressed in one of my new tunics, a black tabard with hidden pockets, and new britches and boots.

Temar was not inclined to let me relax. He prowled around as I bathed, hidden by a carved screen, and as soon as I was decent, he came and sat between me and my view of Miriel, who was the hub of frantic activity; she was being dressed by five maidservants, stitched into a gown ordered by the Master of the Revels. She was to represent the bountiful harvests of peacetime, and was accordingly dressed in gold and orange silks, hung with ribbons of reds and browns, and with long, draping sleeves cleverly-cut to resemble falling leaves. Another maidservant was winding ribbons and jewels into her hair.

Temar snapped his fingers in front of my face to get my attention. He was impatient, even more worried than I was for the safety of those he guarded. The Duke was one of the most widely-hated men in Ismir, and there had already been an altercation: after the formal meeting, in the bustle, some guardsmen of Kasimir's household shouted at Temar and the Duke's servants that their master would see ours dead, and soon, and stick his head on a spike over the gate at Voltur castle. It had been hushed up, but we were all on our guard now.

"How did the greeting go?" I asked. The Duke's household had been far back, but the Duke himself had ridden with the Council, directly behind the royal family. Temar had been able to witness the event first-hand, and I was envious. "How were the Ismiri? What was Dusan like? And Kasimir." Temar held up a hand to stem the flow of questions, but he was smiling. He had chosen me for my inquisitive nature, and he was closest to forgiving me when he saw it demonstrated.

"Nothing of importance happened," he assured me. "Really. All like a play, very flowery speeches. No surprises. Kasimir wore mourning black for his father, but no one expected subtlety from him." He snorted. It was against his own rules to be so blatant, and it offended him to see others break that rule—even if it made his own job easier.

"And the Queen?"

"Jovana? Yes, she was there. In state. All in cloth of gold." I was impressed. Dusan must be taking this seriously, to bring his wife. I knew that Jovana was rarely seen in public now, she was a queen beloved of her husband, but tormented by grief and guilt. Vaclav had been her only son, born the last of eight children, and he had been her favorite, the golden child. Now he was dead, and Jovana's failure to produce more sons for Dusan meant that the throne would pass out of his direct line.

"Tonight, there will be more to see," Temar predicted. "Anyone can keep their face straight for a half an hour, but give them wine and dark corners, and—" He snapped his fingers and I nodded. He held up a little map of the village that he had made for me. "Now. We will watch the masque here, on the plaza. After that, we will withdraw here to eat. You paced everything out like I told you?"

I nodded. As Miriel and the Duke would be sharing a suite of rooms here in the village, Temar had declared it safe enough for me to leave her with them and go inspect the public area. I had taken off my tabard before I went, and put on one of the homespun tunics I had brought with me, knowing that my fine black suit would attract attention. There were too many guards, and they watched too closely. Better if the Ismiri did not know that I guarded Miriel.

It was all very fine in the village, quite as beautiful as the King had written to Miriel that it would be. I had taken notice of the compass rose inlaid in the plaza, with the Warden crest at the east point, and Dusan's crest at the west point. I strolled around and looked up at the buildings that bordered the plaza. A bowman could hide in any one of those windows while the dance went on, and yet—he would be trapped if the guards went in to find him. No, if death came for us, it would be subtler.

Still, I scoped out the hidden alcoves in the banquet hall, noted the way the shadows fell and the lights flickered. Even the chandeliers were shaped with the two crests; I could hardly look anywhere without seeing something gold-plated, jewel-encrusted. The servants must be making a fortune, knowing that no one would notice one less candlestick, one less bauble.

"Do you think we're safe tonight?" I asked Temar.

"We're never safe."

"I know that," I said, nettled. "But...from an assassin. Do you think one would come tonight?" After a pause, he shook his head.

"Not tonight. Not for her." Worry made lines on his forehead, and I knew he was thinking of the Duke—of men so driven that they would not care that their death followed an assassination. "Just mark who watches her."

And so I did. Miriel danced as if she were a tongue of flame, leaping and twirling so that her sleeves fluttered and her hair flew. She whirled down the aisle of the other dancers and then held her hands high above their heads as they danced beneath themselves. It was difficult not to watch her, and for all his pretended indifference, I saw that the King could not keep his eyes from her.

As she and her partner danced forward towards the two Kings, I saw the envoy lean slightly and murmur a few words in Dusan's ear. The Ismiri King raised his eyebrows and leaned forward to watch, marking her as a beauty, as a player in the game for the throne. He murmured something back to his envoy, and I had the uncomfortable feeling that he was giving instructions. At the side of the dais, Kasimir watched, as well, his face impassive. What he thought of any of the dancers, I could not say; his face did not change for the whole of the performance. He looked as if he would see the whole village burned to the ground, and all of us with it—the Heddrians who had what he reckoned his, the Ismiri who did not share his intense hatred.

On the other side of the dais, I saw the High Priest, sitting in state beside his Ismiri counterpart. I laughed to see them together, for while both wore the jeweled robes and heavy gold rings that were the symbols of the Church, they looked out over the revelry as if the extravagance was distasteful to them. I found my eyes darting back to the High Priest as I watched the event; I wondered what it was that he was truly thinking.

With the thaw between us, Miriel had shown me the sheaf of letters passed between her and the High Priest, and I had been surprised, as she had been, at the man's insistence on delaying the uprising itself. I could see from his response that Miriel urged action. She dreamed of a call to the people, a great show of support to show Garad that this was not a movement of violent rebels, but instead of reasoned, peaceful citizens. To her shock, the High Priest swore that it could not be done—not yet. The people had no power, he insisted. They could not organize such a movement. No, the King must be persuaded by his advisors that this was best for Heddred. When I watched him, looking out over the sea of gold and jewels, I wondered just which nobles he thought would be his allies.

Seated between the High Priest and Garad, the Dowager Queen kept a sharp watch on her son as Miriel danced, and she marked who else caught his attention. Cintia was also portraying autumn, her red-gold hair and green eyes well offset by her costume; I saw her smile boldly at the King, and he smiled, easily, back at her. Marie de la Marque wore the colors of spring, so well suited to her porcelain coloring, and she twirled with all the confidence of a beautiful girl who knows that the prize is within her grasp. Another girl with long, fine brown hair, wearing summery green and pink, danced along the aisle and cast a shy smile in Garad's direction. She had a round face and a tip-tilted nose, and her eyes were grey like mine.

"Who is she?" I asked an Ismiri servant nearby, pointing. I used the mountain dialect, and she raised her eyebrows to hear it from a Heddrian servant, but responded readily enough.

"That's Dusan's granddaughter by Iulia." She nodded up to my King. "Now there'd be a match for your King, no?" I shrugged and turned back to the masque. It was ending, with much flourishing and bowing, and the two Kings rose to their feet, applauding and shouting congratulations to the dancers.

And then I saw it. Not what Temar had told me to watch for, no—but more dangerous by far. Miriel, true to her word, cast no looks towards the throne. She was neither petulant nor prideful. She curtsied without flicking her eyes up to the set of thrones at all, and then she turned and took an offered arm for the procession in to dinner. It was one of the boys, dressed in the colors of fall, and they made a beautiful pair. I saw him speak a short, smiling sentence to her, and she laughed. I looked back to the dais, to see if the King was watching her go. He was not, he was speaking earnestly with Dusan and his envoy, but others were watching. I saw Guy de la Marque's smile flicker as if he had just gotten a good hand of cards, and I looked back to the pair.

Miriel's companion, the boy who made her smile so brilliantly and laugh so merrily, was none other than Wilhelm Conradine.

Chapter 14

The days passed in constant frustration for Miriel. Each day had its entertainments: dances and masques and plays so that we rushed from one thing to the next in a roar of ceaseless excitement and laughter, every courtier half-drunk on excitement and half-dead with exhaustion, and me in a frenzy of worry over who might brush into contact with Miriel in the crowd.

I knew that my worry was as ridiculous as it was useless. Even if I could have protected her against some mad courtier with a grudge against the Duke, no one but Kasimir seemed minded to cause trouble here. The courtiers of Ismir were as mad for entertainments and laughter as were the courtiers I knew. They were happy enough to leave behind their grudges and their old rivalries as long as they had banquets and dancing, and the chance for illicit liaisons in the alleyways between the buildings.

Only men such as the Duke and Kasimir carried their grudges and their resentment here, to the village, and the Duke had the good sense to hide his bad feelings behind courtly bows and honeyed words. It was Kasimir, and Kasimir alone, who broke the peace openly. On the first day, he had held his tongue, but since then matters had deteriorated. At dinner on the second night, he had made loud proclamations that peace would be achieved only when ill-gotten gains had been returned to their rightful owners. On the fourth day, he had partnered the Duke in a card game, and had been overheard to say that the King of such a misbegotten country as Heddred should watch his back.

It was inflammatory, and as soon as the court was not hungover on strong Ismiri spirits, and drunk on excitement, they would all be whispering in corners about Kasimir's words. I did not care. For once, I was minded to let Temar watch the nobles and inform me of their whispered conversations. Miriel and I had larger worries. In such a small village, there was no way for her to meet with Garad, and so, when she was not keeping up the pretense of being the most beautiful, the most charming courtier, she prowled around the apartment like a mountain cat, snapping at Anna and glaring at me.

"I know nothing!" she fairly screamed at me. "Nothing. Why does he not send for me? Why does he not want my advice?"

"He can hardly call for you when his every move is being watched by two courts and he is meeting with King Dusan himself," I pointed out, but she would not be appeased.

"Fool. If he wanted to, he could. We've always found ways before!"

"He's been sending letters." I pointed to the two letters on the table, and she knocked them onto the floor with an angry swipe of her arm.

"Only two! And they're stupid letters! Useless! Love letters!"

"How is that useless?" I cried back, and then lowered my voice, mindful of who might have heard us. "He loves you. He's besotted with you."

"Twice a fool!" Miriel had lowered her voice as well, but her anger had not abated. "I get nothing for his love! Love fades, love dies. Pretty words are *nothing*. I need to be the only one he trusts. I need him to believe he can't rule without me at his side! And you told me he wouldn't, but he *is* forgetting me. He *is* learning he doesn't need me." She whirled about to the window, paced, then stopped and clutched her head. "I could go mad. And pick those up." I bit back a retort and gathered the letters carefully, folded each and placed them in a stack on the table.

I did not say so for fear of stoking her anger, but I knew that she was right to be worried. The King stayed closeted with Dusan, shut off from his Council and Dusan's—and from the commanders of the last war—as the two of them spoke frankly about the troubled history of their nations. Only rumors escaped that room, every one easily discernible as a wild fancy to every listener except the one whose land was rumored to be ceded, or sold, or taken by the crown for roads and quarries. Each courtier laughed off the others' concerns, and spoke fearfully of their own. The Bone Wastes were to be conquered, the DeVere land was to be handed back to Ismir—and, triumphantly spread by Conradine and de la Marque servants, the King was planning to cede Voltur back to the Ismiri; despite his good sense, the last had the Duke in a frenzy of irritation and worry.

"We'll go see the King when the court is on the move again," I soothed her. "And you really do have his heart now."

She nodded. "If only someone were to speak against me,"

she said fretfully. "Then he would want to defend me. It would awaken his love and he would want to say that he had spoken for me."

"Too risky." I did not want anyone reminding the King of Miriel's low birth, and reviving the talk about marrying without love and having a mistress on the side. Not with Ismiri princesses dancing about.

"So what do you suggest?" she asked sharply, and I bit my lip. There was no good answer. If she defied Garad's wishes and went to him, he might be angry—he would accuse her, and rightly, of endangering his plans. If she played along with his scheme, however, she became nothing. She faded into the background.

She did not wait for me to make a suggestion.

"I'll send for Wilhelm," she decided. "He'll know what to do." I looked at her bright, flushed face, and had a stab of misgiving.

"You be careful," I warned her.

"Of what?" She frowned at me, then shook her head. "You don't understand the court, Catwin I can't be cautious like you. If I want to win, I have to be the only one he sees; your place is in the shadows—mine is in the light. There isn't any time to waste, and there's only one person who knows the King better than I do."

I raised my eyebrows and said nothing. I did understand the court, I thought, better than she knew. I knew that her friendship with Wilhelm, once a secret acquaintance, was blossoming, and that I was not the only one who had seen it. I knew that an innocent friendship was the stuff of which lurid rumors were made. And Miriel could not afford this rumor. But these were her uncle's rooms. Wilhelm would arrive openly, during the day.

And Miriel needed a way to keep the King's eye.

I pushed down my sense of forboding and nodded. As Miriel sat down to write a response to the King's most recent letter, I sent one of the Duke's pages for Wilhelm Conradine, instructing him sharply to summon the Lord if he was at liberty, and leave him be if he was not. We did not need to court trouble. Then I sent as many of the servants away as I could, sending them each on lengthy errands until only Anna was left.

It was not much later that Wilhelm arrived, tapping on the door and bowing deeply to Miriel. I reflected that this, at least, was a more equal pairing. Wilhelm was half king's blood, half nothing, his ancient lineage undeniable, but more a liability than a help; there were even rumors that his mother had not wanted to marry a

Conradine at all, though she took their side now. Unlike Garad, when Wilhelm came into the room, he had cause to bow low to Miriel; those who rode the currents of the King's favor could lift up others. Miriel and Wilhelm were bound together as allies, or enemies, as they chose. They had always smiled at each other with understanding. Understanding, and somewhat more—but I pushed that thought away.

"Lady Miriel," Wilhelm said graciously. I saw him hide his pleasure at seeing her. His bow was exquisite, his tone courtly.

"My Lord." Miriel curtsied back. The two of them were children, but not. Play-acting, but not.

"How may I be of service?" Wilhelm cast his eyes around the room. They were blue, I noted, pale to Miriel's dark, and he shared the King's fine, sandy hair. His face was well-formed, his cheekbones high, his jaw sharp. He had become a sensation at the court earlier in the year, when the courtiers were minded to think of the Conradines as tragic figures and not potential traitors. Any woman might lose her heart to that smile, but Miriel appeared not to take the slightest notice of it. As she drew him towards the chairs by the fire, she said,

"It is...in regards to the King." Her steady smile did not waver when his jaw tightened.

"Yes?" He had hoped for more, perhaps, after their laughing conversation the other night; he did not want her to call him to her rooms to speak of the King. But he did not lose his composure. Only someone listening closely could have heard the sudden edge in his voice. Then again, Miriel always listened closely, and she missed nothing. For all her feigned distraction, I knew from the quick rise and fall of her chest that she was as aware of him as he was of her.

I had wondered how she would play this, her appeal to the king's closest friend. I had thought that she might make some clever excuse; she was skilled at such things. She surprised me, however. She did not coquet, she was grave and quiet.

"I feel I can trust you, my Lord," she said soberly, and I saw a leap of hope in his eyes.

"You can," he assured her.

"Good." Miriel smiled, but the smile did not reach her eyes, and it dropped away quickly. "Then I will be honest with you, my Lord. No courtly words. I tell you truly—I fear that the King may no longer love me as he once did."

"No." Wilhelm shook his head. His voice was tight. "He loves you still."

"Then how can he bear this?" Miriel whispered. "I am forbidden to be at his side, and so I cannot advise him. I cannot see his smile. How can I help but fear…" She trailed off into the superstitious silence of those who fear that saying a thing could make it true. Then she shook her head. "I am sorry. I do not question his wisdom," she said firmly. "I will not."

"This is too heavy a burden for you." Wilhelm reached out and took one of her hands in his own. "Watching him flirt with other women while he exposes you to such gossip."

"It was necessary," Miriel demurred at once. "He needed the goodwill of his Council." She could switch sides with the most consummate skill; now she lured Wilhelm on. Only I could have seen the flicker of distaste in her eyes, the sad set of her mouth. It was gone in a moment, but I knew that it would come back to her as she lay in bed tonight. Strangely, I was reassured to see it—that the clever lies grew no easier for Miriel, either.

And she adored Wilhelm. For all that she had kept from him, it was plain to see now. She would not want to lie to him any more than I wanted to lie to Roine, or Temar.

Wilhelm, however, saw none of this. He was consumed with his indignation on her behalf. "He is the *King*," he said passionately. "The Council must heed him, even if…"

"Even if?" Miriel leaned closer to hear him, and I saw his fingers clench around hers.

"If I were the King," he told her, "I would not let anyone make me deny my love. I would never hide it. And I would never hurt my love so."

His voice was taut, quavering slightly with emotion; he was no rake, using the careful, intimate tones of seduction, but desire was there. There was only the slightest pause; however I chided her, Miriel had a good sense for danger. The yearning in her eyes was wiped away in an instant, and in its place was a warm smile.

"Ah, my Lord Wilhelm, you will make some noble lady a fine husband," she promised him. "You have the heart of a poet!" He nodded, only his courtly training keeping his shoulders unbowed; his disappointment was plain to see. Miriel laid her hand on his sleeve and smiled. "But the King is not like you and like me," she said. "He is a King. And I am only a girl. Please, my Lord. Help me."

He swallowed. "I will carry any message my lady wishes," he said, chivalry cold in his voice.

115

"Then, please, take him this." Miriel handed him her latest letter, composed carefully by the two of us. It was scented with her perfume, and I wondered if Wilhelm would take it from the pocket of his doublet when he was out of sight of the room, to breathe in the fragrance. "And tell him…"

"Yes, my Lady?"

"Only that I think of him," she said lightly. She was caught in the woman's dilemma, knowing that her love was both ardently desired and yet reviled as weakness. She stared thoughtfully after Wilhelm as he bowed and left.

"You be careful," I said again, and this time she did not reproach me for it. "If the King knew…" She threw a look at me and then crossed the room swiftly, beckoning me into her bedchamber and ushering Anna out, unceremoniously. We waited until we heard her heavy tread cross the room; Anna had long since stopped trying to listen at doors when we talked, after one or two glares from me.

"The King will not know," Miriel said, when she was sure we were alone. "And Wilhelm knows as well as anyone what can and cannot be. Whatever foolish feelings he has, he will have to put them aside." Her face was bland, and I drew closer to her, intrigued.

"You don't mean that."

"No," she agreed pleasantly, "I don't. I mean to hold him. I mean to take his loyalty, and the loyalty of as many as I can— everyone, if I can. And I mean to keep the King's heart, too, and his mind, and then it will be me who rules this kingdom and its lords." She looked straight at me and her deep blue eyes, normally as rich as velvet, were as cold and flat as chips of stone. Whatever love had welled up in her heart as she spoke with Wilhelm, she had pushed it far away.

"You want power?" I asked uncertainly, feeling my way in this conversation.

"Yes. I want power to bend the King and the Council to do what is right for Heddred." I stared at her: this delicate, pretty half-child. I saw the regal bearing, the determined thrust of her chin, the utter, uncompromising conviction in her eyes, and I had the crazy thought that, in the deepest part of her heart, she *wanted* to give Wilhelm up. It was some kind of simple magic, a spell that would make the rebellion all the more precious to her, and free her of her own love for him.

I could hardly see her as the same girl who had traveled to court with me years ago. That Miriel was so insubstantial that a puff of wind might have blown her away. She had been a girl of empty ambition, yearning for advancement without knowing why. She had known no true desire of her own. And now her soul had been sharpened against the grindstones of her uncle's ambition and the court's spite, she had been forged into something altogether harder and more deadly. Her childhood was wiped away, she had gone cold and found a conviction that they could not touch, could not dim.

And I, too, was unrecognizable. I was forged by her need and our shared danger. I would kill now, I knew how, and I knew I could. Last time I had been able to save us both without using my blades, but I knew without doubt that a time would come when I would not have such a choice. I would have to kill—not only to save her, for those who came after Miriel would come for me, too. The Duke had been true to his word: he had intertwined my fate with Miriel's. He had laid the groundwork for our alliance. He had set us down the path to become something more, and something less, than two girls.

I wondered if this was how it was for him and Temar. And then I wondered if Miriel and I could ever change back.

"Things could change," I said. I did not believe it. She might be a child by age alone, but Miriel had seen more of life and pain and fear than most courtiers twice her age. Now she smiled, narrow-eyed, and she looked like her uncle.

"I hope they will change," she said, deliberately misunderstanding me. "I hope the great Lords will remember their duties to the people of Heddred. I hope that the King will remember that the powers granted to him are given by the church—and that the church may one day remember that it serves the Gods and not its own wealth. But that won't happen on its own. The High Priest is turning the church back to its origins, and I am turning the court, and the King. And to do that, I need everyone. And Wilhelm supports the rebellion," she added. "He'll be a good ally for that reason alone."

"You said you wouldn't do more than writing letters until you were Queen!"

"I might not. But I might have to."

"No," I whispered, as much a plea as an accusation. "You said..."

"Don't reprimand me. You're on my side," she reminded me. "You promised."

"I'm on *our* side," I retorted. "*You* promised. And this puts us both in danger." I sighed at the look on her face. "You're not going to give this up, are you?"

"I can't." For all that I knew her to be a consummate liar, a woman who could charm and dazzle thought out of any mind, I could not resist the sincerity in her voice. "Catwin, I swear to you, I cannot give this up. It touches my very soul—I feel that this is why I was born to this earth, to help them." Her steely mask had slipped away, and as I puzzled, trying to see if this was only a quieter, gentler mask, I wavered. She saw my uncertainty.

"Please, Catwin. Can you not see that this is the most honorable cause that anyone could choose to serve? Of all people, I would have expected you to understand. You know that you are no less a person than a noble. You know that you have a mind as sharp, a soul as worthy. Why should nobles rule your life?"

I laughed; I could not help it. "Because I am oath-sworn to protect one of them. And even if not, I am not such a fool as to range myself against those who hold all the power and wealth in the world."

She turned a hooded gaze on me, as lazy as a bird of prey, ready to strike. "You already have," she pointed out. "You and I, we are allies to no one but ourselves. We have powerful enemies."

I wavered again, unsure of myself and cursing my own stupidity. Miriel was a master of twisting an argument, but I had never been the target of her skill before, I could not deny her logic.

"It's different," I said uncertainly. "With a court, you can set the players against each other—they're all working for the same prizes, they'd be glad to see one another fall. But if you fight for this, they'll band together. This strikes at all of them."

"We can still set them against each other," Miriel said confidently. "If we play it right."

"It's too risky." My tried-and-true response.

"Catwin..." Another woman would be frustrated by my refusal of her ideals. Miriel had a gentle, understanding smile. "The idea seems strange, I know. But if you cannot accept this cause yet for its own sake, can you not fight for it for love of me?" The question was so strange to me that even she could see my puzzlement. "You're the closest to a sister that I have," she said. "We're bound to each other, we should work together—why are you smiling?"

"I've never had any family," I admitted. "Only Roine, and I

never even called her 'mother.' It's strange to be a sister to someone."

"We're not quite sisters." Miriel tilted her head to the side. "We're more than that. We're like sides of a coin." Even knowing that she would say anything to get her way, I was drawn in.

"You think so?"

"Don't you?" she countered. "My uncle named you my Shadow, so I am shaped to you just as you are shaped to me. I could not be what I am without you, and you would not be here if not for me. I give you cause to fight, and you caution me—you are my conscience, and I am yours."

I giggled. "Your assassin is your conscience?" She was not pleased that I had interrupted her grand speech, but smiled despite herself, and then jumped when a knock sounded on the door.

"Catwin?" Temar opened the door and came in. He bowed when he saw Miriel.

"Ah, my Lady, I hope there is no trouble. I hear Lord Wilhelm Conradine was summoned."

"Yes," Miriel answered, readily enough. "He carries letters between the King and me. The King's letters are on the table outside," she added, gesturing, "if my uncle would like to read them."

Temar stared at her, and I looked between him and Miriel, as if I might see their mutual dislike made manifest in the air. I had only seen the look in his eyes once before, and then it had been Miriel, staring at her uncle. Temar, too, hated to lose, and he hated Miriel for how easily she evaded his traps. He did not trust her in the slightest, and that made her his enemy. I saw the wedge, now, between Temar and the Duke: the Duke, wanting to believe that he had not made a mistake, wanted so badly to trust me and Miriel both that he did, and Temar thought him a fool for it. Now, Temar only bowed.

"I will ask the Duke," he said, and he left without even a glance at me. I looked after him, and when I turned back, Miriel was standing with her arms crossed and her shoulders tilted. In a moment, I recognized an impression of myself.

"You be careful," she said, in a near perfect imitation of my reprimand. She had even caught the faint traces of my mountain accent. When I sighed, she smiled sunnily, and sat down at the desk to read.

Chapter 15

And then, just as quickly as Miriel had seen the threat, it all began to come apart for her. The Meeting of the Peacemakers had finished, Kasimir declaring loudly at any opportunity that only honorable allies were good allies, but both Kings doing their best to ignore him. Now the village was set to be deserted, and we were all to pack. When at last the King thought to contact Miriel, it was only a single sentence on a torn bit of parchment.

"What is it?" I asked curiously. Miriel was staring down at the scrap of paper, her face unreadable.

"He says he will see me when we are on the road again," she pronounced. "He calls his work here a great victory for us both, and assures me that he is working to make my dreams for Heddred a reality." Her tone made it clear what she thought of his assurances.

Here, I thought, lay the difference between Miriel and the Duke. The Duke gloated in victory, he enjoyed it to the fullest, he was smug when he triumphed. Miriel accepted victory only with a calm that masked relief. Each victory was only a step for her, at best, or more likely another moment of evading her own downfall. And I knew she was afraid: one letter, only, a single sentence in response to the dozen notes she had sent him as we stayed in the village. *Was* he slipping away, as she feared?

"How are we to meet him, then?" I asked, when a servant had come into the room for her trunk of clothing and then hauled it away.

"He will take a servant's clothes and come to my tent."

"Anyone could listen in," I said at once.

"Well, you make sure He doesn't," Miriel said simply. I did not need to ask who she meant. There was only one man she was so wary of.

"He'll hear it all, one way or another. Be sure of it. Especially after Wilhelm visited. He's waiting to catch you out at something and take tales back to the Duke."

"You can't stop him?" she challenged.

"I could, but not without him knowing I did," I explained. I lowered my voice, superstitiously afraid that he would know we were talking about him and come to check on us. "We don't want this fight yet, do we?"

"Well, you don't," she said pointedly. I ignored her.

"Watch your words," I told her. She accepted the advice without complaint and drifted out into the main room, where the servants were carrying away every bit of luxury we had brought with us, to be packed into the Duke's cart. Some would be missing when we returned, I knew, and the guard stationed at the village would be unable to keep the servants from taking anything they could lay their hands on to sell: relics of the Meeting of the Peacemakers.

The minor nobles, those without their own estates, were already petitioning the crown to be allowed to buy the beautiful mansions. They would form their own enclave, rent out the inns, and rake in the sort of wealth that the higher nobles deplored.

As the week was drawing to a close, I saw the courtiers move through the village with drawn faces. They did not want to return home, where their entertainments were only draperies in the great hall, the dancing of men and maids they saw every day, dinners cooked by the same chefs. They wanted the fireworks and elaborate sets and glittering masquerades never to end. This was a magical place, where a courtier or a councilor could forget that the battles of the world forged onward. Life outside was filled with woes.

Of the courtiers, it was the King's Councilors who fretted the most. Like Miriel, they had been locked out of the long discussions between Garad and Dusan. They and Dusan's councilors circled each other warily, all suspecting the rest of knowing some vital scrap of information. They knew that decisions were being made, and treaties, and trade agreements—all the business of the realm that had been mismanaged, to great profit, by the nobles. They had controlled it since time immemorial, and now the King managed it himself. They could no longer claim credit for it, nor reap the profits. All they could do was wait to see how the dice had fallen, and they feared it—every one of them had something to lose.

"You had better hold his heart still," the Duke had said, ominously, to Miriel. She did not betray by a single flicker that she was afraid of the King's love slipping away. She only smiled.

"You saw his letters," she replied. "I hold his heart, and

when I am back in his eye, I will enchant him as I always have done." Her voice was controlled, but I could hear her uncertainty. We rode in silence on the road back home, and on the first night, as we were waiting for the King's arrival, she said to me,

"I have to change the rules." She was staring into the brazier, watching the coals shift. The nights were cold on the plains, and even wrapped in furs, she was shivering. She did not seem to notice. "I have been too sweet."

I was so slow at these things. "And?"

"He withdrew, on his own terms. Now I must withdraw to even it. It will leave a space, to lure him onward." Her voice was dreamy; she was far away, strategizing.

"How will you do that?" I asked, and that jolted her from her reverie.

"I don't know." She squeezed her eyes shut, coming back to the present abruptly. "I've done so well, but now, when it matters most—I don't know. I can't think of anything."

"My Lady?" a voice called, and Miriel rose to her feet, her hands running over her hair, pinching her cheeks, checking her gown. We were not ready for the King to come so early. We had not had time to prepare. A head poked around the makeshift flap: Wilhelm. He took our silence as an invitation, and slid into the room.

"My Lord," Miriel said. She curtsied, as she always did. "Has there been a change of plans? Am I to dress in servant's clothes, then?" She spoke with the flirtatious banter of the court, but Wilhelm remained grave.

"I regret to inform you, my Lady, that the King is going to be detained. He will not be able to see you tonight. He asked me to bring you his regrets." Miriel's nose flared, as if she could smell the danger somewhere in his words.

"Where is he?" she demanded.

"He is dining." But Wilhelm looked down rather than meet her eyes.

"With whom, then?"

"Efan of Lapland, Nils Torstensson and his wife...and the Lady Linnea." He named Nils' daughter, a girl with eyes as blue as ice, skin like milk. High cheekbones, a beautiful smile, and the power of the West behind her. Miriel's eyes flared.

"What are they discussing?" She had no right to know, and neither did Wilhelm. She should not have asked; he should have disclaimed and bowed over her hand. But his eyes were full of pity. He said the worst thing.

"I am sorry, my Lady." There was an uncomfortable silence, and Miriel sank down onto her bed, amidst the piles of furs. Etiquette was forgotten, she was white as snow.

"I've lost him," she said flatly, and I felt her fear. Speaking to the Council was one thing, declarations of interest in crowded banquet halls, open negotiations... But a private dinner, with the King himself in attendance rather than de la Marque—Miriel was right. The King had moved beyond his ploy. He had indeed pushed Miriel to one side, and now he would replace her with a woman who brought connections.

Wilhelm had been watching Miriel closely, now he knelt at her feet.

"My Lady, will you forgive the impertinence of a question?" The look she turned on him was at once hopeful, and chillingly cold. She was impatient, being distracted in her moment of fear, and she did not want him close for fear that her tightly-held composure would fail; but he might yet help.

"Yes?"

"You loved him once, did you not?"

"I loved him as soon as I met him," Miriel said carefully, choosing words that she might defend to Garad. Wilhelm looked her straight in the eye, his jaw set against what he had heard, and I knew it took all of Miriel's self control not to tell Wilhelm that she had only ever wanted to love the King, but that she knew now she did not—and that she loved another.

"And do you love him the same now?" Wilhelm asked her. She did not recover from her surprise fast enough. Her hesitation told him everything. "Then...is it that you wish to be Queen? That is why you fear losing his love?" He spoke as if he did not understand the pull of ambition, and had hoped for better from her.

"No," she whispered fiercely. "And yes. I wanted to heal this country, bring it to enlightenment. What better way, than to have the throne?" That, he understood. He nodded.

"And so you court him and advise him—but you love him not?" His voice was thick with hope. Miriel bit her lip and nodded. "You do this only for Heddred?" Another nod. His voice dropped to a breath. "For the rebellion?" There was no mistaking the leap of joy in her eyes.

"I always hoped that you felt as I did," she whispered. Then she remembered herself. Joy changed to ambition in a moment. She leaned closer still. "I could help them, if I was on the throne," she said urgently. "Will you help me, my Lord? For them?"

"Do you know what it is you ask?" he whispered back. This time, she did not pretend to misunderstand his words. Nor did she flinch from it. She nodded, drawing back and looking down at him, where he knelt.

"Of course. Would you not ask the same of me?" She held his eyes until he nodded, but anyone could have seen his misery. "Nothing matters more than this," she pressed him. "Nothing. If you feel the same as I do, you will know that. And so you must help me."

"I will help you," he said. He had been defeated with hardly a struggle, no match for her conviction and his own honor. Miriel had been right, after a fashion: Wilhelm Conradine knew what could and could not be, and like her, he was driven to help the rebellion. He would pursue that end all the more ardently, for having given her up. "I will do what I can, I will remind him of his promises to you. I will press him to meet with you. I will praise your wit and your intelligence. But I must go now, quickly—my father seeks me. I told him I would be gone only a moment." Without letting his eyes leave her face, he brought her hand to his mouth and kissed it. Then he left without a word, slipping out the opening of the tent and into the night.

Miriel's face was almost laughable. Her lips were parted, she was staring after him longingly after the brush of his lips against her skin. But when she saw me watching, she remembered herself. Her gaze turned to one of triumph.

"I did it," she told me. "I said I would take his loyalty, and now I have it." She saw my face. "Oh, don't say it again." I felt a hot rush of anger at her dismissal.

"Fine," I snapped. "Then I'll say this: his love for you was only embers until you fanned it, and now you've made it a fire. And you're a fool if you think you can hold it in your hands and not get burned. He thinks he's giving you up for a great cause, doesn't he? It's very romantic, dreadfully romantic. Like a ballad. But that'll wear thin. And then, he's going to do something stupid." I thought she would flare up at my impertinence, but instead I saw only fear.

"I don't have any choice," she said. "He's the only weapon I have, Catwin."

"And be careful of yourself, too," I warned her. A shadow crossed her face.

"I don't have any choice," she repeated, and I sighed. There was a moment of silence as she struggled to push away the emotions I knew she wanted to savor. She said quietly, "So what do we do now?" At her sadness, I remembered what I, too, had forgotten in the face of her tryst with Wilhelm: the King's infidelity.

"We could talk to the Duke," I suggested, and at the instant denial, I insisted, "We should. He's going to find out anyway."

There was nothing she could say to that. We padded over to his tent, and it was hardly five minutes later that he leaned back from his makeshift desk and said simply,

"I told you to keep him. I told you that if you could not, we would need to discuss why you could not do such a thing." We froze, both of us, unwilling to believe our ears. First the love of the King, then a sworn ally—the ally whose anger we had counted on, but whose ambition we had never doubted—going back on his word. It could not be so. Not all at once.

"I need your help to do it." Miriel's lips barely moved.

"I cannot enchant him for you," he pointed out. "All I can do is pave your way, and I have done so. Every tool you needed, I have given you. I secured a place at court for you. Now you must do your part."

"Make a bid for marriage." Miriel's face tightened when he laughed in her face.

"Oh, no," he told her, still chuckling. "I won't do that. It would be laughable. Surely you know that. We have merchant blood. We have no army. We make more enemies than allies for him. You are no fitting match for a King."

"But you said…"

"I agreed that if the King was mad enough to defy the Council for you, I would back you. I hold to that. If he is not…" The Duke tapped the desk with his fingers. "I will not make myself a laughingstock to put you forward."

"What will happen to us if he's lost, then?" She challenged him. She got nothing for it.

"I believe you mean, what will happen to *you*," he said coldly. "And the answer is that you will probably be ruined. They're already saying that you let him have you and now he's lost his interest, did you know? If you fail to get him back, the rumor will stick. And if the rumor sticks…" My blood turned to ice. Miriel swayed where she stood.

"What do I do?"

"Get him back," the Duke said bluntly. "For I am not sure you recall the deal we made. But I do. I remember you telling me that if you rose, I would rise as well. But if you are no use to me, then I will be no friend to you. Go."

We fled, back to her tent, and Miriel leaned against one of the posts, her hand clutched to her side as if he had knifed her. She was blinking back tears.

"Are you alright?" I asked her, knowing she was not. "I'm sorry I told you to ask him." I felt the fool, but she shook her head.

"You did right. I would have done the same." She pressed her face into her hands. "What are allies for, if not to help each other?" she demanded. She dropped her hands and stared at me. "He should have helped me. I won't forget this."

"What are you going to do?"

"We," she said wearily. "What are *we* going to do."

"I protect you," I said. "I always know what I'm going to do."

She nodded, looking exhausted. "It's always me. I have to come up with a plan. Always me."

"I would help if I could," I said, stung. "But you know I'm no good at this. All I know is you have to stay the best at things, at everything. *Remind* him you're the best." She nodded, unmoved by my anger. "And you should refuse to see him," I said suddenly. It had been her own idea, only an hour past, but her brow furrowed.

"What—if he deigns to summon me?"

"He will," I predicted. "He's too honest not to." She looked doubtful.

"What do I tell him?"

"That he was right. That meeting him is too risky. That he must give you up, and you do not bear him any ill will, but you cannot bear to see him."

"That might work," she said, struck. She paused, and I wondered if she was remembering, as I did, her first meeting with Garad, where she had told him that their love was impossible, and so dared him onwards.

"You have to find some way to stay out of his reach," I said, echoing Temar's words.

"Yes. And so we start again. I have to make myself irresistible. Again. Don't I? Yes." She sighed. "And find some way to make Linnea less attractive to him."

"They'll push another one up in her place."

"I only need to hold him long enough for him to make me

Queen," she said grimly. "If I can do that, then I am safe."

Our journey back was quiet. There were no entertainments, only the long days on the road. There were no rumors, either—the King kept his dinners secret, and those who watched Miriel knew that she was not sneaking to his tent at night. He still sent her eloquent letters, and Miriel and I composed letters back, beginning her artful withdrawal from him.

We had no way to know if he had even noticed, but far from being defeated, Miriel seemed as sunny and confident as ever. It was part of her charm, I thought: when there was a plan, Miriel believed in it wholly, without reserve. She picked her path, and set her heart to it. She never again spoke to me of her fear; we looked only forward, the two of us, and we spoke only of our goals. As we entered the city, Miriel sighed in relief.

"Now the game begins again," she told me as we rode. "No more waiting. I will win him back." I did not respond. I looked up at Penekket Fortress as its shadow fell across us, and I shivered.

Chapter 16

Miriel was given an opportunity to retreat almost at once. When we returned to court, it became known—with the speed that only rumor can summon—that a man had arrived who claimed to be the envoy from Mavlon. He had come to honor the relationship between the two countries, he explained, just as the King had honored and recognized Mavlon by sending his own envoy. He had asked, very courteously, to take up residence in the building that housed the other envoys and, in the absence of any senior nobles or the King himself, the steward had looked over the documents bearing the seal of Mavlon and had acquiesced.

It was uproar. Mavlon's King Jorge had ceded the throne of his own free will centuries ago, claiming that his countrymen must choose their own leaders and determine their own destiny. Though some had tried, the monarchy had never been reclaimed, and Heddred had ceased to recognize the country as a power in its own right. Garad's choice to send a spy masquerading as an envoy had set off a firestorm. The very Councilors who had approved his quick thinking were now disclaiming their own role in the matter.

Troubled and alone, he sent a message for Miriel to meet him in the cellars, and she sent back a regretful note saying simply that such would not be fitting. It seemed that scarcely had we sent the plain-liveried pageboy away that he was back, panting, with another note: the King must see her, he had need of her advice. Miriel wrote back that she dared not meet with him, and gave the pageboy a silver coin and a dazzling smile for his troubles.

Wilhelm arrived next, looking disgruntled. He had clearly been summoned from his own lessons in combat, for he was wearing loose clothing with the dust of the courtyards, and he stank of sweat. He was embarrassed to be seen in such a state, and not best pleased with Miriel for being the cause of it all.

"My Lady, the King bids me ask you why it is that you will not agree to meet with him." Clearly, Wilhelm himself was confused. He had done as Miriel had bid, and turned the King's mind back to her, only to find that she now refused to meet with him. Miriel bid him come further into the room and smiled her mischievous smile.

"The King is wondering why I will not see him, is he not?"

"He is, my Lady."

"I have him mad to see me now, do I not?"

"Yes, my Lady." Miriel's smile broadened, and Wilhelm could not help but smile back as he followed her logic. He bowed. "Ah. An excellent ploy. Shall we all meet at midnight, then?"

"No," Miriel said sweetly.

"But now that he—"

"My Lord Wilhelm, I will not meet with his Grace tonight. You will explain to him that, although my heart breaks, I accept the wisdom that he and I must part."

"He only meant to pretend—" Wilhelm started, but Miriel held up a hand to cut him off.

"Regardless, that is what you will tell him. And tell him..." Miriel paused, trying to choose her words. Half of her allure—more—lay in the quick change of her tone and the flutter of her lashes. The words she spoke had never been even the greatest part of how she spoke to the King. What words could she now trust Wilhelm to deliver?

"Say that you pressed me to come to him now, and I begged you to leave before my will crumbled. Tell him that I miss him so much, my heart breaks with it, but I will do what is best for Heddred." She looked straight at Wilhelm, and he looked back: uncomfortable, out of his depth. He was an honest man, was Wilhelm Conradine, an honorable man. He lied to his friend only because they were of two minds about the rebellion. To speak openly would be to lose one of his few allies, and yet he was uncomfortable even with his lie of self-preservation.

"Anything else?" he asked. Miriel smiled warmly.

"Tell him that I know he will choose the wisest course for Heddred, because I know how he yearns for peace."

"Yes, my Lady." Wilhelm left, with a wondering sort of look over his shoulder, as if he were not quite sure what had just happened.

I had my suspicions of where this would lead, and that night I made sure that Miriel chose the finest of her nightgowns, and that her robe was laid out where she might snatch it up in a moment. I took it upon myself to order a bath for her, and saw to it that Anna brushed Miriel's dark curls until they shone. Miriel accepted this without comment; she had the dead calm of a woman who has gambled everything and knows that her plans are hanging in the balance.

We went to bed together, and I lay in the dark for a long while, jumping at every little sound. I must have drifted to sleep, for I awoke with a start in the dark of deep night. The room was quiet and dark, the only light filtered in through the shades, from the oil lamps that hung out on the streets.

I lay very still, trembling. I was terrified that I had awoken to something far worse than an illicit tryst. What was the sound that had brought me from sleep? What if my instincts this evening had warned me of the wrong thing, and now there was an assassin in the outer chamber? My heart was pounding so loudly that I feared I would give myself away. Moving carefully so as not to make the bed creep, I stretched out my left arm for the daggers that lay with my clothing on my shelf—

The noise was faint, filtered through the bedchamber door and the door of the privy chamber, and yet I still jumped, every muscle tensing. It was the very lightest knock on the door of the outer chamber. I waited a moment, for the sound of someone moving into place in the other room—I was still not sure that this was not some sort of trap—but when nothing came, I got up as quickly as I could, snatching my clothes and my daggers and padding to the door.

A rustle, and I saw Miriel sit up. So she had been lying awake as well, waiting with me. She slid out of bed and tiptoed after me as I crossed to the door, eased it open, and went into the privy chamber.

"Wait here," I breathed in her ear, and she nodded, moving so that she would be hidden by the door when it opened. I nodded to her, and scanned the room one last time for unusual shadows, the gleam of eyes or hair. Nothing. Satisfied, I lifted the latch on the second door and slipped into the outer room. The knock sounded again, hesitant.

I pitched my voice low, so as not to wake Anna. "Who's there?"

"Catwin?" It was the King's voice. "It is I. Garad." I slid back the deadbolt and opened the door a crack, trusting nothing. It was indeed his familiar face. I opened the door wider and stuck my head out, peering the other way down the corridor; seeing that the hall was empty, I ushered him quickly into the room, and bowed in the darkness.

"Your Grace."

"May I speak to your Lady?" he asked, as I closed the door behind him and slid the deadbolt back into place.

I did not like the tension in his voice, but there was no refusing him this. "Wait here a moment," I said. "I'll wake her. Your Grace." It seemed so fantastical an idea that I should be speaking to the King that I stumbled on his title. He nodded. He looked uncomfortable, he looked pained. But his jaw was set, he was resolute. I did not like where this was leading. I only hoped, grimly, that Miriel had a plan. Then I heard the faint rustle of her gown.

"Your Grace?" She stood framed in the doorway, her hands holding her robe closed at her throat. She had appeared as suddenly as a ghost. I made a hasty bid to get out from between them, and very nearly upset an ornamental chair in the process. Neither of them seemed to hear the scrape of the wood, the thud, or my muffled curse. As I stood in the dark, clutching my toe, they stared only at each other.

In a moment, they were in each other's arms; Miriel did not even hesitate. I watched, blushing, my toe forgotten, as his mouth came down on hers, and I saw her come up on tiptoe to meet him.

"I should not—" he murmured between kisses, and I understood that my fears had been well founded. He had come here to tell her that if she would be neither advisor nor mistress to him, then he would be rid of her. And then, seeing her, he could not resist her. It was as she had said it would be, and I saw that she had not been choosing the words of her message to avoid his anger, but to stoke it. It was a dangerous game she was playing—all the more dangerous as his hands crept to her waist.

Miriel was no less cognizant of the danger than I. She broke the kiss and flung her arms around his neck, laughing and crying as if she were overwhelmed with joy. A wife meeting a returning soldier could not have seemed more overjoyed.

"Oh, my love—I thought I would never see you again and I—"

"I cannot marry you!" he broke in. He pushed her away and repeated his words, and I knew that he was reminding himself as well as her. "I cannot marry you, my Lady." For a moment, Miriel looked as if she had been slapped. Then she flared up. I could see tears on her long lashes.

"So you come here to me—" she broke off, speechless. "I obeyed your wishes," she said to him. "I kept from you. I accepted it.

But now you come here to give me more hope than I have ever known in my life—and then snatch it away from me again in an instant?" Her voice was rising, incredulous, angry.

"I didn't come here to kiss you!" he shouted back. I cast a fearful look towards the bedroom and hoped that Anna would know enough to stay there.

"Then why *did* you kiss me?" Her hands were clenched.

"I saw you—and—" He moved to take her back in his arms, and she did not resist. She was like a little doll, she did not move as his arms came around her. Then, abruptly, she leaned her head on his chest and burst into tears. I heard her words choked out between sobs.

"I swore I would give you up. I accepted that I must step back. I knew I would be shamed. I knew that I would marry without love, and that I would face the pain of seeing you every day with another woman at your side. I had dreamed that—"

"Dreamed what?" he asked when she broke off on a sob. His anger was turning into confusion, dissolving with her tears. He did not know what to do.

"That I could heal Heddred with my wisdom. It is so bitter to know that the best I can do for the kingdom is step aside for another to advise you." I heard the question clear in her voice. It was a challenge: can Linnea advise you as I can? He heard it, and he answered it.

"I cannot do this," he said brokenly. "I cannot face ruling without you by my side." He moved to pull her closer, but she stepped back, leaving him in the cold darkness of the room, alone.

"And I cannot be at your side," she said. "We both know it." He held out his arms to her, pleading, but she sank down into a beautiful curtsy, her eyes on the floor.

"I must have you with me," he said desperately. He had acquiesced, and now he was bereft.

"Your Grace, you cannot. Such would undermine you. It would seem dishonorable. I want to be at your side," her voice trembled, "every moment. But what has been done, is done now. Your Grace has chosen—wisely." To his credit, he tried to reconcile himself to it.

"I would give you up for nothing less than a kingdom," he said, and she nodded.

"I know that. I regret my harsh words. Say you can forgive me, my love?"

"Your love?" he asked, as if he could not believe his ears.

"Always," she whispered.

"They tell me that we will forget each other," he said, unsteadily, and she shook her head.

"Then they do not know us, do they? They have never known a love like ours." She did not wait for his assent. She smiled, her lips trembling. "I know that I will never forget you. I will think of you every day. I will pray for your Golden Age, even when I am far away from your Court."

"You are to go away?" His voice betrayed his anguish.

"I must," she said steadily. "There is only one woman you should ask for advice. There is only one woman you should come to in the night. And that is your wife, my love. And your wife is chosen now. I cannot keep from you, nor you from me. You must be here, and so I will go—so that you may be here, with your wife."

"Then be my wife." He spoke wildly, and Miriel started forward to him, then retreated, holding her hand out to stop him.

"No, please, I beg you—torment me with no false hopes. The marriage agreement is signed, you cannot go back on it. "

"It has not been signed yet," he said quickly, and I saw how cleverly she had drawn the information from him. Now, she lured him on.

"My love—Garad—you cannot do this—"

"Tomorrow, I will tell them that it cannot be done," he swore. "My love—my Lady—tell me that I can call upon your uncle to discuss marriage negotiations. Could I?" Her laughter rang from the rafters and his eyes widened.

"Surely you cannot mean that," she said incredulously.

"I do, I swear I do. Would he allow it?" She laughed again.

"Oh, my love, what could make him happier than being able to wed me to the man I love with all my heart?" Only I could have heard the twist of grief in her voice. Her uncle had not cared, for a single moment of her life, what would make her happy. But her smile was steady, and the King's face warmed. I saw the fact, then, that Miriel never forgot for a moment: above all, a King wished to be loved as a man. She had convinced him both that she shared his vision for the kingdom, and yet loved him only for himself, and now he knelt before her.

"I came to you tonight to tell you that I could see you no longer," he said seriously. "But my heart tells me that I cannot bear to do so. For the good of your King, Lady Miriel, for the good of

---

Heddred—which will blossom under your wise leadership—will you do me the honor of becoming my wife and Queen? You may say yes or no without fear."

"I could not do other than say yes. My heart and my duty are as one," Miriel assured him. She knelt with him on the floor. "Your Grace, Garad, my love—I will be your Queen."

The light creeping under the door gilded her hair as he kissed her, and I heard him murmur, "Then stand by me, wife, and none shall part us."

Unbidden, I had a memory of a face: blue eyes, sandy golden hair. A boy as passionate as Garad, and yet as determined for reform as Miriel. And I had the wish, which I would later regret with all my heart, that Wilhelm could be Miriel's King.

Chapter 17

"He wanted to come to your rooms—and you let him?" the Duke was prepared to be furious.

"Catwin was there the whole time," Miriel said calmly. "She can vouch for me."

"No one will take a servant's word for this," her uncle reminded her. Then he looked at her more closely, at the small, self-satisfied smile on her face, and the glow in her cheeks. "What are you so smug about?"

"He said he wanted to come speak to you," Miriel offered. She smiled at her uncle's stony expression. "I'm getting closer to it than you thought I could," she challenged him. "Am I not?"

"Then even you are not such a fool as to believe this is a done deal," he rejoined.

"Of course not," she said scornfully. "He will renege on his agreement with—who was it? The Torstenssons?" As if she did not know perfectly well who it was. She raised his eyebrows at his flicker of surprise. "You did not know? Ah. Well, I will not trust an agreement. I will think it done only when there is a marriage treaty, signed and sealed and announced to the court."

"You had best think it done only when you have a crown on your head," her uncle said sharply. "This is a man who could renege on anything. So don't you allow him to touch you until the High Priest pronounces you his wife. In public." His eyes narrowed. "You didn't allow him liberties last night, did you?"

"I let him kiss me," Miriel said, untroubled. Of the people in the room, only I knew that she had practiced that line a dozen, a hundred times, in front of her mirror. She raised an eyebrow at the Duke's face, which was beginning to turn red. "And he would have done more, had I not stopped him." She looked as satisfied as the cat that had the cream. Only I, and Temar, would have thought to look at where her hands were shaking in her lap. The Duke was only watching her face.

"If you or he breathes a single word of this to the court—"

---

the Duke's voice was strangled with rage. This was the betrayal he had been waiting for, Miriel making decisions behind his back. It was time for her to capitulate, and I prayed she would know that.

I should not have worried.

"My Lord uncle." Her voice was placatory, sweet as honey. "He came to my rooms because I had refused to meet with him that day. You had told me to get him back, and I had staged a retreat. He came forward to it, he came to my rooms. He had planned to tell me about the Torstenssons, and say that he could not see me again. But—as I had told you I would—I enchanted him, and he swore that he would go back on their agreement. Yes, after he proposed marriage to me, I let him kiss me."

"He has spoken of marriage before. I don't see why this time should be any different." He glared at her.

"Because we were closer to losing him this time," Miriel said simply. "Because my mind alone was not enough to keep him from his duty."

"So even you view his marriage to you as an abdication of his duty?" He was intrigued.

"Not really." Miriel shrugged one shoulder, negligently. "No other woman can advise him as I can. But if he wants an advantageous marriage, from a noble who is well-connected...then, yes."

I had the thought that the Duke might have been less angry if only she had been wrong. If she had made a horrible mistake. He did not want her to be able to choose a gamble on her own and have it pay off; he would prefer that she fail, rather than use her own techniques and win. I wondered if he knew, in some part of his mind, that as soon as she became Queen, she would have him destroyed.

"*If* he comes to talk to me, I will entertain any offer he names," the Duke said warningly. "If. I doubt he will, Miriel. I doubt it very much. By now, he will have remembered his duty. But if he does indeed come to see me, I will speak to him of your marriage. And *you*—you will not let him come to your rooms anymore. You will insist on meeting him at another place, so that you can give me forewarning."

"So you can spy on me," Miriel said flatly, before she could stop herself.

"Exactly so!" His hand slammed down on the arm of his chair. "I do not like this game you are playing. I doubt you can win

---

136

it. And so I—" he jabbed a finger at himself "—*I* will make sure that if you fail at your game, you are not ruined. I will ensure that you keep his ear and his heart, even if you are not Queen."

"Little good that would do me," Miriel rejoined, and the Duke smiled. I did not like that smile.

"Perhaps. Now go. And not a word of this to anyone. If anyone asks you, you are to say that you know nothing of it, that your uncle will surely tell you when a marriage has been made for you. You, Catwin, will say that you have heard no rumors of the King's marriage to Miriel. None. That is all. Go, both of you."

Miriel obeyed him in this, as she always did when he gave her a direct order. She walked through the court as if nothing at all had happened. She was dressed in gowns no finer than she ever wore, she did not claim a place of seniority at the maidens' tables at dinner. She was so sweet and so deferential that it was nearly sickening. She never showed, through a single flicker of her eyelashes, that she knew Linnea Torstensson was her rival.

But within only a few days, the court knew. Somehow, the court knew both that the King was entertaining thoughts of a marriage with someone who was not Miriel—no one seemed to know who—and that, despite it all, his public indifference to Miriel was only a show. There were rumors that the two met secretly in the night, so many wild rumors that even Temar, with all his skill, could not scotch all of them. The court was violently divided between those who thought Miriel was a girl of absolutely, unswerving virtue, and those who thought she was no better than a whore.

It was not long before the court knew, also, who Miriel might supplant. And this time, when the men of the Council knew that the King had been close to a marriage, they backed the family who might have secured the Queenship. This was not Guy de la Marque, ready to flaunt an army, this was a family that had petitioned, as any family might. Linnea was a charming girl, very kind. The Torstenssons were one of the oldest lines, nearly royal in their own right, ancient rivals to the Conradines. And the alternative...

And so the rumor swirled that the King would discard an alliance that came with the goodwill of the entire country, for a smile from an upstart's daughter. The councilors narrowed their eyes at the Duke, who disclaimed that he'd not petitioned the King for such an honor, and they watched Miriel, as if their fury could cripple her.

Miriel affected surprise. She shook her head and parted her lips and blushed. She protested that such a decision had little enough to do with her—a flagrant lie, but then, such an impossibly strange situation needed such a lie. She said that she had heard nothing from her uncle regarding her marriage, and that until she did so, she would assume that the rumors were only that—rumors and lies. She praised Linnea Torstensson as a fine girl, a well-born girl, and said that it would be a fine match for the King—but, of course, she had not heard any evidence that he was considering Linnea, or even herself.

This did not save her from the enmity of the Dowager Queen. Isra would take even a secret marriage treaty over a marriage with Miriel. She would not be pushed aside for a commoner, and yet she had learned that she could not go against her son, not openly. And so she launched her own subtle campaign against Miriel. One day, only the maidens from the oldest families might be invited to dance at dinner, another day, each maiden was to wear cloak pins to show her heritage: her mother's crest on her right shoulder and her father's crest on her left shoulder, so that Miriel alone must wear a copper pin on her cloak, while the other girls wore silver and gold. I heard whispers that the Dowager Queen prevailed upon members of the Council to question the Duke's ability to rule Voltur.

And no matter how the King might protest against it, the Dowager Queen kept alive the talk of mistresses and wives. Each day, it seemed, I heard one man or another jest with the King about the joys a ruler might have. When I heard even the Torstenssons laugh about it, I had a thought to look over at Linnea. She was a pretty girl, indeed, generous and kind. I knew she had not ever been one to join in the talk against Miriel. I did not think that if she got the crown on her head, it would bring her much joy—not if her own family was willing to have the crown on her head and another woman in the King's bed.

Miriel had no time for sympathy, as I had.

"A rival is the same thing as an enemy," she told me, with scant patience. "If you think Linnea would have no joy being Queen, well, help me become Queen instead." I could not fault her logic, and yet, I wanted to ask her if even she would have any joy of being Queen. But we never spoke of that. I only let myself admit in the depths of the night, to myself, silently, that I sometimes doubted that our goals were worth the price we paid for them; neither Miriel nor I would ever question it aloud. We looked only forward to the goal.

It seemed foolish to me that I questioned our plan at all, for the King, true to his word, had indeed approached the Duke. What respect the Duke showed the King when the two of them spoke, I could not imagine, for when he told us of their conversations, my lord was as contemptuous as if he had been speaking to the village idiot.

"He's wavering," he told the two of us bluntly, as we stood before him. The respect Miriel had been shown when she was his new ally was gone; the closer she came to her goal, the less the Duke seemed to think of her. The ornamental chair he had once given her was pushed to the side of the room, but she, who had once stood with her eyes on the ground, now kept her head up and her shoulders back. She looked at him as if she were Queen already.

"And yet, my Lord uncle, he came to you today with new conditions for a contract."

"It's nothing until it's signed," the Duke said flatly. "That woman has every family in the land proposing marriage to him." There was grudging respect in his voice when he spoke of the Dowager Queen; I understood that he might well have used the same tactic. "You are to prepare yourself for him to marry another."

"Never," Miriel said instantly. "I have his heart, he is seeking my advice once more. He undertakes no decision without consulting me first. I *will* have the crown."

"You will prepare yourself for it," the Duke said, his voice dangerous. "I say so, and unless you wish to parade about as if you know better than I do—and as no ally of mine—then you will do as I say. As you promised to do." Miriel colored and looked down. The Duke snorted. "You can go. You, Catwin, you stay."

I heard Miriel's steps pause, and the Duke smiled, predatory. "The guards will see you back to your chamber," he told her, and she had no choice but to leave, her head held high but her face set with sudden fear. What could the Duke want with me? When she was gone, the Duke turned his attention back to me.

"What does Miriel need to lure him on?" he asked baldly. "New gowns? Cosmetics?" I shook my head in confusion. The King was, once more, devoted to Miriel. He spoke to her on every topic he could think of. He relied on her, as she had told me he would. For a moment, stupidly, I could not think how cosmetics would aid her.

"He comes forward now," I said. "He likes her as she is, without adornment. He likes her mind." I was thinking of her words that love talk meant nothing, that her true power would be in his belief that he could not rule without her. But the Duke snorted.

"Is he hot for her?" I felt myself start to blush.

"I don't know, my Lord."

"Then he's not. And he has to be. So you tell me now what she needs, to make that happen." When I hesitated, he snapped, "Must I have you trained by whores as well to be of use to me, girl? Temar told me you could see to the heart of men's desires. Do not show me that his faith in you is mistaken." On the side of the room, Temar settled his chin onto his fist, watching me. He was unmoved by the slur against his powers of observation, he cared only to see what I might say.

"She needs only herself," I shot back, my pride pricked on her behalf. "She doesn't need jewels, she's beautiful in her own right. She can stir his desire without baubles and ornaments." The Duke smiled, he was amused by my indignation.

"You're serving the King's mistress," he observed. "You had best be less squeamish. For sure, she has no such qualms."

"She does! And she's not his mistress," I said instantly. "You told her to be pure, and she is. I swear." *Don't beat her.* But he only shook his head, impatiently. He snapped his fingers at me.

"Do you understand nothing, girl? Have I found a complete dullard to guard my niece? Her idiocy I can at least understand— she has the crown in her sights. But you should have clearer eyes."

As much as I hated to admit my ignorance, I had no choice. I swallowed and looked into his grim eyes, and said only, "No, my Lord. I don't understand."

"Then let me explain it. Once." He came around the side of the desk, and I tried not to flinch, but he only paced in front of me as he spoke. "My niece is to be for the King. She is to enchant him. She is to turn his head. She is to bear sons for him and be his closest advisor. It matters not a whit to me if she is his wife or his mistress." He stopped pacing for a moment and raised his eyebrows at me. "You should know as well as I do that it might even do us more good for her to be the mistress. She would be his forbidden love. It would keep the flame alive for longer."

"You planned this? For her to be his mistress?" He had been correct to call me a dullard, I should have known. Had I not heard him say that if her plans fell through, he had plans to keep her in the King's eye? What else could he have meant? Now, he laughed in my face.

"What else? My niece may be mad for the title, but I have never been so foolish. Do you see Isra, girl? She has a title, and it means nothing. Power slips away from her. The Queen has never been the center of the court, not where there are dozens of pretty girls for the taking. But the power held by the Kings' mistresses…you should study your history again, Catwin. Study it, and wonder whose voice it was that came from the throne."

"And so you would control the King's mistress, and be the power behind the throne in that way." It made sense—and yet, it was such a strange idea that I must say the words out loud in order to believe them.

"Just so."

"But she's still not to let him…" I was blushing again, and he nodded, cool and impersonal.

"Not yet. I will tell you when."

Bile nearly came up in my throat as I bowed. I walked alone back to Miriel's rooms, dawdling all the way. I did not know what to tell her; I did not even want to let the words pass my lips. I wanted only to go to the baths and scrub myself until I could feel clean once more. I had to remind myself, every step of the way, that it was worth it to feign agreement with the Duke, with everyone who disgusted me. He was right: I should be less squeamish. But I did not like it. I did not like it at all.

Chapter 18

Miriel spent the next days in a frenzy of irritation: at me, at her uncle, at the King. As the court circled her, avidly desiring any clue she might let slip, she watched them all through her smiling mask, and then she came back to the room to spit accusations out through clenched teeth. She spoke against anyone I might mention, until I nearly shouted at her to ask if she suspected me, too. She pursed her lips, and eventually shook her head, but I saw fear in her eyes. She feared being a mistress, she knew what spite the court would level at her. She was clever with the rules, and yet—and yet. This was too much for her. She resented her uncle for planning this, knowing that he would not be the one to bear the shame and malice.

"If you want to be Queen, I will help you," I told her.

"What do you mean, *if* I want to be Queen? I have to be Queen now," she said. "Don't you see? If I'm a mistress, he can cast me off any time he wants—and he came back to me from habit. He knows, don't you see?"

"Knows what?" I asked, bewildered, and she stamped her foot at my slowness.

"He knows he can rule without me. He negotiated a peace treaty without me, didn't he? And so now he loves me, but not the same way. He consults me, but it's a habit, not need. Now it's all his heart, he knows he does not need to listen to my advice in the same way. And if I don't hold him somehow, his love will fade and he'll slip away entirely." I had the thought, disconcerting, that this was what her uncle had intended for Miriel. To seduce the King: blind the man with desire, and become once more his only confidant, his closest advisor. If Miriel had known my thoughts, there would have been a storm of shouting, but she was biting her lip and staring off into space. Quietly, she finished her speech.

"If I am a mistress, I will still need my uncle's help. I will only be free of him when I am Queen."

She fell silent, and I had no answer for her. The man who still had her life in the palm of his hand did not care if she was

Queen or mistress. He could sign her over to the King, or he could even insist that the King choose another. As if we had both had the same thought, she looked up at me.

"Find out," she ordered me. "You find out what he and the King speak of. Find out if he truly bargains for me, or against me. I have to know."

"I'll go now. You stay here. Don't go anywhere. Don't answer the door. Don't meet the King." She nodded at my wisdom, too distracted by her fear to snap that she already knew to do so, and I slipped out the door almost at once, making for the cellars and the tunnels. I would wait in the hallway, I determined, with the secret door cracked so I could hear people passing by, and I would see the Duke and Temar as they passed by. The Duke should be in a Council meeting, I knew, and Temar had told me that the marriage might be finalized today.

He had expressly forbidden me to leave Miriel alone for the duration of the marriage negotiations as well, of course. I bit my lip, and then shook my head to clear it of fear. Miriel had ordered me to do this, and I obeyed her over Temar. That was the way my loyalty fell now.

I wandered for most of the afternoon, hovering at the end of the hallway and peering down at the Duke's rooms, asking servants of the Palace proper if the Council was in session, even making my way into the library on a pretense that I must deliver a message. It was close to time for dinner and I was returning, defeated, to Miriel's chambers, when a servant told me that the Council had been adjourned, and the men returned to their chambers an hour past. I thanked him as politely as I could and raced off down the hall, slowing to a walk as I approached the Duke's doors.

"Is his lordship here?" I asked, as politely as I could.

"He's just gone," one of his guards told me, and I nodded.

"Thank you," I said. I walked until I was out of sight, and then broke into a run, making my way down to the wine cellar, and the secret passageways.

I hurried down the steps into the cellar, looked around to make sure no one was about, pulled the door to the tunnels open as quietly as I could—and stopped dead. I had a chance to follow Temar and the Duke, and hear what they discussed. But if I was caught—and who was I trailing, after all, but the best spy in the world?—I would almost certainly be dead. I wondered what Miriel would say to that, and had the uncomfortable thought that she would simply retort, *well, don't get caught, then.*

After a few moments of warring with myself, I stepped into the darkness. This was what I had been trained for. This was why Temar had told me that the greatest skill of a Shadow lay not in killing, but in listening. I had agreed to be Miriel's ally in this world, and that meant using my talents, not staying out of danger.

I sat on the stairs until my eyes grew used to the light. Even here, bits of light filtered down through floorboards and chinks in the rock. Then I got up and crept onwards. Months ago, I had spent a few hours exploring these tunnels, and then a few more nights learning the layout of them so that I could walk them in the dark. Temar had always told me that it was better to creep in the dark without a light—not only more stealthy, but the darkness would make my hearing more acute. I would notice potential enemies before they noticed me, he told me.

I knew the passageways well now, and so I crept through them pad-footed, without hesitation. My fingers trailed along the wall, to catch the markers I had learned, and I was able to devote only a small piece of my mind to finding my way, with the rest being devoted to any noise my ears might catch.

My vigilance was rewarded. Close to the exit that would take me up into the palace proper, I saw the faint glow of a torch and I heard voices. I froze for a moment, gauging the threat, and noted that the light and the conversation were growing fainter. My quick progress had led me into a problem. If they were not minded to move away from the entrance, I would be trapped, and would miss the Duke as he walked by. As I grew closer, however, I realized with a start that my companions in the tunnels were the Duke himself, and Temar.

I was tempted to turn and run. I could move quietly enough that Temar would not hear me over their conversation. I could get back to Miriel, knowing that they would not catch me, and she and I would be safe from their anger. But I had been taught too well, I was too curious. As if of their own volition, my feet moved to carry me forward, and I breathed as slowly and quietly as I could. I had to know what they were saying, when they did not think we would be listening.

"You can't be serious," the Duke was saying.

"She's been right to be confident before," Temar said reasonably. "She got further, faster, than you had anticipated." I frowned in the darkness.

"She got nothing for that."

"Not yet. But she might now, if you can sign the treaty today. It can be signed and sealed and public, and your blood will sit on the throne. I know you did not seek it, but to have your descendants be Kings rather than a King's bastards...worth a little gamble, perhaps?" Temar's voice was so persuasive that my hackles went up. Even the Duke sensed something amiss.

"What are you hiding?" he asked sharply. "And you remember your vow—I wanted the power of the throne for myself, not for that brat."

I had reached a corner of the corridor and I strained to hear them as they continued picking their way down the long stretch, lit by the flickering light of their torch. I peeked around the corner for a moment and grinned at the sight of Temar walking patiently at the Duke's side. He looked like I sometimes felt when I was constrained to walk with Miriel: like a wing-clipped falcon, like a caged beast. He longed to move quickly and quietly through the dark, a skill he had cultivated to serve the man who now hindered his progress.

Watching him, I wondered how the animals of the King's menagerie felt, able to kill any of the puny beings that looked into their cages, yet bound back by bars of iron. I felt a strange darkness at the thought. I had no true cage, save my own thoughts. There was nothing to keep me from lashing out at any of the nobles who walked these halls. It seemed like a very thin barrier all of a sudden.

Shadow. Temar had lied when he told me, *"there is more to this than the part you fear,"* for his training had warped the very core of myself. I stood in the shadows of the corridor and feared that a transformation had begun, and I would not be able to stop it. Then I heard Temar's voice very faintly, and realized that the two of them had rounded another corner.

Shaking my head to clear it, I followed after them. Temar's voice was bland, careful.

"I think only that Miriel and Catwin are correct to be confident. If Miriel is not made Queen, they will believe that you— we—meddled." His voice grew chilly for a moment. "And I remember my vow well, my Lord."

The Duke laughed, and I thought that his mirth sounded unkind. "So I can see. You never forget, do you? As for Catwin and Miriel...they can believe what they like, as long as they do what they're told," the Duke said. "I don't want to hear those words from your mouth again—you've let Catwin blind you to Miriel's failings."

"You know," Temar said, musing, "she almost never speaks of Miriel. And I am well aware of Miriel's failings, but she has quite a talent for manipulation. You should be more wary." No one else could have said that to the Duke and lived, but even when the Duke was irritated, he would listen to Temar. He said, testily,

"I am always wary. I do not trust the girl."

"You think you know her motivations," Temar observed. "And that is a kind of trust."

"You think you know better than I do what she wants?" the Duke's voice was growing dangerous again, but Temar seemed unperturbed. He was deep in thought.

"It's why you accepted the bargain," he said absently. "Any man can use blades, but very few can see into the hearts of others. I can. And I am telling you that Miriel wants something, something very specific, that you do not know of. She has spoken to no one about it. She keeps it hidden. But she is pursuing some goal."

"She'll have told Catwin," the Duke said, and I shrank away, as if he could see me, as if he might know I was there with them.

"Perhaps," Temar said evasively. I felt a moment of warmth that he might not want to question me.

"Enough of this. I have told you a dozen times—you owe Catwin nothing."

"Yes, my Lord." Temar's voice was distant.

"So you will find out from Catwin what it is that Miriel wants."

"Yes, my Lord."

"And you will remember that your choice of Catwin is nothing like my choice of you." Temar did not respond to that at all, and I narrowed my eyes, crept as close as I could to the corner. I barely breathed; I must know what he would say to that. I felt I was on fire, I was so curious. But he did not speak, and so the Duke said, normally,

"So. You think I should sign the treaty, then?"

"Of course." They must have exchanged a look, for Temar's voice took on a persuasive tone. "Say she's unbiddable, then—you need her only as long as it takes for her to bear sons. Then she can have an accident." After Temar's protection of me, his words were jarring; then again, he had always hated Miriel on the Duke's behalf.

The Duke was neither shocked nor offended. He laughed. "True. If she can hold him that long, then why not?"

146

Holding my breath, I backed away, and then, at the second corner, I turned and fled, as silently as I could, to Miriel. More knowledge, more plots—and some agreement between Temar and the Duke. A need, also, to blind Temar before he scented the whole of the truth. I was not such a fool as to think that we could turn Temar. I told myself that as I ran: *I am not a fool, not a fool*. Temar could have loved me and embraced the rebellion with his whole heart, and he would gut both of us at the Duke's instruction. I had always known this, I told myself. But it hurt, even after all these months, and even the strange discussion of an agreement, a hint at last of *why*...that did not dull the hurt, either. Tears stung my eyes, and I was glad that I did not need to see to make my way back.

"It hurts to know that he would kill you," Miriel observed when I had told her. I heard sympathy in her voice, and I sniffled and nodded, wiping my nose on the back of my hand like a child. Her sympathy was gone in an instant: "Well, remember how it hurts, and then be done with it. We don't have time for you to be like this with an enemy."

"You were like this over Garad," I muttered, and her eyes flashed.

"Just so. And I cut him out of my heart when he betrayed me." I thought of Wilhelm's blue eyes, and how Miriel softened at the edges when she was in his company, and I thought that perhaps she had not so much cut Garad away as realized that Wilhelm was the man she wanted to be the King. Then I realized that perhaps she had not realized as much; I said nothing.

Miriel herself had sunk into repose. She was sitting on the window seat, staring out at the street below. The midday sunlight illuminated her pale yellow dress, and for a moment, she looked far younger than her sixteen years: delicate, porcelain-skinned. Then she looked back at me and the spell was broken. Her eyes were cold and hard.

"So I must get rid of him before he can get rid of me," she said simply, and I did not know if she meant her uncle, or the King. I nodded.

It was two days before we heard anything, days in which I began to doubt that the Duke had taken Temar's advice. I did not think the Duke wanted his niece to become Queen. He preferred the side channels of power—he had watched the nobles snarl and fight for too long to trust that titles meant anything. And yet, on the off-chance that a title did give her power, he did not wish her to have it in her own right.

Miriel was, I knew, as suspicious as I was, but she seemed as serene as a priestess. She danced like a forest nymph, sang like a muse, jested elegantly with the maidens, and held court at dinner; she was always the focus, and yet she never seemed to notice for a moment that she moved in a ripple of murmurs. Most of all, she seemed happy, radiantly happy. No one would know that she was using all of her charm to pursue a goal that now sickened her. No one would know that she was exchanging one cage for another, and she knew it.

She used every ounce of self-control each day to walk out into the court with her head held high and a smile on her lips. She knew that half the courtiers she greeted despised her utterly, and that half or more thought her to be willfully ruining the country. She knew that whether she succeeded or failed in her quest for the throne, a torrent of hatred would follow. The rumors alone were hateful, and none else even knew that the King was pursuing marriage with her; at least once a day, I heard that the DeVere girl had taken with child, the King's first bastard. For once, Miriel's tiny body was an asset to us: with the waist of her gown cinched tightly, with the flatness of her chest, she had no need to combat the rumors with words.

She did well beyond belief, but as the marriage negotiations dragged on, it had grown more and more exhausting for her to do so. Each night that I saw her return to the room, I understood a little more why she clung so fervently to her belief in the rebellion. She would hold her smile and the playful turn of her head until the door was closed, until it was latched and the deadbolt had been locked into place; then, the life went out of her like a rag doll and she would slump into a chair. In the last few days, even the blush in her cheeks fled, and she lay as still and white as a dead girl. Each day she walked in fear that the King's love for her was fading, fear that the marriage deal would not be signed and sealed before his gaze strayed elsewhere. When she returned to her rooms at night, fear had drained her dry.

I saw—and it twisted my heart to admit it—that even my friendship could not support her when she walked out into the glare of the court. She knew that I walked close in the shadows, and that I could stop any blade, any arrow. But there were a dozen kinds of pain that I could not save her from: insults, threats, poisoned words. If she had maintained Wilhelm's friendship, she might have spoken to a man who understood the pain she faced. Wilhelm knew the spite of the court. But, waiting for the King's promise, Miriel had retreated utterly from any hint of impropriety. She never, not ever, looked at Wilhelm; the two of them never spoke. If she needed a letter sent to the King, she sent me. And so she must bear the pain of a courtier alone. I was grateful for my cloak of shadows, and grateful, also, that she had an ideal to which she could cling, to sustain her when the darkness of the court seemed overwhelming.

When we were summoned to the Duke's chambers one night, even her surety of the cause could barely rouse her from her exhaustion. It took me several minutes of cajoling, pleading, and promising rest soon, before she could bring herself to lift her head from the table, and I ended up hauling her to her feet. She did not seem to come to life until I half-carried her across the threshold of the room; then, she drew herself up and walked slowly to her uncle's chambers.

He took in her exhausted appearance with scant sympathy.

"Look merry," he instructed her, the irony of his grim tone entirely lost on him. Miriel shaped her face into its usual sparkling smile, and her uncle nodded. "It is my great pleasure to inform you that the King has signed, just an hour past, a marriage treaty naming you as his betrothed. It is to be announced at services tomorrow morning. You will wear white."

It was a moment curiously drained of joy. Miriel did no more than nod. She was too tired now to clap her hands with joy, and from the look on her face, this marriage was more a trap than an achievement. It signaled not her ascendancy, but instead the dawning of a new test. I saw her wonder, as she had not allowed herself to wonder until now, if she had made a terrible mistake. As much as I had wondered it myself, I did not want her to share my doubts now. It was the worst time for her belief to fail her.

The Duke understood none of this. His brows snapped together in a frown.

"Look alive, girl! Do you understand nothing? You have it. You are to be Queen."

"I understand," Miriel said simply. She was fairly swaying with exhaustion. "May I go to sleep now?"

"Is that all you can say?"

She paused to think, and then said, quietly, "I thank you for your aid, my Lord uncle."

149

"Well enough. Then go. Tomorrow you will be witty and enchanting and merry." The threat was clear in his voice, and a few minutes later, as the doors of her rooms closed behind us, Miriel turned to me and said, eerily calm,

"You will kill him for me one day, Catwin."

"Yes, your Grace."

Chapter 19

That night, fearful of assassins, I went over Miriel's bedroom inch by inch: checking in and behind each wardrobe, under the bed, going over the paneling of the walls, even checking the latches on each of the windows, which I bound with wire. Eventually, satisfied that no one could enter the room quietly, I left Miriel to sleep and checked her privy chamber and the public room with the same exacting detail.

I knew that I should sleep, but I was too nervous. I knew the Duke's obsession with privacy, and I knew also that Temar could nearly guarantee that the business had been signed and sealed with no one the wiser. And yet—who was to say that the King might not call his mother to his rooms to tell her? Who was to say that he might not gloat in his success?

And so I sat in one of Miriel's beautiful chairs, by the fireplace, and I let the fire die down, so that no one should think I stood watch. I was wearing my black, and I had wrapped my hair in cloth. I sat and waited for dawn, and I pondered.

If I believed that my dream of my mother was a true telling of a true prophecy—and I was equally sure that I both believed it, and did not want to—then what did the prophecy mean for me, and for Miriel? Poison in my food might mean betrayal, although I could not even be sure of that. But even if it did, then what? A balance would tip, and end would come. What was the balance? What would come to an end?

Near midnight, there was a tap on the door; I jerked awake, and realized that I had slipped into a doze. After checking the room once more, I padded across to the heavy door, and hesitated. If this was the King, I did not want to admit him. I did not want to wake Miriel so that she could resume her endless, sparkling show—and I did not want to know what demands the King might make. But, in answer to my silent question, I heard a breath of a voice, in the mountain dialect:

"Are you there, Shadow?" I drew back the bolt and cracked the door open, peering into Temar's black eyes.

"What's wrong?"

"Nothing. The Duke sent me to ensure Miriel was safe." I looked at him silently, and he held up one hand. "On my honor, Catwin. That, and no more."

I opened the door for him and he slipped inside, heading for the chairs at the fireplace. I followed him and we sat together, in silence. I stared over at his profile for a few moments. This was the closest we had ever come to acknowledging the enmity between our masters, and the enmity, indeed, between us. I was trying to decide whether or not I should say something about it when Temar looked up and said, quietly,

"How is she, then?"

"Tired," I said simply. It was no betrayal of her trust to tell him. He had seen her this evening, it would be nothing he could not see for himself. He shook his head.

"She cannot show it until she has the crown on her head," he warned me.

"I know that." My voice was sharp. "And she does not show it. Can the Duke have any complaint about her manner in public?" He only shrugged, and I fought the urge to demand that he acknowledge Miriel's worth. The Duke's plans hinged on my Lady, and he cared for her so little that even Temar thought Miriel useless.

"Is she in danger tomorrow?" I asked, instead. There was no time for harsh words when we had our masters to protect. "Does anyone else know of the marriage yet?"

"No one that I could think of," Temar said. "I've watched the King's chambers, and he's called no one to him since the Duke returned to his rooms." He looked over at me. "You're not too tired? You would be able to stop an assassin?"

"I was trained by you," I said. "So, yes." In reality, he was touching on one of my greatest fears. I knew every theory and every technique about stopping an assassin, but with both attempts at murder, I had grown less sure of my skills, not more. Saving Miriel's life with herbs and quick thinking, throwing a dagger at an unsuspecting opponent—that was one thing, but being able to step in front of a dagger, push her out of the way of an arrow, protect her when they came in force and knew I was there to help her— that was entirely another. I was afraid, every day, that when that day came—and I was sure that it would—that I would fail.

Preoccupied with my fear, I said what I should not have: "Unless the assassin is you."

152

I could have sworn that the room itself went ice cold. I stared at Temar, and he just looked at me. His eyes, so expressive and so warm when he taught, were as flat as a painting. He stood, and I tried not to flinch, but all he said was, "I will see you in the morning." His footsteps receded across the room, and the door closed with unexpected gentleness.

I sat frozen in the dark room, waiting for him to come back, wanting to call him back, but he did not return, and I did not send for him. *We both know what cannot be.* I sat in silent misery until dawn arrived, grey and leaden, and then I pushed away my hurt. I got up and sent a serving girl for a bath, and went to wake Miriel. She was lying just as I had left her, so exhausted that she had not even moved in her sleep. For a moment, I wanted to let her be. I thought of the exhaustion I saw in her each morning, when she realized she faced another day of dancing and laughing and pretending. Then, sighing, I bent to shake her awake.

She did not speak to me that morning. There was no anger in her, only a bone-deep tiredness. It took all of her concentration and all of her strength to plan her smiles and curtsies for the day, and I did not distract her with idle chatter. I told the new maid to dress Miriel's hair finely and put her in her gown of white, and at the woman's inquisitive look, I lied blithely. A masque after services, I said. Each maiden as a snow sprite. I found that I did not trust even her, the woman the Duke had chosen to serve Miriel.

Against my will, my thoughts drifted back to the night before and my heart twisted. No matter how long he had distrusted me, my own distrust had felt disloyal. I had concealed it behind smiles and half-lies, unable to lie to him, on his own, as easily as I lied to the Duke. I had fooled myself into thinking that, if only I did not tell him that I feared him, if only I did not admit that I worried he would one day kill me in my sleep, my mistrust would be bearable. But now that the truth had crept out into the open, and I had seen his cold anger—and yes, hurt—at my feelings, I felt as if it was I who had crept up behind him and slipped a knife between his ribs. We had always pretended. I was the one who had broken the pact, just as I had been the one to keep the secret of Miriel's success with the King. Always, it seemed, it was I who betrayed Temar.

With Miriel dressed like a winter queen, like a fairy princess, we walked to morning services. She joined the other maidens in their plain morning gowns, and I saw them take in her finery; the whispers spread outward in a ripple, and some of the

Queen's ladies cast looks over their shoulders at my mistress, who affected—as she always did, as she always must—not to realize that she was now a center of the court's attention. Where she walked, a hundred pairs of eyes followed her every movement.

I chose a place on of the side benches, watching the courtiers as they paid homage to the Seven. I was quivering with adrenaline, waiting for the moment when the familiar form of the service would be interrupted by the King's announcement. So far, the whispers had come to naught; I tried to believe that, whatever the courtiers thought of Miriel's fine clothing, none of them could guess the cause. But what would happen when the King spoke? I had cast a look down the row of servants at the side of the room, and had recognized each face, but it would take only one disaffected courtier, one quick-thinking and self-sacrificing servant, and Miriel would be dead on the floor of the Cathedral.

To my surprise, it was the High Priest himself who stepped down from the pulpit and walked forward into the congregation. The relentless drone of his voice as he preached had been transformed into the strident tones of a war leader.

"For every nation," he boomed, "there must be a wise and just leader. He must be raised with respect for the words of the Seven Gods, given the wisdom of the Saints, and taught the lessons of history. At his left hand shall be the finest advisors of the land...and at his right hand shall be the finest of women, who may give him the strength of a godly home, and many strong sons to bring his House glory and honor."

He stopped his procession by the row where the maidens were seated, and then he turned to face the very front of the church, where the King sat.

"Your Grace," he said. "Name your betrothed."

"Lady Miriel DeVere," the King said, his voice ringing out. I saw a flash of surprise on the High Priest's face, hurriedly pushed down. So even he had not known. Had the King lied to him, then? Doubt stabbed through me. The High Priest was a hard enemy, and he could not yet know that his secret letter-writer was Miriel. He could not yet know for certain that she espoused the same cause, and hoped to guide the King to a truce with the southern rebels. Would he now wish Miriel harm?

I would not have guessed that he held her any ill will, for he held his hand out to her, and without hesitation, she rose and went past her companions to take it. He walked with her down the long aisle in a silence that grew deeper and more terrible with every step. Miriel must know without looking that the Dowager Queen had gone whiter than death, and that the heads of a dozen families watched her with undisguised hatred.

There was no longer the slightest portion of uncertainty in the court. They had known from the moment that Miriel stood that this was not some poor jest, that the King had chosen his bride, and that their own daughters had been passed over for a merchant girl, for the daughter of a woman whose own husband had been ready to deny the child. For the heir of the Duke of Voltur, whom every one of them would have seen dead in a ditch.

But Miriel walked as if she were Queen already, as if their hatred could not touch her. Finally, I saw that she had gained enough trust in my abilities that she would have me watch the court. She expected their hatred as a matter of course, she had spent months hardening her heart against it. The exact shape of it was mine to determine, and mine to guard against. She had devoted all of herself to enchanting the man who awaited her at the end of the aisle.

I saw the Dowager Queen start to rise to her feet before one of her bolder, quick-thinking ladies reached to lay a hand on her arm. Isra returned to her seat, but I fancied I could see the air around her boiling with her fury. Her son had defied her, her only dynastic hope was shattered—and with the participation of her closest advisor. However he had been trapped by her son, Isra would resent the High Priest for failing to put a stop to this announcement.

The High Priest laid Miriel's hand on the waiting arm of the King, bowed deeply to his liege, and returned to the pulpit. I barely spared a thought for his words as they rolled over the congregation; few enough people seemed to hear him at all. They were frozen in horror, attentive enough only to realize that, whatever lingering hope they might have held, the King was now irrevocably tied to Miriel DeVere. Even the servants were frozen, there was barely the rustle of cloth, hardly the sound of the crowd breathing.

And so, with the echoes of the High Priest's blessing dying away, and the stunned, resentful chorus of blessings from the court, Miriel walked down the long aisle as the betrothed of the King, untouched by an assassin's blade, but the center—now—of a sharp new division in the court.

Chapter 20

Only months from his success at the Meeting of the Peacemakers, the King was now determined that his wedding must be the most extravagant event the court had ever seen—grander than his father's wedding, or his uncle William's, grander than the wedding of King Dusan, grander even than the Meeting of the Peacemakers. It was as if he believed that if he could awe the court with a shower of wealth, a spectacle of mythic proportions, he could silence their complaints. If only he could command a feast sumptuous enough, he could trick the Lords into toasting to Miriel and forgetting that their own daughters had been passed over. He announced a full fortnight of revels, with the pinnacle to be the Midwinter Feast.

To my disgust, and deep surprise, his ploy seemed to be working. Maidens who should, by rights, have been sulking, were too excited by the prospect of masques and gowns and dancing to remember that any one of them had a better claim to be Queen than did Miriel. Their mothers, ladies in attendance on the Dowager Queen, were flattered by the King's insistence that their grace and beauty must be shown off in their own dance for the court. Their husbands' egos were soothed by the fact that, although their daughters would never sit on the throne, the King had taken the time to assure each and every Lord that he had a particular match in mind for their children—they must come speak to him after the feast, he insisted upon it, and he would take a personal interest in the matter.

The young men of the court were the most amenable to the King's marriage. Their joy was untainted by jealousy, for with the King's marriage treaty signed and sealed, there was no longer a mad rush to the throne. Boys of ancient families who had been overlooked and slighted for months, were now once again feted and sought-after. Marriage agreements that had been conveniently forgotten were once again pursued, and the young ladies of the court had eyes once more for the men who were not of House Warden.

Indeed, the court was a merry place, and only those who

had been thwarted had any time to be displeased. I was grateful to the King for driving them out into the open, these malcontents, for in the childish flush of excitement that gripped the Court, it was easy to pick out those whose smiles were more like grimaces, whose eyes strayed coldly to Miriel or the Duke, and who slipped away to whisper in corners. They thought themselves unnoticed by the court, and indeed, few cared enough to watch.

I was one of those few. I stood in the shadows, and I marked who grudged Miriel's rise, and I named each and every one as my enemy and my target.

Most of them did not surprise me. The Torstenssons were bitterly disappointed, and the whole of the Lapland faction with them. Linnea accepted her fate with barely-concealed relief, but her father and brothers sat quiet and unsmiling through each of the feasts celebrating the King's betrothal. I had heard from one of the servants in my pay, a stable lad, that the men were deeply offended by the slight to their blood, to their land, to their spoken agreement with the King.

This alone would hardly have worried me, but their close-headed conferences with Piter Nilson and Arman Dulgurokov were far more dangerous. Together, these men and their factions controlled the whole of the southeast of Heddred, stretching from the base of the Daelvic mountains to the DeVere lands north of the Bone Wastes; together, they would make a force to be reckoned with. Each of them had a grudge to carry against the King: the Torstenssons believed the King to be forsworn, Arman Dulgurokov was watching his sister as she was she was inexorably pushed from the throne, and Piter Nilson had returned to the capital to plead once more for soldiers to keep the peace in his lands.

The King was aware of Nilson's discontent; indeed, not one man in the court or Council could claim ignorance of the matter. Nilson was shameless in his indignation, willing to corner any man who might listen, and then whisper angrily that the King cared nothing for the security of the south. Why, he was leaving his own nobles to fend for themselves against an uprising that daily seemed both more nebulous, and more organized. He feared his tenants, he mistrusted his own servants. Why would the King not do as he must, and root out Jacces and crush the rebellion?

If the King were not careful, I thought, he would have a second uprising on his hands—for while he did not listen, others did. Arman Dulgurokov and Efan of Lapland, of course, whose lands were close enough to Nilson's, could often be seen in close-headed conference together. But others listened to them, others repeated their words in low voices in the hallways, and worst of all, I saw Gerald Conradine watching them, noting their discontent, his eyes flicking this way and that to see the currents of unrest that ran through the Court. He never spoke against the King, not a word, but he was everywhere, it seemed, that discontent arose, with his sly smile and his sympathetic words. He did not plant the suggestion that the Warlords would never have stood for this rebellion; he was waiting, I knew—but for what? For someone else to come to him with a proposition? I watched him, and as always, I watched with fear.

Nilson's demands for soldiers and force had me looking up to the royal dais often, watching the High Priest. I made sure that I noticed whom he watched and who he spoke to. I had known that the man must be a master of self-control; he had watched and waited for decades already, gathering power, sowing a whisper here, a seed of doubt there. He did not endanger himself by showing his hand now; he did not speak out against Nilson, nor did he preach sermons that might catch the man's ear. The High Priest laid low, spoke little, and watched everyone, and continued to distribute the letters that I, for the life of me, could not trace.

The King, young and impulsive, had none of the High Priest's self-control. His delight in his marriage would turn in an instant to petulance; he begrudged anyone who did not share his exuberance, he was quick to reproach them. But this, even he could not wish away. Day by day, as Nilson's protests grew more widespread, as the man did not wait patiently for the business of the realm to resume, as he did not stay obediently silent, the King grew more and more furious.

"What does he think?" he snarled at Miriel, where she sat on one of the ornamental couches in his chambers. "That I welcome this rebellion? That I show it the slightest lenience? I will end it, can he not wait?"

I saw from the slight pause before Miriel spoke that she was choosing her words carefully. I felt the familiar curiosity to see what she would say, and the similarly familiar rush of dread that she would betray herself to the King's anger. In the corner sat two of the Dowager Queen's ladies in waiting, hand-picked to chaperone the young couple; Miriel's words would be repeated exactly to Isra later, I knew. So far, they had made no comment on my presence; as with other nobles, their eyes seemed to slide past anyone in livery.

When she was the most frightened, when everything hung in the balance—then, Miriel went as still as the summer sky before a storm. She barely stirred now. She stayed exactly where she was, leaning against one arm of the couch to watch the King as he prowled about his chambers, and she smiled at him soothingly.

"He is making trouble, only. Have you not sent declarations affirming the order of the world? Have you not refused to take up arms against your own citizens? That is the mark of a wise man, who does not reach at once for swords and spears like a savage."

He warmed to her praise, but was still sulky. "He says that I care more about peace with Ismir than I care about my own people."

"Foolish of him," Miriel said sharply. "How can he be so blind? The man must see that without the threat from Ismir, we are stronger. With peace, we are not losing our wealth and our young men to battles in the West."

"Yes!" The King swung around, staring at her intently. "That is it exactly, my Lady. The alliance with Dusan makes Heddred stronger. And do you know why?"

Miriel might well have retorted that she had just told him why, but she had learned that he liked to hear himself talk. Only when his thoughts were let loose could she have his attention and begin to change his mind. She smiled sweetly and waited. He, too, was smiling, but savagely.

"Because with Dusan's help, I can crush this movement so that it shall no longer appear in any part of the world. Before, either one of us might have supported these men, to sow discord in the other's kingdom—but now we are as one. We will act as one. I will write to him at once, he must aid me, as I will aid him, to keep this heresy from spreading to his kingdom as well."

Miriel's eyes flickered at the mention of heresy, and I saw her take a slow breath to calm herself. She kept quiet as the King spoke, and as we swept out of the room, I saw that she was already planning what she would say to him at their next meeting. The King's will was like a live beast, twisting out of her control and only barely tamed by her words. Now, with his heart turned to her and the Queenship almost in her grasp, she had every reason to be cautious, and yet all her heart was turned to the rebellion. She could not afford to fail, and fear made her hesitant even as it stirred her temper.

Every day, she returned to her rooms from her meetings with the King, and composed letters to the High Priest, and I delivered them as inventively as I could: baked in loaves of bread, slipped between items of laundry. Once I even snuck into the rooms behind the Cathedral and laid the letter on his table, my heart in my throat the whole time, but full of the excitement that only sneaking and evading gave me. I retrieved the letters as well. Each of them was laid on one of the pews in the cathedral, and it was near impossible to obtain them without being spotted by the High Priest or one of his minions. Each time, I brought the letters back and gave them to Miriel, still trembling with the feeling of matching wits with someone.

"Oh, no," Miriel said one day. The latest letter crackled in her fingers.

"What is it?" I was at her side at once, peering over her shoulder at the words. It had been a particularly difficult letter to retrieve, this one, so closely guarded that I had resorted to dressing as a chorister and stealing it right before morning services. The High Priest was growing ever more desperate to learn whom the letter-writer might be, and despite my pleas to Miriel that she was in danger as long as she kept her identity a secret to him, she was determined to reveal the information only when it would do her the most good.

"Look." Miriel pointed to one of the paragraphs. "He says that he is going to begin distributing letters again in the south."

"Isn't that good?" I asked cautiously. The rebellion had been dormant for so long that I could only imagine she would be pleased to have more adherents joining the cause, but she shook her head.

"Not now, it's too delicate. I'm still working Garad around." She pursed her lips. "I keep telling Jacces to wait, but he will not heed me. I can't tell him I have the King's ear without him figuring out it's me, but I must convince him to keep quiet. I can persuade Garad eventually." I considered; I could see her reasoning, but I doubted her. Miriel could convince a man of almost anything, but I did not think that even she could convince Garad of this. No matter how irritated the King was with Nilson, his irritation would not spread to Nilson's cause—they were of a like mind on the matter of giving up their own power.

"You knew that this would come sooner or later," I pointed out, trying to soothe her. "It's just sooner, that's all." She looked up at me, and her eyes were filled with fear.

"I need more time," she whispered. "He's not as in love with me as he was. I need to turn him back to me, and then when I'm his Queen, when I'm carrying his child, then he'll be in the first flush of the marriage—he'll listen to anything I say. But even now, I have to make sure he doesn't find another girl he likes better. He defied the Council to have me, he can defy the law again to have another girl if he wants. I can't spare a single moment to do anything other than enchant him—I can't afford to say something that would anger him. My hold isn't strong enough."

"Isn't there anything you can do?" I asked, worried by the bleak picture she painted, and she shook her head. Then she bit her lip.

"I could ask Wilhelm. He might have advice. The King might have spoken to him about what he likes, and what he doesn't." Alarm bells went off in my head, a great clamor like the tower bells at the Winter Castle, warning of a raid. I thought of trying to forbid Miriel outright to speak to Wilhelm, and knew that it would not work. Miriel was headstrong; she always had been.

"Be careful," I said finally, and she looked at me sharply. I felt a great weariness come over me at this dance. "Don't. You know why I'm telling you to be careful."

"Say it," she challenged softly, and I knew she needed to hear the words.

"You're in love with him," I whispered back. Her color rose, but she only stared at me steadily. "And he with you. You're about to marry a man you hate." I was at a loss for words. I did not know how to say that I feared Miriel, with her supreme self-control, would do something stupid now, at the worst time. I only said, helplessly, "Just be careful." She swallowed, and then her shoulders slumped.

"It's so hard," she breathed. "Every day, he's there. We think the same thoughts, I know just what he'd say to the King, what joke he'd make—"

"Stop it," I said brutally, and her eyes went wide. "If you think like this, you'll destroy it all—you know it can only come to ruin." She stared at me, stricken, but she nodded. I took her by the shoulders, as Roine would me, and stared into her eyes. "You told me that above all, you wanted to lead this country. Well, you can—but you have to give something up. Like I did."

Miriel met my eyes, and I saw that she understood the feelings I could hardly understand myself. She knew how much it hurt for me to hide things from Roine, from Temar, and she knew how it hurt to become the shadow I had hoped I would never be. She would never apologize for asking me to give up my innocence, give up those I loved—no, Miriel reckoned that worth the cost. But she understood the price I paid, and she was fair enough that she would not shrink from giving up something equally precious. At last, she nodded again, and I tried to smile at her.

"Do not think of him," I advised her. "You have to give him up. You only have to bear it for another month, that is all—when you're married, he will go. He will go off questing, or go run an estate. Let him go, then. And this will fade."

"Will it?" She was not angry anymore. She looked lost. She wanted to believe me. I bit my lip and nodded, hoping beyond hope that I was right, and at last she whispered, "I understand. I will give him up." I gave a sigh of relief, but it was too soon. She nodded to me, regally. "Go summon him, then. I will seek his advice."

"But you said—"

"I said I would give him up. But we need this information." Her voice sharpened. "Can you think of anyone else that has it? Anyone we can trust?" Finally, regretfully, I shook my head, and she nodded. "Then go. Summon him to me before I lose my resolve to be cold to him."

I went.

Miriel was cold, indeed, when Wilhelm arrived. She bade him be seated, and then she paced, her voice clear but her face turned away. I alone knew that she could not bear to see his eyes when she asked him how she could better enchant the King. Wilhelm himself looked stricken—he doubted her love for him, and he yearned for it. Even as I would not wish him pain, I hoped that he might doubt for a little longer. If Miriel could only keep him here, caught between hope and doubt, she could use his knowledge, but if either doubt or hope won out...Wilhelm was as passionate as Miriel. Who could say what he might do?

"My Lady, his Grace much admires the Lady Marie," Wilhelm offered. "His mother, the Dowager Queen, Gods save her, has much remarked upon Lady Marie's...pleasant... nature."

"Pleasant," Miriel repeated. She had not moved from where was she standing, staring out the window, but her shoulders were rigid. I could see her anger rising.

"Not that you are not pleasant," Wilhelm hastened to assure her. He started to rise, to go to her, and then caught sight of my stare. I shook my head, and he sat down, slowly. "My Lady, everyone knows that the Lady Marie has no opinions on statecraft. She is well-taught, but she does not share her own thoughts. She speaks only of embroidery and—" He broke off as Miriel turned to him at last. Her eyes were cold and hard.

"Indeed," she said. "I see what I must do. Thank you for your advice." She stared at him for a moment, then turned back to the window. "You can go," she said, over her shoulder, and Wilhelm's eyes widened. He had never seen her like this before—no yearning glances, no sweet smiles. He hesitated, but she did not turn back to him, and eventually he left, giving an awkward bow to her back, and a nod to me.

When the door closed behind him, Miriel turned to look at me. Her face was screwed up with determination.

"That was good, right?" Her hands were balled up.

"It was." I nodded and stepped closer, and she swallowed. "It's not for much longer," I assured her, and she looked away.

"Yes," she agreed, in a small voice.

Chapter 21

Miriel was pleasant. She was sweet, she was kind, she rarely raised her voice except to laugh at the King's jests. She hung on his every word. Most importantly, she never debated him as she once had. She was still clever, citing old philosophers or court sages, but she never pitted herself against Garad—her lively conversation was always, always in agreement with him.

As he grew more and more irate at the letters from Jacces, and convinced that he must send troops to restore order, Miriel never once wavered in her agreement with him. Even I, who knew her the best of anyone, never saw her eyes flash, and never heard the strain in her tone. She could not have been a more devoted ally—whatever he wished to hear, he heard it from her lips.

It was only barely enough for her to keep him, for the thing she feared had come to pass: Garad's interest was wavering. Had the marriage treaty not been signed, he would have been slipping away from her; but then, had the marriage treaty not been signed, he would not have been so irritated with her. Having stood defiant against his guardians, his mother, and the Council to pick Miriel for love, Garad was now determined that each of them should see Miriel as the perfect match, and it was a futile effort. Queen, Guardian, and Council alike were determined to stop the folly of this ill-advised betrothal, and whenever Garad found that they did not yet love Miriel, the blame fell on her shoulders.

Once, I had thought Miriel foolish to worry so, but her detractors were always working to persuade Garad to break his word. I do not know what sly words Guy de la Marque poured into the King's ear, or what impassioned pleas the Dowager Queen might have made. All I know is that, in those weeks before the marriage, the King was alert, as he had never been before, for imperfection and impropriety in his betrothed. Miriel could be charming and well-mannered, yes—even deferential. But she could not rival Marie de la Marque's birth, or Linnea Torstensson's, or Maeve of Orleans,' and he punished her for it, snapping criticisms of everything she said and did. If he had been any other man, or perhaps if she had been a princess born, she could have shaken some sense into him; he was the King, no one could do such a thing. No one had ever said no to him, not even his mother—her bright, sickly child had outlived his childhood, and now no one knew how to control him.

So when the King commented critically on Miriel's gown, or her jewels, she could only apologize. When he spoke of his grand alliance with Dusan, she could not disclaim that the tensions with Kasimir were as bad as they had ever been, his spies gathering evidence of assassination plots and warmongering raids on the Voltur mountains; she agreed that Garad had led the country to peace. When he spoke of the rebellion, of rooting out the insurgents and hanging them in the marketplaces, Miriel only nodded and concurred. If she wished to get herself on the throne, she could do no less.

Her only comfort was the friendship of Wilhelm, and even if I knew that such friendship was to tempt fate, it would have taken a heart of stone to deny her the only joy she had in the world. Her burning belief in the rebellion, and her desire to escape her uncle's tyranny, were poor comfort—and whatever we shared, it was underscored, always, by ambition. We kept each other to the difficult path we had chosen, and we lent each other strength, not comfort. And so, as Miriel's resolve to be cold to him failed, I could not bring myself to remind her of her duty as harshly as I had before.

As Miriel feared that the King's love waned in the face of regret, it was Wilhelm who could comfort her. It was Wilhelm who kept the King steady by singing Miriel's praises to the court, and Wilhelm who provided her with updates on the King. When she read his letters, I could see the tension melt out of her shoulders. More than I could, it was Wilhelm who could convince Miriel that even if the first flush of love faded, even as the King was forced to defend his choices every day, his heart yet belonged to Miriel. And, more than I, it was Wilhelm who could plot with Miriel on how best to turn the King's mind to the rebellion, even as she struggled to keep his affections.

"You cannot truly doubt him," I said to Miriel one night, as she undressed. "Wilhelm is right—the King loves you still, he defied Guy de la Marque for you today without pause."

There had been an explosive Council meeting before dinner, where de la Marque had accused the Duke of using Miriel to seduce the King, so that the Celys family might rise above their station. At such a chillingly accurate accusation, the Duke had only laughed and entertained the Councilors by recounting how surprised he had been to learn of the King's infatuation with Miriel. With the King laughing, as well, de la Marque's supporters had chosen to sit silently rather than come to de la Marque's defense. Even the truth, it seemed, would not sway the King from Miriel.

"And he is honorable," Miriel said, biting her lip. "He gave his word in front of all the court. If I keep faith with him, then he will keep faith with me. And then..." She trailed off and looked down. I knew what then: then she would spend the rest of her life walking the same fine line of enchanting the court and holding the heart of a man she did not love, forever wondering what might have been if she had given up her ambitions for Wilhelm. That her uncle would have had her killed would be of no consequence to her heart; she would spend each day imagining the ways she and Wilhelm might have escaped, or persuaded the King to let them marry.

Miriel's thoughts must have run nearly parallel to my own, for she said, "At least I will be free." Her maidservant would not understand, but I did. This was Miriel's great gamble, the goal she had had before she discovered the rebellion: become Queen, and she was free of her uncle forever. Becoming a Queen was the only way that Miriel could ever have a fighting chance against those factions that tried to use her as a pawn.

Miriel and I had both reckoned that this was the only way to keep her above the fray, and Miriel knew now that this was her chance to help the rebellion as well. In the aftermath of an attempt on our lives, our horror fresh and our instinct high, we had banded together and reckoned the bargain worth making. It had seemed a better deal then than it did now, living each day with the constant wear of vigilance and uncertainty.

And so, when Miriel asked me to arrange a meeting between her and Wilhelm, alone, I did not deny her request as I should have done. It was the week before the wedding, and Miriel had endured countless hours of being fitted for elaborate gowns that would overwhelm her tiny frame, being stuck with pins and criticized by the Dowager Queen—who oversaw the preparations— for her lack of figure. When she was not being pulled about like a doll, she must endure countless lectures from the Duke regarding his views on any number of subjects. Miriel had just returned from one of these.

"Another lecture. So that I will know what to say if the King decides to speak of grain shortages on our wedding night," she said acidly. I stifled a laugh, but I frowned at her face. I could see her exhaustion, and it was a mirror of my own. It required twice as much vigilance and three times as much sneakiness to keep watch over Miriel now. With so many people watching her, I must be careful that no one noticed me. I, too, was worn down with work and worry.

"Please," Miriel said, "I must see Wilhelm." Seeing the exhaustion in her eyes, I did not even argue. I sent a page running to give a note to another page, to take a note to one of Wilhelm's servants. By now, the matter of a clandestine meeting was hardly difficult for me.

The meeting was all wrong from the start. A servant with any sense would have invented some pretext to haul Miriel away, but I, bone-weary myself, did not heed my own instincts. No matter how many times I chided myself for my stupidity in the days that followed, at the time I only stood and watched them. They stood a few feet apart, awkwardly, but anyone could have seen that they yearned toward each other. The artful show that Miriel put on, the way she could convince the watching court that the air fairly crackled between her and Garad, was not necessary here. They were head over heels in love, and yet their conversation was a marvel of stilted formality.

"Is he still determined, then?" Miriel asked, and Wilhelm nodded. When Jacces' letters resumed, Garad had been quite as enraged as Miriel had feared, and she had begged Wilhelm to put aside his habitual caution and speak for leniency. Apparently, he did not have Miriel's silver tongue.

"I told him that his legacy would be enough to crush Jacces and his philosophy," he said helplessly. "And he told me that the rebellion is a rot at the heart of Heddred, and he must root it out before it spreads."

"A rot!" Miriel curled her hands into fists.

"We have to be patient," Wilhelm advised her, and I raised my eyebrows. As well as tell Miriel to grow wings and fly. Indeed, she flared up.

"How can I be patient?" she demanded. "There's no *time* to be patient if he's going to send my uncle. You must do something!"

"What *can* we do?" he asked practically, and she nearly sneered at him, beloved though he was to her. She drew herself up.

"I made myself from nothing into a queen in waiting," she asserted. "I can set my will to this, too. And you are no less intelligent than I."

"Perhaps you could tell him that you do not want your wedding overshadowed by bloodshed," he suggested, and she shook her head violently.

"*I* cannot say anything until I have a crown on my head and I am carrying his heir," she said flatly. He winced at the thought, but she did not stop. She went on, her little scowl the only sign of her determination and her own pain. "Until then, it only you we can trust to speak for them." He shook his head, but she held out her hands, pleading. "I know that you have lived your life in the shadow of the throne, but please, surely you can risk this for the rebellion? If not, for love of me?"

"For love of you, I must speak of a rebellion the King despises so that *you* can have a clear path to his bed," Wilhelm said bitterly, and Miriel hesitated, then nodded.

"I should hope that you would not hesitate to ask the same of me," she said softly. "I do not ask anything of you that I do not ask of myself, every day. Just as you must give me up, so I must give you up, so that I can advise the King and guide Heddred to a better future."

"You seem happy enough about it," he shot back, and she went as pale as if he had slapped her. Neither of them could bear the other's pain; and, more the pity, they could only take their hurt out on each other.

"I am not happy," Miriel said fiercely. "I am not, I swear it. On my honor, Wilhelm, I gave you up because we would never have been allowed to marry—my uncle would have killed me for it. I thought my love for you was nothing but infatuation, I swear I thought that it would fade, for us both. And now that the King wants me, there is no way out for us."

"There is," he said urgently. "You fear his love is slipping away, Miriel—then let it go. We will go away together, anywhere. We can help the rebellion. Anything you wish." For a moment, she was going to say yes. I saw it in her eyes. She was torn, but at last she shook her head, resolute. It was too great a change, she was too uncertain.

"Neither of us would survive it. Your family and mine would be shamed, your friend would be shamed. And is there any better way to help the rebellion than to have the King's heart, and turn him slowly to the rebellion? I would know all of his plans, I could have given them information no one else would know. Can you think of any place better for me to be?"

She waited until, slowly, he shook his head.

"You said this cause was your own," Miriel reminded him. "Should the good of the Kingdom mean less to us than our own happiness?" Again, defeated, he shook his head. "Then you know what we must do," she said, and he nodded.

"I don't know how I'll bear it," he said, his voice choked, "to see you marry him."

"Or I—to do so," Miriel responded, with a flash of wry humor. She sobered almost at once. "But I must find the strength."

There was a pause; it would have been long enough for me to stand, make a noise, break the spell. But I did nothing, and as if in a dream, they moved towards each other. He bent his head and she stood up on the tips of her toes to meet his mouth. I averted my eyes courteously, and so I only heard only a gasp from Miriel and a cry from Wilhelm as the door to the cellar creaked open.

"Very interesting," said Garad.

I turned my head sharply, and I was on my feet in a moment. He held a hand out to me, commanding, and I stopped. He was my monarch—but Miriel was my Lady. I could not bring myself to lift arms against this man, but, confident that he would not, could not, stop me, I walked slowly to her side, my hands out to show I meant him no harm. He followed me with his eyes.

"Your Grace," Miriel whispered, and his eyes flashed.

"No," he pronounced. "Do not speak." His face was cold and hard. "I can hardly believe what I saw with my own eyes. Do you know, my mother warned me of this, and I argued with her. She told me that your low breeding would show, and I told her that you were the finest of the ladies at court. And now, I see that she was right." His face twisted. "You have betrayed me."

"Your Grace, the fault is mine alone," Wilhelm said. Miriel's face went blank; having exhorted him to take a risk for the rebellion, she was now forced to watch him try. "I have always admired the Lady, and I see now that while I believed she might feel the same, she was trying only to—"

"No. I will believe no pretty lies. I know what I saw." Garad stared at Wilhelm with such hatred that even I shrank back. He might be shamed by Miriel, but the betrayal ran deeper with Wilhelm. Wilhelm, who had been his only friend in the long years of his illness. Garad's eyes narrowed. "Now I know where your interests lie."

"I know you will break off the betrothal," Miriel said quickly, "and I swear to you that I will make no complaint—"

"Oh, I'm not going to break the betrothal." He had gone cold. He snapped his fingers and I heard the tramp of guards. I thought later that I should have grabbed Miriel and run, and left Wilhelm to face the King alone. They would never have killed the heir to the throne. But instead, like a fool, I stood still, caught in the King's gaze, obeying him as any subject should do, and in a moment, we were surrounded. "I'm going to destroy you," Garad said softly. "Starting with the rebellion you hold so dear."

Chapter 22

I remember very little of what happened next. There was crying, and shouting. I should have been in the fray, between my Lady and the guards, but the King was no fool, and he had prepared his men for this encounter. I was the first one to be hit, hard, in the back of the head. The world faded to black around me, and I knew no more.

I came to my senses alone, in a small, dim cell, the only light filtering in from a window barely as large as my hand, and the flickering torches out in the hall. I could smell the stink of a hundred prisoners who had gone before me and hear the cries and clanking chains of those in the other cells, and in that moment, I was overwhelmed with fear. Was I here awaiting execution? And where was Miriel?

I struggled to see reason. The King would never execute Miriel—she was half common blooded, but also half noble, and executing young noblewomen was something one just did not do. And if the King wanted me killed, he surely would have ordered it done at once, with no witnesses except his guards. How better to make an impact on Miriel? No, if I was still alive, it was because he thought he could use me further; I was to be an instrument of Miriel's punishment. He wanted something of me yet. That sent a fresh wave of panic through me, and it only grew stronger when I heard voices in the hall. I curled into a little ball on the floor and squeezed my eyes shut as the voices came closer. When the key turned in the lock, I was sprawled just as I had woken up.

There were footsteps, then silence. I knew that they had surrounded me.

"Get up." Garad's voice. Cold. "Wake up, girl. I know you should be awake by now." Someone nudged me with the toe of their boot. I considered the matter, decided that their next move would likely be to kick me, and reluctantly opened my eyes.

"Yes, your Grace?" Pleasantries were ridiculous, but I had no idea what else I might do. He scowled at me, and crouched at my side.

"Tell me of Miriel's involvement in the rebellion." It was a sharp order, and his guards shifted so that I might hear the clank of their weapons. I felt fear begin to tighten my muscles, and tried to remember the lessons Temar had taught me: focus only on what I would say, not on what I did not want to say; slow my heartbeat; push away fear. And, unluckily for Garad, I had been practicing my response to this question for months. If I had planned to use it on the Duke, well, no matter. I stared up at Garad and delivered the lie as best I could.

"Oh, Miriel, is not involved, your Grace. She only has sympathies."

"How can she have sympathies, when she knows they mean to destroy me?" he demanded. Then his face hardened. "Of course…I know now that she does not love me. Did she ever love me at all?" Wary of contradicting whatever silver-tongued lies Miriel had been employing since I saw her last, I ignored that question entirely.

"Your Grace, you know my Lady—she has ever been kind to her servants. She sympathizes with the common people, who wish to have a say in their kingdom, as any noble might have."

"That is madness!" the King exploded. He stood and whirled, began to pace. "What do commoners know of ruling? How should they rule my kingdom?" I kept silent, watching him pace, until he rounded on me. "What of her passing information to the rebels, then?"

I froze, considering. Then I remembered what Mirel had said in the basement. If that was all the King knew… I tried to think what Miriel would do. "Oh! What she said!" I laughed outright, in his face, trying to mimic Miriel's innocent expression. "Oh, your Grace—Miriel has no mind for that sort of thing. She said it, but I assure you, she could never manage it." He sat back on his heels, surprised by my apparent mirth.

"She couldn't?" This was where the true test of my skill began. He still loved Miriel, and he desperately wanted to believe me that Miriel could not deceive him, but he was not stupid—if he set his mind to it, he would quickly begin to doubt. So I must fix his mind on something else: me.

"Of course not," I said scornfully. The guards bristled at my tone, and Garad narrowed his eyes. "Surely you can't be so blind as to—" The kick came from behind me, and even expecting it, I cried out.

"You forget to whom you speak," the King pronounced. "And whatever you claim, I know what I saw. I will give you one more chance: tell me of Miriel's involvement in the rebellion."

"There *is* no involvement," I insisted. "Can you truly believe that she would undermine her own uncle's work?"

"It is not his work any longer. He has been removed from command until I can determine his loyalty to me." I had a thought of the Duke's shame in the eyes of the court, and his cold anger, and I was seized by fear. If the King did not hurt Miriel, the Duke surely would.

"Where is Miriel?" I asked. "Please, your Grace—"

"Miriel is somewhere you cannot find her," the King pronounced. The corners of his mouth curved slightly. "She will not have your aid. I want her to be as blind as I have been, all this time."

"Your Grace, please—"

"No. And no more chances. You can rot in here until you feel like telling me what I want to know. Or until I kill you to teach Miriel a lesson." In a moment, they were gone, and a key turned in the lock. The guard grinned at me through the bars as he pocketed the key and walked after the King, whistling.

Trapped. And Miriel in danger. I knew that I had seen the glint of doubt in the King's eyes, and I could only doubt that I had bought Miriel even a little extra time. But there was no time for me to focus on that now. As I had lain, curled on my side, I had felt the contour of my packet of lock picks, still in their pocked in my tunic. Now, trembling with excitement and disbelief, I checked for each of my weapons. Every one of them was there. Whatever the King knew, no one had checked me for weapons. I had everything; it was better than I could have dreamed.

Caution kept me still. *Always have a plan. Have two plans.* Before action, planning, and for planning, I needed an objective. Freeing Miriel was one my goal, but freeing her to what? If the Duke had lost command, he would be angrier than I had ever seen him. Miriel could not be released to him, but where else could she go? Who else was her ally?

The High Priest. If Miriel had wanted to wait for a time when an ally would be of the most benefit, this was it. There surely could not be a time when she needed help more than now. And—at last a plan fell into place in my mind—if I could get to the High Priest, he could tell me the mood of the court, perhaps the mood of the Duke. It was even possible that he might know where Miriel was.

Now for the details of it. Chains first, then the door lock. Then run. I did not have time for bribery and persuasion—I would need to be quick and stealthy. And while I knew that I should wait to see how often the guards did the rounds, I did not have time for that, either. There was no time to waste, and no time to spend wondering where Miriel might be, and what disaster might have taken place. We would figure this out. We would. Our first objective had always been to survive, and now she needed me for that.

Trying to let my chains clank as little as possible, I withdrew the lock picks and set to work. The locks were laughably simple, and in a few moments I was free. I stood and stretched, and took an inventory of my injuries. The back of my head was still tender, and the guard's kick might leave a bruise, but the rest of my stiffness was from lying in chains. I ran through some stretches, trying to prepare myself. When I escaped my cell, I would need to run, and run fast.

Carefully, I approached the bars and peered both ways down the hall. I had heard no sounds since the King's party left, and there seemed to be no one about. Now I snaked one arm through the bars and began to work on the door lock. The lock fell into place as I heard a sound: careless laughter. There was a flicker of light now. Guards, on their rounds.

I looked behind me, and saw the shackles open on the floor. No time to hide them; the guards were not yet upon me, and I reckoned that I could make it to the other end of the hall before they could catch me. I could make it if I went now.

My heart in my throat, I eased the door open and slipped out. Then I turned and ran, ran as fast as I could. As I neared the corner, I heard a shout behind me, and the sudden clamor of drunken guards roused from an easy round. I cursed, and tried to run all the harder. I did not look back; my world narrowed to the corridor ahead of me. I skidded past branches in the corridor, trying to take the ever-larger corridors, running as much by instinct as by any skill. I had never known this part of the palace. I did not know where I might be.

After what seemed hours, but had likely been only a minute, I was rewarded with stairs. I took them two at a time, thanking Temar and Donnett silently for their endless drills. I thought the sound of the guards was getting farther away, and I was barely breathing hard. I got up the stairs and tugged at the huge door at the top. Locked. I fumbled for my picks again, and dropped them. The voices were getting closer, and I tried to force the lock with trembling fingers. The beatings the Lady had given me would be nothing to what would happen if they caught me—

Finally, the click. I shoved the pick into a pocket, opened the door, and found myself aboveground at last. Being stared at by a score of guards, ready to go on duty.

"What a fright!" I said brightly. "I thought I'd lost my key."

"Who're you?" One of them asked, standing up slowly. The others turned from their places at dice tables. I tried not to swallow; I only had to make it to the door on the other side of the room. If I did not let them see my fear, they might let me pass. As much as every instinct was screaming at me to run, I leaned back against the closed door and crossed my arms.

"I serve the Earl of Mavol," I said loftily. "His Lordship has...business...with some of the prisoners brought in from the Norstrung Provinces. And he will not be pleased if you detain me."

They fell away, uncertain, and I pushed myself up and walked as calmly as I could through them. At the far wall, I heard my pursuers reach the door at last. As the guards swung around to see what the clatter might be, I shrugged at the few who still watched me, turned the corner, and took off as soon as I was out of sight.

This was the armory. I should have known. It was time to use one of the strategies I had noticed for making my way through a crowd quickly. Accordingly, I pelted through halls, calling, "Message! A message for his lordship!" and, "Make way! A message!" The guards and soldiers obligingly fell away to make room, and I was hard-put not to laugh. They paved the way for my escape, and closed up in my wake. I could hear a clamor behind me, and could only hope that the soldiers were not so obliging to my followers.

Now my heart was pounding. At least two detachments of guards after me, and not an ally in the world. I headed for an exit and raced for the Cathedral in the Palace proper, preparing my speech in my head. If Jacces could see that it was in his interest to persuade the King to keep Miriel...

It was a short dash across the frozen alleyways, and I disappeared quickly enough into the Palace, but I was cautious, still: I made for the servants' corridors at once. I had snuck enough messages into the High Priest's chambers that I could have walked these corridors blindfolded. I hurried, trying to compose a speech in my head—anything that would gain his sympathy. He was a ruthless man, he had tried to kill Miriel at least once. But now it would be different, I told myself.

All of a sudden I felt light-headed. The thoughts that I had pushed away with my fear rushed back now. Where was Miriel? Was she alright? Had she already been held up to shame, the betrothal broken? What if she had been given back to her uncle? She would be sent back to Voltur, I knew that, or some other remote manor the Duke owned, and it would not be long until there was a story of an illness, a fever that had carried her away... This could all be for naught, and even if it was not useless, she was the one who was good at these speeches, not me. I was silent. I was unseen.

I took my courage in my hands and emerged from the servants' corridors in an antechamber of the choristers' rooms. From here, I only needed to make my way behind the chancel, and I would be in one of the rooms that led to the High Priest's apartments. I crept, conscious of how loud each footstep seemed in the vaulted chambers, and at last I raised my hand and knocked on the fine wood paneling of Jacces' doors.

I could hear a conversation cut off abruptly, and the door swung open almost at once. A man glared at me suspiciously.

"Yes?"

"I need to see the High Priest at once," I said, swallowing. "It's on behalf of one of the gentlemen of the court." He began to close the door. "Wait," I cried. "Please. Tell the High Priest I have another letter for him."

"Let her in." The abrupt command confirmed my hopes: the High Priest had been just inside. The servant stepped back reluctantly, and I slipped around him to look closely, for the first time, at this man who was as much enemy as friend. A man who recognized me, and gave a satisfied smile to know my identity at last. He had been seated behind his desk, now he stood and held out his hand.

"You have a letter?"

"I would speak with you alone," I said desperately. He looked me over, taking in my heaving chest, the fear on my face, and then he made a gesture, and his servant left the room silently.

"Yes?" he said. I tried to find words, overwhelmed to be in the presence of a man who was second only to the King in importance, by virtue of his title, and the rival of the King, by virtue of his cause.

Trying to catch my breath and gather my thoughts, I looked around the High Priest's chambers. They were small, and after the richness of the Palace, they seemed as cold and unwelcoming as my prison cell. The High Priest was doing his work at a table no finer than the one Roine used. A pomander sat at the edge of the desk; else, the whole surface was covered with books and papers. A small fire burned in the grate, and the only other furnishings in the room were heavy drapes, and a chair by the fireplace. The High Priest was indeed the ascetic they spoke of.

"You can guess now," I said clumsily. All of my speech had disappeared from my head, and I was left with only my wits and my fear. He said nothing, only looked at me with his deep-set, far-seeing eyes. "She was afraid you might doubt her," I explained. "That's why she didn't tell you. She began to learn of the rebellion after...well..." The High Priest raised an eyebrow.

"After I sent an assassin for her?" He smiled at my nod, a smile without happiness, only satisfaction. "How intriguing. How very intriguing. And she became a sympathizer? Tell me truly, don't think of lying to me."

"I'm not lying," I shot back. "And if you ask me, it's crazy." He smiled.

"And yet she's the noble, and you are the servant. Most interesting. So why are you here now, on her behalf?" The world shifted, uncertainty rocked me. I stared at him mistrustfully.

"You don't know?"

"Know what?" He leaned forward to me, and his eyes narrowed when I did not respond at once. "Catwin...what should I know? Is the Lady Miriel in trouble?"

"Yes." Too distracted to wonder how he might know my name, I crept closer, looking around myself fearfully, and he nodded to me to draw up a chair close to him. We leaned together like conspirators. "Miriel and—a friend—were speaking of the rebellion, and the King heard them. He had me imprisoned, he promised he would destroy her—I don't know how long it's been, and I don't know where she is now. You mean the Court does not know?"

"No." He shook his head. "Who was the friend?" When I hesitated, he raised his eyebrows. "If you want my help, you'll need to give me what I ask. Who was the friend?" He was right, I did need him. I sighed and said a silent apology to Wilhelm.

"Wilhelm Conradine."

"Ah." The High Priest smiled, and I was relieved to see that he did not seem surprised in the least. "Yes, Wilhelm is a sympathizer. I have spoken with him of it." His gaze sharpened. "Does he know of...me?"

"No, we did not tell him. We did not tell anyone." I shook my head, and the High Priest nodded, pleased.

"Well, then. So what is it you want from me?" I stared at him, wondering if he was joking. Was it not obvious?

"Your help. For Miriel's sake—because I swear to you, she would be a good Queen, she would aid the rebellion, and bring about the changes you seek. But we need your help, or the King will break the betrothal. He has sworn to crush the rebellion, out of anger at her. He must be persuaded to keep the betrothal, and not destroy the rebellion."

"And you want my help," he said, his voice expressionless. "To save the Lady and the rebellion. That is your goal—her safety, and the changes the rebellion would bring."

"Yes," I said impatiently. "I am loyal to her, and what she wants most is for the rebels' cause to become reality."

"Is it." I sighed. Why was he doing this?

"Sir, if you do not help us, the rebellion will be lost. I swear to you, he will stop at nothing now. I know you've spoken to him before, and not persuaded him—but now you must. And please—please, you must convince him that she has done nothing wrong." The High Priest clasped his hands together and stared off into the distance.

"I'm not sure I can convince him of that," he said thoughtfully. "But if you say she wants above all for the rebellion to be safe...that, I may be able to accomplish. Now, you must go. Find your Lady—the King gave out that she had a fever, she may be in her own rooms. We have much to do, both of us." I nodded and stood, then bowed and withdrew from the room. I put the High Priest out of my mind; I would come back to inquire as to his progress later. In the meantime, I needed to find Miriel, and help her escape.

I turned from the door and was setting off into the palace when Temar stepped out of the shadows, blocking my path.

Chapter 23

He smiled easily.

"Hello, Catwin."

I froze, uncertainly, and Temar was on me in an instant, his hands sliding up my arms, his breath in my ear; I was pressed up against the wall, my arm twisted behind my back and his face inches from mine. I saw the pain in his eyes, the fight of divided loyalties, and had a moment to wonder what it was he felt, with his mouth so close to mine and our gazes locked together. I saw his gaze flicker, and then he shook his head slightly, as if to clear it.

I had always known what would win out if it came to a choice between me and the Duke. I faced into the thought, as bravely as I could, gritting my teeth against the fact that I understood his choice—I would have made the same choice for Miriel.

"So where is she?" Temar asked, conversationally, the brief moment of conflict forgotten. He was his usual self once more.

"Don't give me that," I said, to buy time. I was thinking furiously. Temar would never ask me if he knew: he would ask me what I was doing here. He would taunt me that I did not know where she was. He would ask where I had been. He must, in truth, not know. Which meant that Miriel was *not* in her rooms.

The grip on my wrist tightened and I bit my lip to keep from crying out in pain. "Answer me, Catwin. Where is Miriel? Her rooms are locked and quiet."

"The King has her," I said, with as much dignity as I could muster. "I would have thought you would know that."

"Has her where?"

"In his chambers," I lied blithely. Temar frowned.

"Doing what?" At my hesitation, he tightened his fingers once more, and I twisted desperately, dropping and then lashing out. We ended up in a sprawl on the floor, fingers locked on each other's throats, cold fury in his eyes and matching anger in my own. Slowly, by mutual agreement, we loosened our fingers and backed away from each other. I crouched, wary, back against one wall, and curled my fingers. My legs were still tensed to spring. He looked back, his eyes betraying nothing; only the faint hunch of his shoulders showed that he, too, was waiting for a fight.

"Nothing improper." I weighed the options. If he did not know that Miriel was in trouble, he surely would soon. And when the Duke knew that Miriel did not have the King's heart wholly in her grasp, his response was always the same: *get him back*. That would give me the freedom I needed to find her, and formulate some sort of plan. "The King is angry with her," I explained.

"We know that well enough," Temar snapped. He was rotating his arm gingerly, where I had wrenched it. "Since the King took away the Duke's command in the South. What in the name of Nuada did she do?"

"Nuada?" I asked, baffled. His face flickered.

"Nothing," he said tersely. "*Answer* me."

"He thinks she's sympathizing with the rebellion," I said wearily. I had not wanted to tell Temar, for fear that this would give him the final key, but I could not think of a lie quickly enough. Indeed, I saw recognition flare in Temar's eyes, and I could only hope to recover for this. "He has it all wrong," I said, trying to mimic the tone of muted frustration. "He never *listens* to her, he thinks—"

"What's the truth of it?" Temar demanded. He was coiled, ready to grab for me, and I held up my hands.

"Oh, leave off! I'll answer you. She doesn't…she's angry at the Duke for treating her like she's nothing. It's true! You know it is. And you had to know she'd resent it. Well, she thought she'd teach him a lesson and get the King to give command to someone else. Only, he took it wrong. He thought she meant not to send soldiers at all, and now he thinks…" I sighed, as if weary, and hung my head. *Please*, I thought. *Please let her be Queen by the time the Duke has a chance to get back at her for this.*

"So she tried to betray her own family—" Temar's disgust was plain as day "—and in return she's stripped the Duke of his power and lost her own? You know, Catwin, I'd laugh if it weren't so—"

"*Shut up.*" He stopped, surprised. Even I was surprised. I would not have expected such an outburst from myself, but all of it had crashed in at once: the fear, and the guilt, thinking of his feelings and wondering if he ever—*ever*—thought of mine. Wondering what it meant that when he forgot himself, he smiled at me, and yet I saw my death in his eyes.

"What?" His voice was cautious.

"I said shut up." I scrambled to my feet, and he followed suit, uncurling with his feline grace and standing ready for another fight. Once the words had started, they would not stop. "You hate her, and you always have. I don't have to know why, but I'm sick of it, and I don't have time for you to tell me, anyway. We're *fixing* it. I went to talk to the High Priest to have him go talk to the King, and now I'm going to go get her a gown so that she can go to the King and apologize and make it all right. It's a lovers' spat, he'll be more in love with her than ever by tomorrow morning. So get out of my way and let me set this to rights."

Temar had gone quiet, he was looking at me with an expression I could not read. Before I could demand again that he move, he stepped out of the center of the hallway, leaving the path open. He made no move to stop me with force, but as I went to step past him, he held out his hand.

I looked up at him, and saw his eyes go cold and hard. I felt my lips part at that, the breath leaving me in a rush. At last, as I watched the last traces of emotion bleed away from him, I could see what I had missed, all these months. It was gone so quickly that I could hardly put a name to it—regret? Guilt? Sympathy? It was there no longer, and I could take no joy in knowing that something trace of friendship had remained; I was terrified. Now, in Temar's face, there was only resolve. And I knew what Temar was capable of, if he set his mind to it.

"Be warned, Catwin," he said, softly. "You've upset my plans, and if you ever stand in my way again, I will kill you." His voice sounded far away, the echo of himself. He did not wait to see if I understood, only dropped his hand and walked away, leaving me looking after him with tears in my eyes.

I hurried to Miriel's rooms, biting my lip until it bled, angrier than I had ever been in my life. He had cared for me, I knew that now. I had seen that when he had defended me to the Duke, and now he had let me go when he could easily have hauled me off to the Duke's rooms—or, at least, tried to do so. But none of that caring had stopped him from remembering that he was my enemy, and if any of it remained now, it would not stop him from hurting me. I believed every one of his parting words.

How many times? I demanded of myself, mouthing the words silently, biting my lip against the start of a sob. *How many lessons will it take?* I had been given chances, dozens of them, to cut this weakness out of my heart; and the Gods could have borne witness, in this moment, that I wished I had done so. We were assassins, Temar and I, we were killers; it was foolish for us to love, and more foolish still for anyone to love us. I, of all people, should know better than to hold such sentiment for him.

But I, of all people, had seen also that he was caught between logic and instinct—and that was the crux of it. My steps slowed, and I leaned against the wall, hunching over as if the pain in my chest were true, a wound of flesh and blood instead of emotion. As long as I saw that struggle in Temar, I could not hate him; I could not even blame him, however much I might believe that I should. If ever there had been a chance of that, it had been in the moment when my anger spilled out, and it had been wiped away when I saw him press down the guilt he carried with him. I could not hate him, and without hatred, I could not cut away the rest.

Logic against instinct: the cold truth that an ally with doubts and divided loyalties was no more than an enemy in disguise, and the instinct that led the two of us not to glare, and posture, but instead to smile, to search out the spark of empathy in each other's eyes. However misplaced it might be, we had a bond that none other could share. I closed my eyes for a moment, feeling the cold of the wall seeping into my skin, and I prayed that Temar had not pushed his instinct beyond reach.

I opened my eyes, and had a moment of confusion. Looking around myself, I realized that my feet had brought me not to Miriel's rooms, but to Roine's. I hesitated, caught by the desire to run, and avoid her censure, but I found myself moving forward inexorably. She might still be disapproving, she might barely speak to me anymore, but I needed nothing more, in that moment, to see her and remember who I had once been, before the Duke named me a Shadow. I stopped for a moment, wondering who reminded Temar of his past, then I shook my head, and pushed open the door.

She turned from her work table to regard me. Her eyes took in my tears, and she was at my side in an instant.

"What's happened?" she demanded, her voice low and urgent.

"I can't tell you." A mumble. A look away. Roine would not understand. She would tell me that to love an assassin was foolishness—and to explain that I could see beneath that, see what Temar was and had once been, was to remind her that I, too, was an assassin. Roine never wanted reminders of that.

She looked into my eyes for a moment, and then she sighed, brushed the hair away from my eyes, and enfolded me in a hug. At this, I began to cry. I stood there, frozen with the fear of everything crashing down around me, and I tried to find words for what had gone wrong. "I have to go help Miriel plead with the King. Again. And lie. Again." I gulped and pulled away to blow my nose into my handkerchief. Roine sat back, watching me, her brow furrowed. "I'm sick of lying," I said thickly. "I don't think it's worth it anymore."

"Then let Miriel fight her own battles," Roine said quickly. She swallowed. "Get out now, Catwin. Run away. Right now. You don't want to be a part of what's coming. Go." There was real passion in her voice, and I shook my head regretfully.

"I can't," I said. "I took a vow to Miriel, that I would protect her. I have to go to her now. It's just…it's hard," I finished, lamely. I looked over to her, and saw not her anger, which I expected, but a deep sadness. "You're not angry?"

"No," she said. She shook her head. "I knew how you would choose." She took a deep breath. "Go, then. I won't keep you." I nodded; there was no time to waste, and certainly no time to talk to her of Temar. She would never understand that kind of loyalty, I thought, as I hugged her and left.

I was cautious as I approached Miriel's rooms. No guards waited outside, as I had been afraid they might—the King, knowing of my escape, must be searching for me—but the door, to my surprise, was locked. I rattled it, and then, confident that the deadbolt was not in place, set to picking the lock. It was evening, with most of the Court at dinner, and so few enough people were about. Still, I was lucky that no one rounded the corner as I opened the door and slipped inside.

A sound caught my ear, the tiniest sound, and I pushed my way through the privy chamber and into her bedroom. Nothing. Not even Anna was here. I was just about to leave when I heard it again: a little scratching sound, coming from the wardrobe. Cautiously, seized by a sudden, superstitious fear, I drew my dagger. I yanked the door open and leaped back—

"*Miriel?*" Her eyes were wide in silent appeal, her mouth bound with a strip of cloth and her hands tied behind her back. I sheathed my dagger and set to work on the knots. Clever. Damnably clever, to hide Miriel in the last place the Duke would think of looking for her. Hide her, and know that if the Duke and Temar

183

came looking for her, she would keep quiet out of fear of them.

"He said if I gave anyone a hint I was here, he would have me killed," she whispered, when her gag fell away. "But I thought…I know how you walk. I had to try." Her mouth twitched in an attempt at a smile. "I know you could kill anyone that had come in with you, anyway. Where were you? They took you away…" Her voice trailed off as she realized that she was babbling, and she took a deep, shuddering breath. I helped her up and then, on a whim, wrapped my arms around her in a hug. I felt her arms grip me as she hugged me back, both of us wordless in our relief to find the other unscathed.

"They took me to the dungeons under the armory," I said. "But I got out. Listen. Your uncle doesn't know what really happened. Promise not to be mad?"

She drew back and eyed me narrowly, but nodded. "I promise."

"The King gave out that you were sick," I explained. "But the Duke knew it was false. He sent Temar to find us, and…well, he found me. I told him that the king thinks you sympathize, but it was all a misunderstanding." She opened her mouth to speak, but I shook my head. "I said you were angry that the Duke hadn't given you enough credit, and so you tried to get his command taken away—but the King thought you didn't want him to go because you were sympathizing with the rebels." Miriel was staring at me as if I had gone mad and I shrugged, helplessly. "It was the best I could do," I pleaded with her. "The Duke will be angry, but I couldn't think of anything that *wouldn't* make him angry. His command was already taken away—he knew something was wrong."

"So, I'd better get the crown on my head or he'll kill me," Miriel said grimly, her babbling relief forgotten. She was all business. She waved a hand at me, distracted by her thoughts. "It was a good enough lie," she said absently, and I sighed with relief. I had known it, but it was another thing entirely to hear her say it.

It was good that I had not earned her anger in addition to everything else. We did not have time for blame, and a shouting match—for I knew, if pushed, that I would yell at her that she had gotten us into this mess to start with. I would not need to; she knew it well enough. And in truth, I did not blame her. The best either of us could do now was move forward.

"Also…" I swallowed. "Look, I know you wanted to wait, but we needed an ally." She looked over at me wordlessly, and I sighed.

"I told the High Priest who you were." She bit her lip, then nodded.

"Fair. What's he going to do?"

"He said he wants the King to support the rebellion, too," I said grimly. "He's not sure he can persuade him, but I convinced him that our interests were the same."

"You know, I do look forward to meeting him someday," Miriel said. "Now that he knows I'm an ally." She looked almost hopeful, but then she sighed, and the hope drained away. "Gods. I have to go to Garad, don't I?" The bitterness was so sharp in her voice that I took a step back, and she smiled sadly.

"I don't even want to anymore," she said, and I heard the twist of powerless anger in her voice. "At first, I thought I just had to get him back. And then I was sitting there, alone, and I thought...what if I do win him back? What then? I'll spend my whole life with a man who tried to destroy everything I love. How can I do that?" We stared at each other for a moment. I had no answer for her, and she knew it. She knew from my silence that I had wondered much the same thing.

"But is there any other way?" I asked. It was the most important question. It was the question that held us trapped. She shook her head.

"Not if we want to survive at Court." She pointed to my cot. "Very well, then," she said grimly. "Sit. Tell me what we know. If we have to get him back, we need a plan. A very good one."

"We need the best lie we've ever told," I said, the words bitter in my mouth, and she tilted her head to the side, at once looking thoughtful.

"You know..." she said. "Now that you mention it, we might not."

"What do you mean?" I frowned, and she gave a wondering sort of laugh.

"What's the one thing we haven't tried? The truth. We've never just told him the truth." To her credit, the fact amused her.

"You're going to tell him—" I started, and she cut me off.

"That I don't love him? No. Not that truth. But what if he knew that he had hurt me. That my uncle had nearly killed us after the audience, that someone had come to kill us with poison...what then?"

"He would feel guilty," I said slowly, beginning to see her plan.

"And so then it wouldn't just be me who had betrayed him,"

she said grimly.

"No," I agreed, with the sinking feeling that this could work. We might come out on top again, and Miriel would be right where she had been: within inches of the crown. I was trying to untangle just why that thought was so repugnant to me when Miriel clapped her hands.

"I have it," she said. "*You* will tell him about my uncle, and that he—Garad—has made me enemies, and kept me in fear. Then I will step in and have you stop yelling at him, and he will listen. He'll be surprised, you see. No one's ever told him he was wrong. It will give us an opening."

"What will you say?" I asked curiously, and she shrugged.

"I'm not sure. I'll think while I get ready. Go guard the door; we can't let anyone in." Wearily, I went to obey. We had faced ruin and disgrace, and now our only choice seemed to be to forge ahead, ever pursuing a goal that would bring us no joy at all. I could only hope that when Miriel had the crown on her head, the game would change. I was not sure how much more of this I could stomach, and from her own outburst, I knew she felt the same.

Chapter 24

"Are you ready?" I slipped into the bedroom and raised my eyebrows in surprise at Miriel's attire. Instead of one of her fine, jeweled gowns, Miriel wore a nightgown and a robe, her hair falling loose in a wealth of dark curls. She wore one of the finest of her robes, embroidered with silver thread and seed pearls, but the effect was deceptively simple. It was innocent, very far from the tiresome elegance of the Court; it was how Garad had first seen her in their meetings. She shaped her mouth into a smile, but her eyes were frightened.

"I'm afraid it won't work," she confessed. "I can't stop thinking that we've lost. I don't want to go, I want to run away." When Miriel was in the spotlight, when she was performing, there was no room for doubt in her mind—only absolute, uncompromising conviction. It was always strange to see her fear when the mask came away.

"Do you want to run away now?" I asked her curiously, a strange seed of hope in my chest, and she considered the question for a moment. Then she shook her head.

"No. I don't think it will work, but I have to try. If I don't, I'll always wonder what might have been, because I'll know I crumbled."

"We might not have a chance to run later, if this goes wrong," I warned her, and her brow furrowed.

"No. We have to go. Do you agree?" Silently, I nodded. There was no other choice, no safe place to escape to. Even when our hopes lay shattered, there was no way but forward. "Then don't make this harder for me," she pleaded, and I took a deep breath.

"Let's go, then."

Our journey through the depths of the palace was quiet. Miriel was preparing herself for the most important act of her life, and I was twice as vigilant as normal, steering us along a circuitous route that even Temar would not think to check. I did not speak in part for fear of scaring Miriel. My heart was pounding so hard that I thought I might be sick, and I remembered how I had felt when I first came to the palace: like I was trapped in a story, where nothing was quite right. Was this how heroes felt in stories?

A ridiculous thought. Had any true hero ever accompanied a lady as she tried, once more, to pull the wool over the eyes of the King she had already betrayed? No, fairy tales were simple—a lady and a knight, no difficult loyalties, no lies. Heroes did not betray their families and their Kings.

"Did we ever have a choice?" I asked Miriel, before I could stop myself. To my surprise, she stopped her progress to consider.

"Yes," she said finally, and I felt the sinking feeling that she was right, that we had walked into every deception with our eyes open, and always the choice to walk away. Despite how many times we had told ourselves that we were trapped, we never had been. "But you know," Miriel said, "I don't think we did wrong. What could we have been if we ran away? What I wanted for Heddred was noble, and what you wanted…Catwin, what *do* you want? For you?"

I winced and looked away. Unwittingly, she had touched on the sorest point, one I had meditated on as she had gotten dressed. Miriel had schemed and lied and betrayed because she believed she could rid the world of injustice and reshape the court and the country for the good of all. I had no such lofty goal. I had lied and betrayed as much as she had, but to no good purpose. More, what *could* I ever want? Temar?

Useless even to think it.

"I don't know what I want," I admitted in a strangled voice, and I felt tears come to my eyes when she reached out to lay her hand on my arm.

"If we get through this, Catwin—you've been my friend when I had none other, you're the only one who ever believed that I could help the country like I wanted to, and not just because I could help you to your own ends. Whenever you find what you want, I'll help you like you've helped me." I said nothing, blinking back the tears, and she squeezed my arm. "Are you ready?"

I sniffled inelegantly and nodded, then wiped my eyes, and we set off once more. When we emerged from the side corridor, I drew my old boot knife out and slid it across the floor to the guards. If they searched me, they would find the others, but as I had bargained, this appeased them. They were new guards, I noted, and I was pleased to see that they did not know of Miriel's disgrace, only her status as the King's betrothed. With curt nods, they swung the doors open to us, and closed them again once we were through.

"Your Grace?" I called, and there was a rustle from the direction of the King's bedchamber.

"Who's there?" There was real fear in his voice, and for a moment, I truly felt pity for him. What good purpose could any visitor have? There had only ever been two people who would visit him for friendly purpose, and now he knew that neither loved him with an undivided heart, and neither shared his vision for Heddred. In the world of a King, with ill will on all sides—Kasimir's threats, and Nilson's, and those who would see the throne itself torn down—Garad had never been quite alone, until now. He was afraid—and I was sick to my soul at the thought of this new lie, our continued deception of this young man.

I felt the shadow welling up in my heart, undeniable. Garad was no friend of ours: I could not blame him for not caring for my happiness, but he had closed his eyes even to Miriel's best interests, and he had put her in grave danger time and again. Right now, he was our enemy. *When you play to win, everyone is always your enemy.* Miriel might soften towards him one day, as might I. He might become an ally. But tonight, there was no time for sentiment, no time for my foolish qualms.

"It is Catwin, your Grace," I called, and I held out my hands, palms forward, so that he might see I meant him no harm. "I have brought Miriel."

The King emerged from his bedchamber scowling.

"I do not wish to speak to the Lady," he said coldly. "And *you*. You defied my wishes, you went and freed her, then." I did not point out that it had been laughably easy; however much he might have cautioned them, his guardsmen had not believed that two girls could outwit them.

"I swore a vow to her," I said simply. Even if this was a piece of our plan, I was proud to say it, and I was glad to speak the truth at last. "After they tried to kill us, we swore to each other that we would be on the same side. If it is in my power, I will never let her be alone and imprisoned. And, see, we came back," I added.

"Who tried to kill you?" he asked suspiciously, seizing on that, taking the bait. I bit my lip.

"We still don't know. Do you remember her 'illness' after the official audience? That was not illness, it was poison in her food and mine."

"Someone tried to kill her, and you did not tell me?" he

demanded. As Miriel had predicted, such news distressed him. He was angry, and still he loved her. I wondered what she made of this, watching from the shadows, but I did not have much time to spare for such thoughts. I had not her skill at weaving illusions, even when they were made of truths.

"We were afraid," I admitted to him. "We did not know who we could trust. To call attention to it might have brought her more danger." I drew a deep breath and took the plunge. "We even suspected the Duke, her uncle. We have asked him, and he has not denied it—but you see, I think it is just to keep us in fear. When Miriel arrived here, he told her that she must obey him and behave with absolute purity, or he would have her killed. When he knew that she had been going to see you without telling him, he was…" I took a moment to remember the Duke's rage after that audience with the King, so that fear would show on my face; I was not Miriel, who could create the illusion of emotion from nothing. "He was very angry," I finished softly.

"I knew nothing of this," the King exclaimed. He saw the truth in my face, and was stunned. But seeing his wide eyes, his horror, I found that I had no sympathy. This was not only an act for me.

"You never *cared* to know," I shot back. "Miriel begged you not to tell the court, do you remember that? She knew that it would make her enemies she could not fight, she knew it would enrage her uncle. But you did not listen to her. You put her in terrible danger, and ever since—"

"Catwin." Miriel's voice was soft and sweet. She walked forward out of the shadows and put her hand on my arm to stop my tirade, and even knowing that this was a part of the act, I wanted to shake her hand off and go on, rail at the King for his blindness. He was shocked already, staring at me open-mouthed. No one had ever yelled at him in his life. He turned to Miriel, who smiled at him tremulously.

"Is this true?" he asked, and she bowed her head.

"You could not have known." She was whispering, but she knew this room; her voice echoed off the beautiful, cold marble.

"I hurt you?" he asked, disbelieving. "I?"

"I swore I would not be angry." Tears stood out in Miriel's eyes. "Not then, and not when we disagreed. I told myself—you were the King. You were born a King, not an ordinary person. You could not understand, and that was as it should be—you *should*

190

not." There was a moment of dead silence while his face showed his uncertainty, and then he scowled.

"You betrayed me," he said flatly. He knew, now, that what he had seen was only a part of the story, but it was an inescapable truth. Involuntarily, I looked to Miriel, who nodded, squaring her shoulders.

"I did," she admitted, looking him straight in the eyes. "I crumbled. I looked into the brightness of your love and I was afraid—of what I am, of what you are." I could never have delivered such a line with a straight face, but Miriel could. "I was afraid I would never be worthy of being your Queen...and now my fear has cost me everything."

"Yes," he said. "It has. And it has broken my heart. I will never forgive you." I felt a wave of elation and despair. So it was over. The thing we had lied and cheated and betrayed to achieve—it was snatched away, out of our reach forever. There was no recovering now, we had gambled everything and lost...and now we were free. I was not sure what I wanted, but I let myself realize, at last, that it was not this life of lies.

Miriel was far from defeated; she would not be turned back so easily as that. She played on without a break: swallowing, nodding, looking down at the ground for a moment. Then she clasped her hands before her, twisting the fingers, and looked back to him.

"I thank you," she said simply, "for your honesty. I had come here to ask you for one more chance to be the Queen you deserve." She drew a deep, shuddering breath. "I know I did not even have the right to ask, but I could not go without knowing. Now I do. And I vow, you will have no argument from me and mine when you break the betrothal. I will admit what I have done if you wish it. And you need not tell my uncle. I will do so." He stared back at her, swallowing. At her retreat, he was at a loss, torn between pride and love, and for all that I wanted Miriel to win—there lay our only path to safety—I was torn as well. I could not wish it with my whole heart.

"He will kill you," the King said uncertainly, and I realized that he could not hold out. Not against her. Miriel saw it, too. She let no triumph show in her face, but she knew she had him. She swallowed, as if in fear, and there was a moment of pure silence.

Silence. I looked around myself, confused. We might have slipped into another world—I could hear nothing around us...

All at once, my hackles went up. Something was wrong—I might not know what, but I did know that every instinct screamed for me to run. I looked around myself wildly, missing whatever whispers the other were exchanging, and at last I put my finger on it. All this time, and not a sound from the hall. The guards should have changed—I knew their timing. And I remembered their faces now: men I had not seen before, their uniforms ill-fitting.

And now, faintly, so faint I thought I might hear only the frantic beat of my heart, I heard the tramp of a whole squadron. I waited for a moment, and heard it grow louder. It was all I needed to know; whatever form it took, death was coming. Panic washed over me.

"We have to leave," I broke in. "Right now. Are there tunnels here?"

"What?" The King was bewildered, and I heard the tramp of soldiers growing ever closer. I did not hesitate. I grabbed Miriel's hand and ran, yanking her after me, skidding to a stop and running back to pick up her cloak from the floor, and then running once more, making for an antechamber.

"Something's happening," I whispered fiercely over my shoulder to the King. "*Run!*" He did not follow us, he was frozen, looking to us and then the door, and I had no time to keep him safe. I turned, and took stock of the room: one window, too high for Miriel to climb, a table and a chair, and a wardrobe. As I began pushing the table beneath the window, I heard a shout outside the door, and the unmistakable thud of two bodies. "Get in the wardrobe," I panted.

"What's happening?" Miriel's eyes were wide.

"I don't know. Get inside!" The big double doors slammed open, echoing through the main chamber, as I heaved the table into place. It would have to do. I grabbed Miriel's cloak and followed her, shutting the door behind us to a crack as quietly as I could, and crouching down next to her. We were hidden by the thick folds of the King's cloaks, and I laid hers over our head so our eyes would not gleam and give us away.

"If they find us," I breathed, "I'll hold them off. Get on the table and climb out the window. You'll have to break it. Then run, and get help." She did not respond, and I could hear her breath coming in little sobs. Tentatively, not wishing to hurt her, I put my hand out to cover her mouth. Whoever was out there, we could not let them hear us.

192

"Who are you?" the King asked, his voice like a whiplash. "Why are you here?"

"Your Grace." It was a voice I had never heard before, accented strangely. "I bid you good evening."

"What is this?" the King demanded.

"This is the end, your Grace." There was barely a pause, and then there was a choked off cry. I heard Miriel gasp in fear; my own mind had gone blank. Then the voice said, cold as deepest winter: "Sweep the rooms, kill any you find. His betrothed and her servant may be here—they must not be allowed to escape."

Miriel was sobbing into my hand now. I could feel her tears wet on my skin, but she made no sound. We waited, breathless, as we heard the men tramp about. The minutes passed; I could feel every muscle tensed, beginning to scream with pain. I was finally beginning to believe that they had forgotten to search our room when I heard the leader's voice.

"What about that one?"

"Yes, sir." *Oh, Gods.* The door to our chamber opened, and footsteps approached. I readied myself as well as I could. If I could silence this man before he could call out—

A clamor in the main room, and both Miriel and I stiffened, the fear we had so tenuously controlled rising up until I thought I might vomit. There was the sudden sound of another group, and the clash of steel on steel. A was a jumble of voices, and Miriel and I curled closer together as our hunter exclaimed and hurried out of the room. "For the Gods!" I heard, and the clash of weapons. Above it all, a young man's voice: "Garad!"

I do not know how long that battle took, how long we waited in the darkness for the fight to cease. I pictured Wilhelm, battling his way to Garad, to free his cousin from the grasp of the soldiers; I pictured the warrior that had such a cruel, cold voice. Huddled close to each other Miriel and I clenched each other's hands and waited, hardly knowing what to hope for. It seemed to be hours before it ended, and yet at the same time, that it was over as quickly as it had begun. There was a silence: complete, stricken. And then the sound of broken sobbing. Fear began to creep in. What awaited us in that antechamber?

I had hardly begun to form the thought, when I heard another voice, choked with grief.

"Wilhelm Conradine, rise up." The High Priest. So he had come with Wilhelm, to plead for clemency. I swallowed. Gods, if he had only come sooner...

And then the full importance of his words broke on me like a wave. *Wilhelm Conradine, rise up.* There was only one reason for the High priest to speak those words. In my head, I could hear Garad's cry of pain—and a whimper of fear so complete that I thought I might cry out, myself, in shared terror. It had not only been the cry of the helpless, of a man held restrained as the soldiers swept the rooms for us. The gasp, Wilhelm's grief, the ferocity I had heard in the Royal Guard, as they fought these intruders—all of it could mean only one thing. I felt my breath leave me in a second; I could hardly understand the thought.

Wilhelm, even as he must see the truth with his own eyes, did not seem to understand it. "Why?" he demanded. His voice broke on a sob.

"Ye must, milord," a guardsman said gruffly, and I heard the clank as—to a man—the soldiers knelt.

"The King is dead," the High Priest said, his voice carrying high above his pain. "Long live the King." And to a man, they echoed him:

"The King is dead. Long live the King."

Chapter 25

Long live the King—
—Wilhelm Conradine, rise up—
His betrothed and her servant may be here—
The last phrase stuck in my mind. It was shock, I knew it, but I could not think of anything else. The phrase rolled around and around in my head as Miriel and I crouched, frozen with fear and stifling even our breathing. *His betrothed and her servant may be here.* Had they only suspected that we might be here, knowing that Miriel and the King were inseparable? Or had they known? Had someone told them? Who had known that we might be here tonight? Who had we told? The High Priest might have known. The Duke might have known—

"Catwin." Miriel tugged on my sleeve. "We should go out."

"No." I gripped her arm to stop her from pushing the door open. "Not yet."

"Why not?"

"We don't know what's going on."

"What do you mean?" Our heads were craned together, our voices barely a whisper, but still I made a shushing noise. I could sense her glare even in the dark; she must speak it, she must make sense of it. "Those men came in here—"

"Yes! Those men. Who were they?"

"I thought—the accent—Kasimir?"

"But do you *know*?" Miriel stared at me, and I realized she did not want to know. She did not want to think, because the more she thought, the more she realized that she had been seconds from death. When she thought, she would remember that Garad's body lay on the floor, and that even if she could bring herself to forget the horror of the murder, the rest of her life lay in ruins as well.

"I don't know," she said in a small voice. "I don't know anything. I—"

"Shhh!" Her voice had been starting to rise, and I clamped my hand back over her mouth. We sat for a moment in silence, both of us terrified that we had been heard; I knew that I did not want us found here, not even by our supposed allies. And what would the court say if ever they knew that Miriel had been in the King's chambers when he was executed, and survived?

"What do we do, then?" Miriel asked finally, her voice the barest hint of a whisper. I could hear her breath coming short, but her voice was deathly calm, the cold rationality of shock. I had to get us out of here before we both descended into raving madness. I thought, and came to the only option:

"We have to go to the Duke."

"*What?*"

"Quiet! We have a lot more to lose by hiding from him than going to him. If we run away now, he'll think *we* had a hand in this. And anyway, no matter how angry he is, it's safest—he had the least to gain from any of this." That, at least, rang true, but a little voice in my head whispered, *and he was also one of the only ones who knew you were going to be here. And you told that lie, and now he hates you.*

"He'll kill me," Miriel whispered, a morbid echo of Garad's words only—what—ten minutes past. This felt unreal; I wanted to wake up. I could feel my mind slipping away into shock, and I shook my head as violently as I dared, trying to clear it.

"We just have to get out of here..." I murmured. "We have to wait until they go." Miriel made no response, and so we did wait, in silence, our muscles aching more and more as we stayed curled, frozen in fear. We waited while the King's body was loaded onto a bier to be carried to the Cathedral, and I thought unexpectedly of Isra, being woken in the night to hear that her only child was dead by murder. My throat tightened.

When the way was clear, and the room empty, I pushed the door of the wardrobe open. We emerged, stumbling on cramped legs and blinking at the light of the oil lamps in the next room, and I wrapped Miriel's cloak around her shoulders, for in our silence, the shock had hit her in earnest: she was shivering violently. For the first time, I gave thanks for Temar's insistence that I learn to push away my fear until I had the safety to stop and think. I stooped to look into Miriel's eyes until at last they focused on me.

"You need to close your eyes," I told her. I was not sure she could see what lay in the room outside without breaking down entirely. I guided her through, mindful that she held her gown out of the way of the pools of blood, and got her into the servants' corridor. "Can you wait here a moment?"

"Why?" Her teeth were chattering.

"I need to look at the…" *Bodies.* "…soldiers. I'll be back." In the room, I spent a moment looking over things, trying to commit the smallest details to memory, and then crept to the body of their leader. He wore armor that would look, to any casual observer, like the uniform of the Royal Guard; they had disguised themselves to sneak into the palace. Oddly, I was relieved—this was not a detachment of the Guard itself, then. Carefully, I pushed his braid aside and studied his neck, his hands, his wrists, looking for tattoos. Nothing. His dagger was finely wrought, though, made with ripples in the metal. Hastily, suddenly afraid of being found here, I grabbed the knife and left. I paused outside, seeing the two new guards who had greeted us earlier; their throats had been slit, and I wondered now if they had been accomplices, sacrificed for the illusion of two factions.

That was a very interesting thought.

I guided Miriel carefully through the darkness, knowing that I should speak to her and yet too preoccupied with my own thoughts to concentrate. When we emerged into the main hallways by the Duke's rooms, I heard the strident tones of his guards, and the clipped speech of a Royal Messenger. I pushed Miriel back and closed the door behind us as the man went past, and when he was gone we darted out and around the corner. Seeing our white faces, the Duke's guards did not even ask why we were there; they swung open the doors without comment.

The Duke was pulling on his coat as we came into the room, and Temar was hastily slipping his minor arsenal of weapons into the various concealed pockets of his suit. Both of them stopped what they were doing when they saw us. I saw their instinctive anger at the sight of us, but even the Duke was cautious—they knew from our faces that something was terribly wrong, and I judged from their own that the Royal Messenger had not divulged the earth-shattering news of the King's death. I tried to find the words to speak, but Miriel broke the silence first.

"The King is dead." Her voice trembled.

"*What?*" It was Temar. He had gone whiter than I had ever seen him. The Duke was frozen in shock. I found my tongue at last.

"Assassinated," I said. "Someone sent a detachment of soldiers, dressed like the Royal Guard. I heard them coming and hid Miriel in an antechamber."

"Are they still in the Palace?" The commander in the Duke

awoke. I saw he was ready to call for reinforcements, knew that he was bent on vengeance. I shook my head.

"No. The High Priest came with the true guard. They were...too late. But they were able to kill the soldiers who were there already." Temar and the Duke exchanged a look, the glance between Light and Shadow, the sharing of something far beyond words, beneath conscious thought.

"I must go," the Duke said abruptly. "I have been summoned to a Council meeting." Slowly, his face changed. His jaw tightened. "The King," he said softly, bitterly, "has called a Council meeting." He had not realized, until then, how completely his chances lay in ruins. Another King, years more of courting favor. "You two, stay here." He made for the door, but as it swung open, he turned to look at us. "You swear you had no part in this?" he asked dangerously. Miriel gasped, but I held firm. I would have wondered the same of him, if his surprise had not betrayed him.

"We swear," I said, my voice even. He nodded curtly.

"I'll make a plan when I return. Do not leave this room, and for the love of the Gods, do *not* open the door to anyone. If they have any sense, they'll come for Miriel, too."

"The Council, or the assassins?" I asked. It was Temar who answered.

"Both."

The Duke waited a moment more. "Do not think this erases your betrayal," he said, softly. "I will deal with you when I get back. Do not even think of running." And they were gone, the two of them as grim as I had ever seen.

I managed to get Miriel to a chair and myself to another before my legs gave out. I wanted to laugh hysterically. The Duke could never have realized how little his anger meant to us now. What we had seen in that chamber was more horrifying by far. After a while, I realized that I was rocking back and forth wordlessly; Miriel was crying. Her sobs had gone hoarse, and she was muffling them into her hand as if she were still hidden, still listening to the footsteps of the soldiers coming closer and closer to our hiding place.

"It's so much worse," she choked out, and I nodded, not trusting myself to speak without crying, or vomiting on the Duke's polished floors and fine carpets. It was worse—far worse than when the man had come to poison Miriel, worse than when we had found the poison in our food. To be so close to death, and spared for no reason—chance had placed us there, and luck alone had saved us, and it made no sense. My mind could not accept that I was still alive. I had only to close my eyes for the feelings of terror to rush back and choke me.

"Someone's trying to kill us," I heard myself say. Miriel looked up at me, her tearstained face blank. "You remember when the soldier said to check for us? I think they were there for us, too. This wasn't just about the King."

"But why—" she had to stop and catch her breath around a sob. "Why us? Who would bother to kill us if he was dead? Anyone with sense would know that—"

"I don't *know*," I nearly yelled back, and her eyes went wide. "I don't know who, and I don't know why. We didn't know why last time, either! We never know! We never found out!"

"Catwin, listen." Miriel's voice was strengthened by her own desire to believe that we had been safe. "They just wanted to make sure that no one had seen anything, so that they couldn't be tracked." Her words were eminently sensible, and yet I could not shake the feeling that those men had been sent for us, that they would have found us and killed us wherever we were in the palace. In my dreams, my mother had told my father to kill me, and spare me the betrayal that would follow me all my days. Superstition. I always said it was superstition. But it was becoming harder and harder to ignore.

"I don't think so," was all I said, and Miriel frowned and fell silent.

Time passed slowly. We were hungry, but too afraid to send for food. Exhausted, but frightened into wakefulness. Sometimes we paced, and sometimes we huddled in our chairs. We were still awake, both of us wide-eyed and frightened, when the Duke and Temar returned at last. The Duke was grim as he swung his cloak from his shoulders.

"They say the soldiers were Ismiri," he said. "One of them carried orders signed by Kasimir." I forgot that I was not to speak in the Duke's presence unless prompted.

"That seems...incautious," I commented, tentative. He was too preoccupied to be angry. He only nodded, but Temar said,

"Kasimir is incautious as well." I nodded, my mind working furiously. No rational person would send soldiers with a letter, something that could be found if everything went wrong. Surely. But Kasimir was not rational, not about this. And I remembered the

Duke saying that a full-scale invasion of Ismir would fail—was Kasimir more calculating than he had seemed? Was he trying to tempt us to make a foolish mistake?

"I don't trust it," the Duke said bluntly. "Too many people benefit. The Conradines, for one." At this, Miriel stirred to life. She raised her head and stared at him, her eyes red-rimmed.

"Wilhelm would *never* be party to murdering Garad," she said. The Duke raised his eyebrows at her vehemence.

"Perhaps," he conceded. "But I'd not be such a fool as to trust Gerald." I thought of Gerald Conradine's slippery smile and shuddered. Had he been planning for war, as Dusan claimed? Had he grown tired of waiting?

"You two will be sent back to Voltur," the Duke said suddenly, and we both looked over to him. We had forgotten, for a moment, that his anger would be waiting to spill out.

"What?" Miriel asked disbelievingly.

"You need to be seen to grieve," he said. He had been planning this out in his head, I saw. He was making the quick, hard decisions on which his survival had depended—first on the battlefield, and now at court. "And I don't want everyone watching you and spreading rumors about your behavior." His voice hardened. "*And* I cannot afford another crisis, or another betrayal." I waited to see where he was taking this, but Miriel flared up, forgetting my lie in her anger.

"My betrayal? After you were the one who would have sold me as a whore?"

"You would have been favored beyond your wildest dreams," he spat at her. "But you had to have your own way, and you have destroyed it all. Everything you *touch* turns to ashes. You have ruined my plans for this family, just as your mother did before you. Did you think I would not learn the whole of why the King was displeased with you? Your Shadow would have hidden it, but I know of your disgrace!"

Wilhelm. I froze, but Miriel was undaunted.

"You should be glad of it." She was as quick on her feet as he was. "I'm beloved of the King now, as well as before! You want me on the throne? I could still be!"

"I never wanted you on the throne," he snarled back. "I only wanted the keys to the Kingdom, and you took that from me. And you will pay for that. You will go back to Voltur, until I decide how best you can be played. Until I decide if it's even worth protecting you against whoever is trying to kill you now!"

I looked over to Temar, and saw him hunched in a chair, the very picture of despair and furious resolve. He was not even paying attention to the fight that raged between Miriel and the Duke, and tentatively, I walked over to him and placed my hand on his arm. I could almost forget the fight between us, to see him so sad; there was always sorrow behind his eyes, but he had held it inside himself until now. At my touch, he stirred and looked up at me. For a moment, he barely saw me, and then he shook his head to clear it. His eyes focused, and I saw him running through the conversation he had only half-heard in his head.

"Oh," he said, seeing at once what I would want to know. "There was poisoned food sent to Miriel's rooms. Her maidservant was sent to bring it from the kitchens. She must have eaten some— she's dead, you know."

Chapter 26

I might still be frozen into shocked stillness by the King's death and the reality of another assassination attempt, but the Duke was as quick to act as ever. He did not waste time. Miriel's gowns were packed within a scant few hours, an honor guard readied from amongst the Duke's most loyal men, and supplies hastily commandeered for the journey. I was forbidden to go about the palace, but even the Duke's anger could not keep me from saying goodbye to my few friends.

When no one was watching, I slipped out of the courtyard where the carts were being loaded, and headed down the corridors to Roine's rooms. Already, the news was making its way through the buildings: runners were darting to and fro, and I could hear the faint shouts of soldiers. I tapped on Roine's door and slipped inside, glad to be out of the bustle before someone could recognize my tabard, stop me, and ask what the Duke thought of the news. It was dark; the day was so young that even she was still asleep. I shook her shoulder to wake her, and at the sight of me her face was troubled. I saw relief and wariness as she pushed herself up.

"What is it?" she asked, her voice neutral, and I saw that she had been waiting for bad news. I felt a pang of guilt. For three days, I had not come to my lessons. The King had given out that Miriel was sick, but Roine had not been summoned to attend to her; she would have known something was wrong. I had come to her crying, and left without ever telling her what was wrong. And now this: me coming to her rooms in the middle of the night, while she could hear the pounding of feet and the shouts of disturbance in the halls.

"It's okay," I assured her, before remembering that it was not okay. Nothing was okay. I did not know how to say that, or tell her that I was leaving. I was going far from her, and she would be commanded to stay behind, away from the very girl she had come here to protect. Roine had never wanted to serve nobles in the palace. "I had to wake you. Look, everyone will know soon—the King is dead." Her face barely changed, she was looking at me almost with fear, and I could not bring myself to tell her that I, too, had nearly been killed. "The Duke is sending me and Miriel to Voltur," I offered, clasping her hand in my own. "We'll be back soon." That was true; however angry the Duke was, I knew he would not let the chance to use Miriel pass him by, especially when he knew that the King was enamored of her.

"You're going away," Roine said softly. She was looking away from me.

"We'll be back," I assured her once more. I tried to smile, but her words had opened up a gulf at my feet. I had never gone anywhere without Roine. She had always been there to reassure me, give me advice, hold me while I cried. How could I bear to be parted from her now, when I had been so close to death? I was deeply afraid, now, and I did not want to leave the one person in the world I could call my family. I felt tears in my eyes and gulped them back.

"At least I'm going, right?" I asked her. "Like you wanted."

"It's too late for that," Roine said sadly. "I wanted you to go before you were caught up in everything here. Now you're a part of it, come what may."

"I'll be safe," I promised here. "But I have to go now. I love you."

"I love you, too." Her voice was muffled into my hair as she embraced me. She looked into my eyes and tried to smile. I could see her heart breaking as well. "I'll see you soon, I'm sure. Go on, now." Blinking back tears, I stood and left, and back in the hallway, I squared my shoulders and set off for the armory.

The guard rooms were a mess of yelling, men calling out curses on the Ismiri and offering to kill Kasimir themselves, others muttering about Conradines and Warlords. I managed to push my way through the crush to the Guard Captain, a man heartily drunk off a night of toasts to Wilhelm and drinking to the death of the Ismiri, and he shouted in my ear that Donnett was off on his rounds. This sent me out onto the winding streets, shivering in the midwinter cold. When I found Donnett at last, his companion swore at the apparition of a young girl in men's clothes, and pointed his lance at me; Donnett put out a hand to steady him, and raised his eyebrows at me.

"What is it, then, lad?"

"I won't be at lessons for a while," I explained awkwardly. "Miriel and I are going back to Voltur." Mindful of listening ears, I added, "She can't talk for crying, she's beside herself, and she's taken it so hard that the Duke fears for her health. He wants her to be with her mother for comfort." As if the Lady could provide anyone with comfort.

"Why's she grieving?" Donnett asked warily, and I realized that, out on watch, he and his companion had not heard the news. Softly, I repeated the litany that was being whispered through the corridors of the palace.

"King Garad is dead, may the Gods protect his soul. Long live King Wilhelm."

Both of them stared at me, dumbstruck.

"Yer jestin,'" Donnett said softly, and I shook my head.

"I'm not. The Guard Captain can tell you more, he knows. Donnett?" I drew him aside, and looked up into his eyes. "You were right, I'm sure of it. It's happened again, someone coming for us."

"D'ye know—"

"No. Not yet. But if you hear anything..." He understood, and nodded.

"Run along, lad." He clapped me on the shoulder. "Gods keep ye."

"And you," I said. There was so much more I wanted to say: a thank you for his training, the details of my imprisonment, the simple fact that I would miss this gruff man. But I only gave a lopsided smile, and a nod to his companion, and I left.

When I got back to the courtyard, all was ready for our departure. In the bustle, only Temar had noticed my absence. He gave me a look, but there was no real anger in it. He was preoccupied still. I walked over to him; I knew this was a poor time, both of us exhausted and shaken, but I did not know when I might see him next, and I wanted to clear the air between us.

"I am sorry for lying to you," I said bluntly. He looked at me, but said nothing. I felt as if he was far away, hardly caring for my words. "Are you sorry you chose me?" I asked him, trying to spark a reaction, anything to bring life to his eyes. He only considered.

"That's the wrong question."

"What's the right one?"

"I can't tell you that." He hiccupped, and I realized that Temar was drunk. I raised my eyebrows at him.

"How did you know about Miriel and Wilhelm?" I asked, trying to bring back the Shadow in him.

"The Royal Guard." He did not seem to care if I know, and finally I was angry. Seven Gods, he had lied to me, and deceived, and hidden truths from me. He had been loyal to the Duke before me, and then hated me for my own loyalties; he had no right. Gods above, he had told me that he would *kill* me. And he would not even accept an apology.

"Temar," I said sharply. I was not sure if I had ever called him by his name before, and his eyebrows lifted in surprise. At last he seemed to see me, but his face had hardened.

"You'll be back to Court," he said. "Soon. And all this begins again. You've meddled in something greater than you could dream, Catwin, and I'll not tolerate it a second time." Anger rushed over me. It beat a rhythm in my temples, I felt my hands clench. I stared at him coldly, any sympathy for his sadness gone.

"You made me what I am," I said coldly. "And whatever grand thing it is you're planning, if it means sacrificing Miriel, I *will* meddle."

"Then you'll die," he told me, and his mouth twitched.

"Maybe." I giggled, and Temar stared at me, confused by this sudden turn. "You see," I said, trying to stop the hysteria welling up in my chest, "a lot of people have tried that already. And it hasn't worked yet."

"Move out!" came the call from the front of the wagon train, and I did not even say goodbye. I turned on my heel and left, running and jumping to get into Miriel's covered wagon and not looking back.

We rode all day, barely stopping to eat or drink. I lay with Miriel in the darkened wagon and we slept, sometimes, comforted by the sound of the guardsmen talking and the jolting of the carriage. At times, I would slip into the nightmare of the soldier coming closer and closer to our hiding place, and I would awake terrified and crying, with Miriel holding my hand and shaking my shoulder to wake me. Other times, it was I who heard her crying, and woke her; neither of us asked the other what we saw in our dreams. The horror was too fresh for words.

As the days passed, we pushed aside the hangings from the windows of her carriage and looked out at the countryside around us. We sat in silence together, still recovering from the blank horror of what we had seen, and as the carriages rumbled through the countryside of Heddred, I was starkly reminded of our last journey through this land, to the Meeting of the Peacemakers, and of the journey before that: coming from Voltur, years ago. I had been a child still, full of trust in the world, blushing at Temar's smiles, with no greater worries than Miriel's pout and Roine's scowl.

We drew closer to Voltur and the roads grew less well tended, the countryside sparser. The pretty fields of corn and wheat were replaced with untended prairie, and stands of twisted trees. I realized that Miriel and I, mountain children by birth, had grown used to the lush landscape of the eastern plains. I viewed this prairie not as a forest of greenery and a tangle of growth, as I had when I first rode here, but as a water-starved wasteland.

When we had set out for Penekket, I had noted that Miriel seemed to grow more and more depressed with every mile we traveled. She had been afraid of what awaited her, and I knew now that she had been right to fear. There had been knives waiting for her, and poison, and hatred. I wondered if she regretted it, but I did not have the heart to ask her.

"He'll wait for me," she said one day. She had been looking out the small window, and she turned back to look at me. "Won't he?"

Wilhelm. The only thing left of her former life. I nodded, but I was not sure. Garad had not been raised to take the throne, but he had been born to it. Since he was a child, everyone he met had sought his favor with smiles and compliments. Wilhelm had been half-outcast since he had been born; how would he behave now that he was the most sought-after bachelor at the court? He loved Miriel, of that I was certain. But what would Gerald Conradine do, with a chance at power? I had watched the man for weeks, waiting for just such a move as this—why had I not seen it at once?

Miriel saw my hesitation, and did not realize the source.

"You don't think he'll wait," she accused. "Do you know something I don't?" She had scrambled across the carriage and was staring at me fearfully. I shook my head, holding my hands up.

"I don't, I don't know anything. He'll just be very unsure right now, and..." An idea took form in my head, and Miriel saw that, as well.

"No." She was horrified. "Oh, no. Catwin, don't doubt him."

"Who had the most to gain from this?" I said. Miriel was shaking her head, but I could not stop myself. It was unlikely, but it was undeniable. "It wasn't Kasimir, was it? Garad is dead, and the warlords are back on the throne. If Kasimir wanted a war, he'd do better to have Garad in command." Miriel had her hands over her ears.

"I'm not listening. I won't listen to this."

"I'm not saying Wilhelm planned it," I said. I thought of Wilhelm's discomfort with lies, his straightforward gaze. "I don't think it's likely that he planned it," I added. "But maybe it was his father. We just can't ignore it." She swallowed, and looked away, and I knew that she had also marked Gerald Conradine's attempts to sway the Lords to his side. She knew that he was not only a soldier, but a courtier as well. He was not a man to be turned away from his goal once and relent. Whether or not he had been behind this, I could say without reservation that he would have done it.

With a pang, I remembered Garad's words: "I thought the bad blood between Warden and Conradine was done with," he had said. His friendship with Wilhelm, I had never doubted. But the bad blood remained; it was in the gaze of Gerald Conradine and his wife, it was in the hisses and whispers that had followed the Conradines for generations. The court knew what Artur the Betrayer had not: a rival faction should be cut down. None of the Conradines should have survived the coup, and Artur's superstition might well have ended the Warden line.

And, I realized, of all of those who could have wanted Garad dead, Gerald was one of the few who might have wanted Miriel dead as well. To anyone else, she would be a nobody, a half-widow, powerless. But Gerald Conradine might have learned that his son was besotted with Miriel. Wilhelm, the honest fool, might even have told his father outright. And for a man planning a coup, planning to put his son into place on the throne, few things could be more inconvenient than the son's foolish love for a girl with no political connections. It occurred to me that I would not be surprised to hear of Wilhelm's marriage to Linnea Torstensson—although I would never have told Miriel of such a thought. I stole a glance over at her, and she looked back at me.

"There's no proof," she said finally, and I sighed.

"We've never had proof of anything. But, Miriel, why was Wilhelm there at all? Why did he think to come with soldiers? It doesn't add up."

"Don't you dare accuse him," Miriel said fiercely. "I mean it, Catwin, I won't believe it of him. Wilhelm is honorable. Above all, he is honorable. He would never have stolen Garad's throne." Contrary to the core, I pushed back.

"Not even for the rebellion? Not if it would save the rebellion and bring you back to him?" Miriel blanched. Then she straightened and shook her head, confident once more.

"Not even for that. He'd do anything else for the rebellion, but he never would have sacrificed Garad's life. He has too much honor for that. He'd go to Garad and plead openly for the rebellion, and go to the block as a traitor, before he'd have hurt his friend."

I shrugged. "Maybe." At her furious, red-eyed glare, I relented. "Alright! I don't think it of him, either. It's not him I fear. But I'm telling you, it doesn't add up." Miriel softened, and then leaned against the wall of the carriage. She had barely slept in days.

"We'll be back soon," she said. "My uncle has to bring us back. And then I can ask him. Yes, Catwin, I'll ask him. Are you happy now?" It was the first touch of her temper I had seen in days, and I was in no mood to respond to it. At my noncommittal shrug, Miriel gave a little sigh and looked out the window once more.

"We're getting into the foothills," she said, and I craned to see the gentle swell of the land, belied by the sharp slabs of rock that thrust out of the ground all around us. The Voltur Mountains were an unforgiving home.

I felt a strange pain, to see this familiar land. It was not that I disliked it, or that I feared it. I had been born and raised here, looking out over the land and seeing the world in the piercing sunlight above the clouds. I had weathered the mountain storms and endured the bitterest of winters here, and I fancied that my heart sang to see my homeland. No, the hurt stemmed from the fact that I knew, beyond doubt—in my very bones—that I no longer had any place here. In truth, I was not sure if there was anyplace left that I *did* belong.

Chapter 27

The wind whipped around the edges of the castle, moaning as if it could call the warmth out of our very bones with its ceaseless wail. I shivered and stirred the fire, repeating to myself for the thousandth time that I hated mountain winters. I never said it out loud, for it sounded soft to my ears—a plains girl, a city girl, might complain of such things, but a mountain girl had no business being so weak. I told myself that as I lay awake each night and gritted my teeth against the sound of the wind. It never stopped, it never relented of battering itself against the castle walls; I thought sometimes that I might go mad.

Three months. Three months stuck in this Godsforsaken castle at the edge of the world, with only sorrow and loneliness for our companions. Between the moan of the wind and our nightmares, we hardly slept, and our waking hours were spent in constant fear of border raids. Our seventeenth birthdays—Miriel's, a feast with strained good cheer, and mine, a sweet roll and a hug from Miriel, and an extra round of duty on the walls from the Lady—had been tainted by the threat of war. It did not matter whether or not Kasimir had sent the King's assassins—war was coming, inexorable, catching all of us up like a wave, to batter us against our foes. We saw the guardsmen carried back bleeding, and we heard the clash of steel carried eerily on the wind. We knew. Sometimes, I wondered if we had been sent here to die on Ismiri swords, tokens to sympathy for the Duke.

And—worst of all—at last I understood the cruelty of the Lady's exile. I did not miss the whispers and spite of the Court, but I, too, now knew the loneliness of moving from the ceaseless bustle of Penekket to the utter isolation of the mountains. If there was no intrigue, well, there was no laughter, either; the halls of the Winter Castle were dark and deserted. There were no spiteful whispers at dinner, but that was because there was no one at all in the hall save Miriel, the Lady, and the few servants who attended them. There were no sly servants looking for silver coins when they brought bathwater, and pouring secrets into your ear for another copper, for there were no secrets to whisper, and the servants gave no special service. Everyone in the Winter Castle did their duty, no more, and no less, and they did it with the dull eyes I had recognized from those who are simply trying to survive. There was nothing to fight for here.

Miriel and I had arrived here in shock, terrified of the faceless enemies we had made and grieving the death of our King. I was consumed with guilt. Now that he was dead, I could not stop picturing the mischievous smile of the boy we had met, disguised, in the hallway. I remembered, with awful clarity, the way his face lit up when he described his Golden Age; uncomfortably, I recalled how Miriel and I had laughed at his grandeur when he named the Meeting of the Peacemakers. An act of monstrous vanity—yes, it had been that. But Garad had kept to his ideals in the face of interference by his Council. And in the end, he had seen the pain he had caused Miriel.

Miriel, never before overly devout, had spent the first days of our stay in the little chapel. It was freezing cold there, and Father Whitmere still scowled at any sinners who might dare cross the threshold. But Miriel went, and she knelt before the altar and stayed there for hours, her face upturned, her thoughts and her prayers locked away inside her head. I went with her, but there was no comfort for me in facing the Gods. When I prayed, the words were bitter in my mouth. I could not help but believe that it was my tangled fate that had brought the King to his death, and Miriel's maidservant as well. If ever I could have forgiven the Gods for giving me the fate of betrayal, I could not forgive them the death of innocents.

By silent agreement, Miriel and I never spoke of this murder attempt, just as we had barely spoken of the last. Each of us could reason well enough, we could name those who would have wished the King dead, and we could name some who would have wished us dead. What I did not understand—what I could not understand— was who, other than Gerald Conradine, would have taken the chance to have both the King and Miriel killed. Surely Kasimir would not have cared enough, and that went for Nilson as well. Nilson, indeed, had no reason to suspect that if he killed Garad, Wilhelm would provide him with the soldiers he needed to fight the rebellion. The High Priest, even if he were brutal enough to kill Garad—and he had loved Garad like a son, I had heard his grief when he saw the boy's body—would have wanted Wilhelm to have a wife who would affirm his devotion to the rebellion. Guy de la Marque might have wanted Miriel dead, but why would he have sacrificed a tenuous hold over the King for no hold at all over Wilhelm? And Isra might likewise have sent those soldiers for us, but she would never, never have killed her own son.

Round and round our thoughts went, but there was never any conclusion, save the worst one: that it had been Gerald Conradine, with Wilhelm himself as an accomplice. As the weeks wore on without a single letter from the capitol, without the tiniest whisper of new information, I found that I was torn between my surety of Gerald's guilt, and the uncomfortable prickle of Donnett's words, spoken months ago: *the one who betrayed ye is one ye wouldn't suspect.* Would Gerald have acted, knowing that Wilhelm would be the first one suspected of murder? Would Wilhelm have snatched at the chance to save the rebellion, and known to kill us before we could name him?

I never spoke those words to Miriel. We had little enough chance to talk during the days in any case. The Lady wished Miriel to be at her side, and she had ordered me away from her presence. I was commanded to join the Guard, walking rounds on the windswept walls, and although none of the guards were quick enough to have caught me if I had decided to abandon my work, I did each round I was assigned, stubbornly gritting my teeth against the bitter cold. I wondered sometimes if this was part of the guilt I carried for the Lady's loneliness, understanding it as I did, or if I walked these walls because I felt close to Aler here. I had asked after the burly guardsman when I returned, and was met with a sad smile. *He died, lass, a year or more past. Didn't you know?* I had not. And I had never gotten to say goodbye. When I walked my rounds, it was as if he was there at my side.

Although I was banned, also, from sleeping in Miriel's rooms, I always found my way in and we lay in silence together in the darkness. Sometimes we told each other of our days, making a dry joke of the monotony; it was one of the only times we smiled. As the days wound on, and our link to the Court began to fade, I noticed the strangest thing: even as we sank into dull routine and hardly spoke—for what was there to say?—we turned to each other for comfort. We had become allies in the face of danger, and we had weathered countless more threats, always pursuing the goal of triumphing over our enemies at court and becoming players in the game, instead of pawns. Now that our goal lay irrevocably out of reach, and there was no game to play, we still faced the world together.

So it was that when soldiers arrived from the Duke, I found another guard to take my round and ran for Miriel. She and her mother were already receiving the Guard Captain as he gave them the Duke's message, and it was only Miriel who saw me lurking in the shadows and gave me a tiny nod. I went to wait for her in her rooms, and it was not long before I heard her running down the hallway to me.

"We're to go back to Court," she said breathlessly. "He's moving mother to a castle on the plains, and we're to go back. But the man didn't know anything more than that." We stared at each other for a moment, and then to my surprise Miriel came closer and perched on my chair, leaned to whisper into my ear as if this was the deepest of secrets: "You don't want to go back, either, do you?"

I drew back to look at her, shocked beyond belief to hear such a sentiment from her. "Don't *you*?" I whispered back, and after a pause, she shook her head.

"Not...really," she admitted, in a rush. Now I wondered just what it was that she had been thinking over, in her long hours spent in the chapel. "I mean—I don't know. I do. I want to see Wilhelm." Her face warmed at the thought, but she bit her lip. "But I don't want to face them again. All of my dreams for Heddred since I was a little girl—I didn't realize it then, but all of it leads to the rebellion. I know I need to be at court to change things...but to be at court is to see everything I despise. They'll hate me when I come back and hold power over Wilhelm, too. Anything he does will be compromised by it. I know that I have to fight for what's important, but Catwin, I hate it. I've always hated it." I remembered her passionate outbursts to me when she had realized she was her uncle's pawn, her sheer exhaustion at maintaining the charade of love in the face of a Court that wanted to see her fall to nothing.

"We could run away," I said, the old litany. She smiled at me, and leaned her head on my shoulder.

"Is that what you want?"

"I don't know," I said honestly. "But I don't want to go back, either. There's nothing...good, there."

"We'll make it good," Miriel promised me. "And we'll find out what it is you want."

"I want not to have this stupid prophecy about me," I said promptly, and she smiled.

"I have to get back to my mother. She says you're to pack my things." I sighed.

"She would. I'll start."

I struggled with Miriel's gowns for most of the afternoon, swearing at the billows of fabric and trying to determine how to wrap what little jewelry Miriel had brought with her. At length, the gowns had been fit into her two trunks; I rather suspected that whatever maid unpacked these would be horrified, but I had done the best I could. All in all, I was rather pleased with myself by the time Miriel returned.

I knew at once when I saw her that something terrible had happened. There were tears in her eyes, and her face was blank. She was stunned, she walked as if numb, one hand trailing along the wall to hold herself up.

"I'm to be married," she said. "One of the guards gave me this, to give to you. It was from Donnett, and...I opened it." I shrugged. I would have shown it to her in any case, as she had always shown me her letters from the High Priest. "It says I'm to be married." The paper was shaking in her hand, and I knew without asking that her marriage would not be to Wilhelm. I went across the room and took her hands in my own.

"It will be okay," I promised her. "We'll find a way out of it. I promise. Wilhelm will put a stop to it, maybe."

"He won't," Miriel said. I could hear a sob lurking at the back of her throat, and all of a sudden I knew the rest of the news. She said it anyway. "He's married. He was married last month. To Marie de la Marque." And with that, her face crumpled. It was the first time I had seen her cry. She had been passionate, she had yelled and screamed that she could not bear her life; she had been exhausted, and despairing, and on the verge of tears. Certainly, she had been terrified into tears when we were close to being found, in the wardrobe all those weeks ago. But she had never once broken down and cried out of grief.

Now she sobbed, and I wrapped my arms around her and held her and felt tears in my own eyes. I found myself praying, angrily—had she not suffered enough? Had she not paid, in fear and pain, for every lie she had told?

My prayers, such as they were, turned to curses. As we made ready for the journey home, Miriel propped up with wounded pride and little else, I realized that there was nothing, now, for me to lose. What could the Gods do to me that they had not already done? They had threatened me with death, they had let innocents die, they had allowed Miriel to be beaten to within an inch of her life and poisoned. I knew my fate, and I knew it to be a bitter fate no matter how pious I might be. Why should I swallow down my anger and hope that they took pity on me?

So I cursed them when I saw Miriel's exhausted determination, the same lost expression I had seen when we set out for Penekket the first time. I cursed them when I realized that I would be returning to the Duke's service as he played whatever game he had formulated, and I would be set against Temar—the man I might have loved, the one thing I might have told Miriel I wanted. I cursed them as we rode down the winding mountain path and through the village; I did not look around me, and I did not look back. I looked around at the thawing prairie and I swallowed down bitterness so that I did not say the words aloud, and at my side Miriel rode through the half-frozen wasteland like a little ghost.

And then one day on our journey, the sun broke through the clouds and the roads became nearly impassable. For the first time since she had told me the news of Wilhelm, I saw Miriel smile; we had stopped, to pull one of the carriages free of the mud, and she and I had gotten out to stand in the fresh air. Miriel was looking up at the sunlight and feeling the breeze on her skin, and I saw her face lift out of fear.

"Can we ride?" she asked one of the guardsmen, and he shrugged. There were spare horses, he said, and if we thought we could master them, we could ride along. His tone said that he did not think much of our chances, but he was too tired to care, and Miriel agreed eagerly. When the carriage was free, we were both lifted into the saddle, and we set off in the fresh air.

I watched out of the corner of my eye as Miriel's mood lightened. Her fingers eased on the reins and she rode with an air of contentment. As we cantered, she began to sing, and threw a smile over at me: her trademark invitation. My voice, light, untrained, joined with her smoky alto, and we sang of winter nights, and summer days that seemed very far away.

Then Miriel glanced around, wrinkled her nose mischievously, and launched into a tavern song so bawdy that even I had only heard it once before. My voice faltered; I looked ahead at the Guard Captain. He was in close-headed conference with one of his men, he was paying no attention to us; he would have no story to carry back to the Duke. All around us, the guardsmen were smiling, in on Miriel's joke. I laughed, incredulous, and then sang along recklessly. As soon as the Guard Captain turned his horse, Miriel changed the song, without a falter, without a changed note, and we were singing a song of harvest when the man fell in with our party.

"We'll ride until nightfall, my Lady," he said respectfully. "We're a few days out yet, but tomorrow night, Gods willing, there will be an inn for shelter."

"Thank you," Miriel said calmly. "I am sure that my uncle will be pleased with the good time we're making." When he was gone, she gave me a sunny smile.

"What's gotten into you?" I asked her that night, as we donned our nightclothes.

"Check outside," she said simply, and I cautiously peeked out of the tent wagon. No one was nearby; the men were cooking dinner. I nodded for her to speak, and she drew a deep breath. "I realized I don't have to go back," she said simply. "I don't. I know we always said so, but I had never believed it. And when I realized..." She laughed at my stunned expression. "I wouldn't expect it of you. You don't have to. But...would you really run away with me?" she asked.

"Yes," I said. It was the only word that came to my lips. "Yes. Oh, Gods...Miriel, I didn't want to go back."

"Yes." She came and clasped my hands, bit her lip. "There's nothing for us there," she explained. "I think you knew that. I just...hadn't."

"Nothing, even for you?" I asked her curiously, thinking of her gowns and her jewels. She saw what I was thinking and shook her head. There were tears in her eyes, but she was smiling.

"No. I'll give it up. You see...Wilhelm's marriage set me free. There's nothing at all for me there, not now." I squeezed her hands, but she was not looking for sympathy. She never saw things one at a time, did Miriel. She saw the whole, a jumble of possibilities, and she saw it all sideways. I marveled at it. Now she gave me the same mischievous smile. "You know where we could go," she said. I felt my eyes widen.

"That's dangerous."

"It's all dangerous. You know my uncle will be looking for us. But..." She swallowed and her smile dimmed a little. "I'm sick to my heart of Courts, Catwin. I thought we had set ourselves apart from my uncle, but we were always playing the same game. I never really thought about what I wanted, I never wondered if there might be another way. And all of it, the lies...it was twisting me. I was turning into something dark."

"I know." I whispered back. I did know, I knew the shadow creeping up in my own soul. We stood in silence for a moment and then, surprisingly, she laughed.

"I feel like I've been set free," she said wonderingly. "Can we really do this? Take supplies, go tonight?" I thought.

"Tomorrow night." I decided. "At the inn. More noise to cover us." She smiled, she could not help it, and it was the happiest I had seen her in months.

"Tomorrow," she agreed, and we went to take our dinner with the men.

And so it was that the next night, Miriel and I snuck down into the stable, slipped the hostler a few coppers for his silence, and set out, riding hard, for the Norstrung Provinces, and freedom.

Epilogue

"Now she's escaped us entirely." The voice was accusing. "Surely you could have foreseen this."

"I? It was not I who had her in my grasp and let them slip away! One girl against twenty men! Some elite force that was!"

"Ill luck. And the men achieved their first objective."

"Little good that does us without Catwin! I have told you, time and again, what she means to us. There are stories about her."

"And I," the first voice said, "begin to doubt you. Prophecies and visions, repeated by peasants and bored nobles—the girl's mother was no seer! How could she know what she saw?"

"It was a true prophecy, I know that in my bones. Everything we have gained from this can be undone in a moment, if we do not secure it with her death." The words were a hiss into the darkness.

"Does it not trouble you? Killing this girl?" The first voice. Curious.

"It is her fate. I do not—I will not—question the Gods."

"The Gods? Has it not occurred to you that they will damn us both for this?"

A pause, then the second spoke: "For this prize, I will accept damnation."

####

Thank you for reading the *Shadowforged*! If you enjoyed this book, read on for an excerpt of *Shadow's End,* the conclusion of the trilogy! Whether you liked the book or not, I encourage you to take a few moments to leave a review—not only will your feedback help other readers to make an informed choice, but it will help me to improve my storytelling! You can find more information about my books, including upcoming works, at my website:

http://moirakatson.com

Shadow's End
Light & Shadow, Book III

On the first night, wrapped in our warmest furs and still shivering violently against the cold winds of the plains, Miriel and I confronted the fact that there was no going back. We had not stopped for hours, desperate to get as far as possible before our guards knew that we had gone. They would follow us—they would have to, they would be desperate to find us before the Duke ever found out that we had slipped through their fingers. Whether we wanted to go to Penekket or not was of no concern to them, and I had no illusions about my skills at combat: if it came to a fight between me and a score of guardsmen, they would likely win. So we pushed the horses as far as they would go and then sought shelter in a stand of trees, vainly listening for the sound of pursuit even as the howl of the wind blocked out any noise but itself.

"Catwin, do you know how to get to the Norstrung Provinces?" Miriel asked, finally, after we had sat in silence for an hour or so. For some reason, the question struck me as incredibly funny, and I laughed so hard, and for so long, that I could not catch my breath. When I looked up, I saw that Miriel was laughing, too, stifling her much-practiced giggle behind a perfectly manicured hand, and holding her side as she shook with mirth. We laughed in disbelief at our own recklessness until at last we had exhausted ourselves, and then Miriel leaned back against a tree and asked simply,

"What have we done?"

The last vestiges of humor disappeared at once. I looked at her and saw her not as she was to me—ally, friend—but as she was to the world: the betrothed of the last King, a young woman of uncertain birth, wearing a priceless gown and cloak and sitting in the middle of a field on an early spring night. A runaway. A woman who could be anything she wished if she chose to work her magic on the new king, or nothing at all if her uncle wished to punish her for her actions.

"We ran away," I said wonderingly. *We ran away.* I felt the shape of the words in my mouth and, oddly light-headed, wondered if this was a dream. For a moment, I drifted, until the realization that all of this was real slammed down, and I felt a wave of nausea and pure terror. I wondered, wildly, if there was any lie we could tell to go back to the warm, well-fed, half-safety of the palace and the Duke's patronage. I was ashamed of myself even for wondering, but I was terrified. I was taunted by my own mind, the little voice that said, mockingly, *you said you wanted this.*

And there was no going back. The nausea grew stronger, and from the look on Miriel's face, she had come to the same realization: this was nothing we could deny or explain away, it was an irrevocable breach with the Duke. We could not pretend that we had done this in his best interests. We had said that we did not want to lie and dissemble anymore, and here we were: honest at last. And filled with fear.

This was a terrible, terrible mistake.

"Oh, Gods," Miriel said, biting her lip. "We ran *away.*" I only nodded, numbly, and she rubbed her face, then sighed and looked up, "So what do we do now?" The golden light of dawn gleamed in her hair and gilded her face, and I realized that it had been growing steadily lighter. Exhaustion counted for nothing; our rest was over.

"We keep riding," I said, and with the first decision, my confidence began to return. "We're not far out of Penekket, so we should start veering south now. We need to stay off the road. And you should change." I had procured a serving girl's spare gown for Miriel, but we had left so quickly that she has not yet changed. She was sitting on a pile of bracken, wrapped in her warm velvet cloak and wearing silk and jewels.

"We're still going south?" Miriel asked, wide-eyed. Even now, with no one to see us, she used her beautiful, practiced mannerisms. She had made her mask so well and so completely that she might never strip it all away. I could not have said how I felt about that—even in our disgust at how our masks and our true faces had become intertwined, at how the twisted darkness had crept into our very hearts, I would have lied if I said that Miriel's mask was not exquisitely beautiful. It was so finely crafted that it would almost be a shame to see it broken down and destroyed.

"We have to go," I said, judging by her fear that I should not say, *and there is no other choice.* I understood her fear; I could not revile it. "You're going to be a great leader for the rebellion, after all." I was trying to coax her away from her terror, and her face warmed at the thought, though she looked pained.

"I feel a fool," she admitted, as she took the rough, homespun dress from one of our packs and shook it out.

"Why?" I looked at her curiously, and she took a moment and chose her words carefully.

"Because I'm doing this for Wilhelm." She saw my face and hastened to explain. "I know it's useless. I don't hope to win him back." She swallowed and curled her hands into fists, so tightly the knuckles went white. "I shouldn't have to. He should have waited for me. I know I should be angry and forget him. But when I try to be angry, and cut him out of my heart, I...can't." She swallowed and blinked away tears. "I think: I told him that he must do whatever he could, risk everything he had, for the rebellion. I told him I'd do the same. And so even if I think he's betrayed me...this is to keep faith with him. Even if he's turned from me, I have to believe that he's still true to this, or I won't survive. So I am true to it, as well."

I did not respond; I had no words to speak of hope, they would have choked me with jealousy. Miriel could still believe that Wilhelm kept true to their cause, and I...

If you meddle again, you will die. Bad luck to adore the man who had turned me into a Shadow, and worse luck that my love had not disappeared when he became an enemy. When I thought of him now, it was not only with hatred and fear and the sense of a coming fight—it was to wonder what his kisses might be like, it was to think of the body that I knew, after years of sparring, almost as well as my own. My heart betrayed me every day, and it was bitter indeed to have none of the comfort that Miriel took from her hope.

I had the thought, so overwhelming that bile came to my throat, that the prophecy had spoken of betrayal—and who could betray me in this world more completely than could Temar?

"Please tell me you don't think it's—what are you *doing*?" Miriel's voice rose to a shriek and she clapped her hands over her mouth. I held my braid out in my hand and shrugged. Distracted by my misery, I had not hesitated, only sawed the hair away with one of my daggers; I could feel the rest drifting, ragged, around my head like so much honey-colored silk.

"Better to seem like a girl and a boy than two girls," I said. "In case anyone sees us." I had been staring down at my hair, and now I looked up and my voice trailed off. "Gods be good," I whispered.

"What?" Miriel looked down at her dress, checking for stains.

"You look…" *Beautiful.* I should have known better than to expect that clothing alone could make Miriel less noteworthy. The rough cloth only set off her beauty all the more. In fine gowns and jewels, her looks were only a piece of a perfectly-polished puzzle, but now they were jarring. Her hair seemed darker, her eyes bluer. "Don't let anyone see you up close," I advised, trying not to let my envy show. But she saw it anyway, and smiled.

"Beauty hasn't done me any favors," she pointed out. "I'm not Queen, everyone hates me but you, and the man I love…" She swallowed. "And anyway, do you really think *you* can pass for a boy?"

"You'd be surprised," I said drily, thinking of the dozens who called me, "lad," or, "boy," every day, their eyes seeing no further than my britches and tabard, their gaze moving on before they saw the hint of curves under my clothes. I knew for a fact that no one had ever noticed me at all, for the Court was so mad for rumors of Miriel that if anyone had ever noticed me, it would have been all over that the Lady Miriel was accompanied by a girl dressed as a boy. But their eyes had only ever slid over me; another servant in livery. "Are you ready to go?"

"One moment." Miriel picked her way over the frozen ground and took my dagger. She pointed to the pile of bracken. "Sit."

"We don't have time."

"We have a moment." She stared at me until I sat, reluctantly, and then she took the locks of my hair in her hands and began to trim the chopped mess of it. Her hands were gentle as they cut it all to evenness, so that my hair no longer stuck out from my head but smoothed itself into a neat, golden cap. She ran her fingers through it, nodded decisively at her handiwork, and then she flipped the dagger about and presented it to me, haft first.

"Thank you," I said, awkwardly, rising up. I checked her saddle, and then lifted her up and guided my horse to a nearby boulder so that I could jump up myself. I surveyed the road in both directions, then sighted our direction from the sun. I wished that I had a map, but hoped that I could remember well enough where we were that we would not run into any major towns. Then, seeing our way clear, I urged my horse out of the trees and led the way southeast, away from the road.

We rode until noon, checking over our shoulders frequently, but we never saw any signs of pursuit. We had gotten away cleanly, and I dared to hope that it had been fully light out before the guards realized that we were missing. I tried to tell myself that even if the men rode their horses to exhaustion, they would never think to veer off the road as we had—but still, I craned my neck to look behind us so much that I developed a crick in my neck.

As the first day drew to a close, we began to search for another copse of trees. Soon, we would sweep south into the fertile marshes and forests of south Heddred, but for now our horses were still picking their way over dormant, half-frozen fields, and cover was rare. At last, we found a few trees on the side of a hill, and I set about gathering wood for a fire. Donnett, whatever he thought of my chances in a fight, had taken it upon himself to teach me survival skills for living in the wild, remarking more than once that if my archery did not improve, I would need all the help I could get.

As I began to build up the fire, a thought came to me, unbidden: Roine, her hair plaited for sleep, her dark eyes worried, embracing me and telling me not to fear my exile. *I'll see you soon*, she had told me, and I had agreed. But Miriel and I had been so terrified of facing the Duke and the Court, so preoccupied with the fact of running away, that I had not thought of Roine until now.

"We have to tell Roine," I blurted out, and Miriel looked over at me. Regretfully, she shook her head, and when I opened my mouth to protest, she held up a hand to quell me.

"We can't," she explained gently. "There's no way to get a messenger to her. My uncle will be having her watched. I closed my mouth and looked down, and Miriel added, "And who's the first one he'll question when he knows we've gone?"

"He'll question her?" My voice came out in a squeak. Panic closed in, and rational thought fled. I could not bear the thought of Roine being questioned for my sake. "We have to go back. Right now."

"No!" Miriel laid her hand on my arm. "We can't go back. And he won't be angry with her, what could she know? He's smart, Catwin, he'll see that. And she wasn't born yesterday, you know— she'll be alright."

I swallowed. Miriel was entirely correct. I could picture it clearly if I set my fear aside: the Duke, furious, and Roine sitting calmly, asserting in her low, clear voice that she did not know where I was, she had not known I was missing until the Duke came to speak to her. In the corner would be Temar, watching. I had to believe that he—and the Duke—would see the truth of Roine's

223

words. And I must believe, or go mad, that the Duke would not think to use Roine against me.

Miriel was right: the best thing for Roine would be to know nothing. Ignorance would be her shield. No messages would arrive for Temar to intercept, no knowledge would show in her eyes. But she would think that I cared for her so little as to go without even telling her; she might not know how it had been, that we had made our plan in less than a day, and had no chance to get word to her. She would not even know that we were safe.

"You know…they may think we were kidnapped," I said, struck by the thought, and Miriel nodded.

"They won't think so for long, but it could buy us time before Temar figures out where we've gone." Her face twisted, as it always did when she spoke of Temar. Not for the first time, I wondered just why it was that they hated each other so instinctively, each of them ready to believe that the other might ruin everything. I was trying to find a joke to make about it when Miriel said,

"He's dangerous, Catwin. Have you ever thought…." Her voice trailed off as she saw my face. She knew this was not something I wanted to hear. As much as I could, I had resolutely refused to think of Temar in our months at the Winter Castle, and I did not want to think of him now. Worse, feeling disloyal, I admitted to myself that I did not want Miriel to speak badly of him. But we did not have that luxury.

"What?" I tried to keep my voice even, to speak reasonably instead of walk away. I knew I did not want to hear whatever she had to say. But Temar *was* our enemy; I never forgot it.

"I used to think he was just loyal to my uncle," Miriel said, "but I don't think so anymore."

"He's loyal. He'd kill either of us in a moment if the Duke wanted." That was the fact I always chose to remind myself of where Temar's loyalties lay, because it was the fact that hurt the most. I reminded myself of it whenever I could not help thinking of him—I hoped that the pain of it might break me free of my foolish infatuation.

"I think he's playing his own game," Miriel posited. She did not tell me to think on it. She knew that, now that the theory was out, I would not be able to rest until I found the truth. For a moment, I hated her for knowing me so well. "Good night," she said, knowing as well that I would not welcome any further conversation, and she wrapped her cloak around herself and curled up.

"Good night," I said moodily. I lay back and stared up at the star through the bare branches of the trees. Exhausted as I was, I knew it would be a very long time until I would be able to sleep.

36608661R00140

Made in the USA
San Bernardino, CA
27 July 2016